A PERILOUS PREDICAMENT

Josephine was lying in the bed at the inn that Mr. Villiers had paid for. And she was snuggled up warmly against Mr. Villiers' person, her head against his shoulder, her nose against his neck, her arm about his waist and her leg pushed up against his.

However had she got herself into such a dreadful state of affairs? If she had sat down at home and dreamed up the very worst predicament she could possibly get herself into, she could not have imagined something quite as bad as this.

But perilous as Josephine's position was, it could only get even more dreadfully dangerous. For if she moved or even if she didn't, the strange man in bed with her most certainly was going to wake up . . . .

D0761336

SIGNET REGENCY ROMANCE
COMING IN NOVEMBER 1990

Irene Saunders
Lady Lucinda's Locket

Vanessa Gray
Best-Laid Plans

Leigh Haskell
The Vengeful Viscount

AN UNLIKELY DUCHESS

Mary Balogh

A SIGNET BOOK

SIGNET
Published by the Penguin Group
Penguin Books USA Inc., 375 Hudson Street,
New York, New York, 10014, U.S.A.
Penguin Books Ltd, 27 Wrights Lane, London W8 5TZ, England
Penguin Books Australia Ltd, Ringwood, Victoria, Australia
Penguin Books Canada Ltd, 2801 John Street,
Markham, Ontario, Canada L3R 1B4
Penguin Books (N.Z.) Ltd, 182-190 Wairau Road,
Auckland 10, New Zealand

Penguin Books Ltd, Registered Offices:
Harmondsworth, Middlesex, England

First published by Signet, an imprint of New American Library, a division of Penguin
Books USA Inc.

First Printing, October, 1990

10 9 8 7 6 5 4 3 2 1

 REGISTERED TRADEMARK—MARCA REGISTRADA

PRINTED IN THE UNITED STATES OF AMERICA

BOOKS ARE AVAILABLE AT QUANTITY DISCOUNTS WHEN USED TO PROMOTE
PRODUCTS OR SERVICES. FOR INFORMATION PLEASE WRITE TO PREMIUM
MARKETING DIVISION, PENGUIN BOOKS USA INC., 375 HUDSON STREET,
NEW YORK, NEW YORK 10014.

*For Pat Jackson
with fond memories of a Pelly winter
when she shared a basement apartment
with these characters and me*

1

"She is a good country-bred girl," Lord Ainsbury explained to his grandson. "She will suit you well, Paul—quiet and sensible, and doubtless accomplished at running a home."

"Yes, sir," Paul Villiers, Duke of Mitford, was standing looking out of the window of a salon in his townhouse on Berkeley Square. "She sounds suitable."

"And we know she is of good lineage," the baron continued after coughing and glancing at his daughter, the duke's mother, who was quietly stitching at her embroidery. "She is Rutland's granddaughter. I've known him all my life. So her grandfather is an earl and her father is a viscount. Her mother was old Findlay's girl. Good blood wherever you look, my boy."

"Yes," the duke said, clasping his hands behind him and watching Miss Hancock and her mama enter the house on the opposite side of the square. "She sounds very suitable."

"I know you don't admire town beauties," his grandfather said. "I know they are too flighty for you. When I met Rutland at Bath and we found that we were both taking the waters and could take them together, it struck me that one of the grand-daughters he spoke of would suit you fine. They have been strictly brought up, you know, boy, and never allowed the frivolity of a Season to turn their heads. Rutland jumped at the chance when I broached the subject with him."

"You decided on the eldest daughter?" the duke asked.

"It is only fitting when you are a duke," Lord Ainsbury said. "She is twenty, Paul. Just the right age. She will be past any silliness but not yet long in the tooth."

"Yes," his grandson agreed, "it sounds like a suitable age."

"Rutland returned home when I did," the baron said. "They will be waiting for word."

"Yes." Mitford watched the Hancock ladies reemerge from

the house opposite. Obviously, Mrs. Paisley was from home. "I suppose they will."

"Well?" Lady Newman paused in her work and looked up at her son for the first time. Her voice was tense. "What do you think, Paul?"

"Think?" he said, turning from the window to look at her. "I think it sounds like a very suitable match, Mama."

"You will agree to it, then?" she asked. "You will write to the Viscount Cheamley to make an offer for his daughter?"

Mitford rocked on his heels and considered a moment. "If it is the right thing to do," he said, "then I suppose I should. And it seems to be the right thing to do."

"You are eight and twenty," she said, "and you owe it to your position to marry and set up your nursery, Paul, dear. Unfortunately, when you are a duke among other things, you cannot always think of personal inclination. It sounds as if Papa has chosen wisely for you."

"Yes, it does," he said. "I shall write to the Honorable Miss Middleton's father, then, without further delay."

"You will not be sorry, dear," his mother said, folding her embroidery and smiling at her son. "Duty is its own reward, as I have always told you."

"You could not do better, boy," Lord Ainsbury said. "Rutland always was a capable fellow."

The fourth occupant of the room spoke up for the first time. She was a small and placid-looking girl, made dumpy for the present by the effects of an advanced pregnancy.

"But, Paul," she said, looking with affectionate eyes at her brother, "do you not wish to see Miss Middleton first before you make any decision about marrying her?"

"She don't have any deformities," Lord Ainsbury said, "and she has all her teeth. And she don't have any pock marks."

"But is she pretty, Grandpapa?" Lady Angela Vaughan asked.

"Any young lady dresses up pretty provided she don't have any of the things I checked about," the baron said. "Besides, prettiness don't count for much when one is choosing a bride. Not when one is a duke, anyway."

"And is she tall?" his granddaughter persisted.

"It don't signify," her grandfather said. "Most females aren't very tall in my experience."

"But is she taller than Paul?" The girl glanced fondly at her brother, whom even the most generous of mortals could not describe as being one fraction of an inch above average height.

"It don't signify," the baron said again, his voice becoming irritable. "What does that have to say to anything, pray?"

"Paul would be mortified to have a wife who is taller than he," she said. "Would you not, Paul?"

Mitford rocked on his heels and smiled at her. "I reconciled myself to my height when I finally admitted at the age of twenty that I was not going to grow any more, Angie," he said. "I am not even sensitive on the topic any longer."

"Besides, dears," their mother said, "there are qualities far more important than looks and height. There are birth and breeding and training. It sounds as if Miss Middleton has all three. And it is evident that Paul does need those qualities in a wife. He is so very proper himself. And so dignified for one so young. He deserves an equally dignified wife."

She smiled warmly at her only son and extended a hand to him. He crossed the room, bowed over it, and raised it to his lips.

"I shall go and compose my letter immediately, Mama," he said. "I shall suggest going into Northamptonshire as soon as I receive a favorable reply, in order to meet Miss Middleton and pay my addresses to her in person."

"My dear boy," she said, lifting a hand to his neck and drawing his head down so that she might kiss him on the cheek. "I know you will be happy with your decision. You always have done what is right and proper. You will be rewarded with many sturdy sons and lovely daughters, take my word on it."

His grandfather was on his feet, waiting to shake his hand. "I'm proud of you, boy," he said. "I knew it would be a perfect match as soon as Rutland mentioned granddaughters. And I will always be able to congratulate myself on the fact that I was the one who arranged it all." He beamed his satisfaction as he shook his grandson heartily by the hand.

Lady Angela Vaughan had also risen to her feet, though slowly and awkwardly. She linked her arm through her brother's. "I will walk to the library with you, Paul," she said. "I get so breathless when I sit for any length of time. And so breathless when I walk any distance. Poor Adrian has to set aside ten full minutes whenever I wish to climb the stairs at home. I really don't see how this child can do another whole month of growing."

"Women are greatly to be admired," Mitford said, patting her hand on his arm. "I really don't think I could stand going through that, Angie."

"Well," she said, smiling and transforming herself instantly into a very pretty young lady, "it is a good thing we females can, because we really do not have any choice in the matter once we have accepted a marriage offer, do we?"

"Do you wish you did have a choice?" he asked with sympathy, closing the library door quietly behind them.

"Heavens, no," she said, chuckling. "Imagine the humiliation, Paul, of not being able to present one's husband with offspring. Besides, imagine the personal disappointment."

"It was not a mistake, then?" he asked. "Marrying for love, I mean, when you had known Adrian for such a short time. Mama was anxious for your happiness."

"It was not a mistake," she said. "Marriage is not easy, Paul, especially when one is increasing and feeling wretched after the very first month. I really do not know how it would survive without love, for Adrian and I did our fair share of snapping each other's heads off for the first few months, even though we love each other to distraction. Paul, don't do it."

"Marry Miss Middleton?" he said with a smile. He knew her well enough not to have to ask what she referred to. "It is time I married, Angie, and this seems a suitable match."

"How can you say that," she said, exasperated, "when you have not even set eyes on Miss Middleton? Even Grandpapa has not. She may be some sort of monster."

"I think not," he said. "The Earl of Rutland is an old, old friend of Grandpapa's. He would not play such a trick on him."

"She may be six feet tall," she said.

"Well, then," he said, a genuine grin on his face for the first time that afternoon, "she will be a good five inches taller than I."

"Paul," she said, "how can I get you to be serious? Or rather, how can I get you *not* to be serious? You have always done everything that you were taught was proper and right. Duty and decorum are the guiding lights of your life. Is it not time you did something to please yourself?''

"But one could do a lot worse than live one's life according to those principles," he said. "And how can I please myself, Angie? How can I ever know any woman's true feelings for me? No woman can look at me and see anything else but my ducal title, not to mention the eight other lesser titles. Women fall in love with me routinely. Yet who, not knowing of the titles and the property and the wealth, could look at me and want me?'' He spread his hands out to his sides and smiled rather ruefully at her.

"Dozens," she said with conviction. "It is true, Paul, that you are slightly short and rather slender. And I suppose your face could not be described as outstandingly handsome. And your hair will curl and will not hold to any style. But you are not by any means ugly. You have a very pleasant good-humored face.

He laughed. "I was settling in to hearing the list of my good points," he said. "Is it over already? No matter, my dear. Miss Middleton is a country mouse, it seems. She has been brought up to decent country virtues and never exposed to the vices of town. She will be pleased enough, doubtless, to have any husband, even if he is rather short, and even if the best that can be said about him from the shoulders up is that he has a pleasant, good-humored face. And doubtless the titles and the consequences she will acquire will help her swallow the pill.''

"I wish I could say something," she said, "to make you realize the mistake you are making. I curse all those titles of yours, Paul, and the fact that Papa was foolish enough to stand under that tree during a thunderstorm before he could inherit more than one of them. And I wish Grandfather had not died before you could even reach your majority. He might have lived until he was at least seventy. You were too young at seventeen to take on all the responsibilities of the dukedom. Paul, dear, you have never had a chance to live.''

He crossed the room to her, smiling, and leaned across her bulk to kiss her cheek. "Go and find some beggar in the streets—they are not hard to find, Angie—and ask him if a man

who owns five large estates, not to mention other, lesser
holdings, and who draws in forty thousand a year from rents
alone, and those least significant title would earn him a place
of prominence in the *ton*, is a man who has never had a chance
to live.''

"Oh,'' she said, "you do not understand what I mean, do
you? And you are going to do it, are you not? You are going
to marry that dreadfully dull girl and live the rest of your life
in dreary propriety.''

"I might reject your adjectives,'' he said. "But yes, Angie,
I am going to do it, as you put it. And now. I never put off
what must be done, you know, for then it might never get done
and I would have neglected a duty. Shall I give you my arm
and take you back to Mama?''

"No,'' she said with a sigh. "I think that commotion in the
hallway must be Adrian arriving to take me home. I shall go
and cry on his shoulder and he will tell me as he always does
not to try to interfere in my family's affairs. For it is a hopeless
task. You and Mama and Grandpapa—all of you bound and
determined to do what ought to be done. Well, I am thankful
that Adrian found me when he did.''

"And so am I,'' he said with a smile. "Don't be cross with
me, Angie.''

"Well, I am cross,'' she said. "I love you, and I want you
to be happy.''

"Don't be cross,'' he said again.

She paused in the act of leaving the room and walked back
to his side to kiss his cheek before laying her own against it.

"He is the Duke of Mitford,'' the Earl of Rutland repeated
for surely the dozenth time, "and the Earl of Newman, and
a half dozen other things. And estates strewn all over the
kingdom. And forty thousand a year. You will be made. Our
own little Jo, a duchess. My own darling little puss.'' He opened
his arms and enfolded his granddaughter in them, also for the
dozenth time.

"Yes, Grandpapa,'' the Honorable Miss Josephine Middleton
said meekly. "I am much obliged to you for arranging it.''

He looked down at her and beamed with goodwill. "Did you
think your grandpapa would not have an eye to your future?''

he said. "And I will do as well for Sukey and Penny and Gussie when it comes their turn, see if I don't. Though I cannot promise them each a duke, I suppose. But I could not settle for less than that for my little puss, now could I?"

"You are very kind, Grandpapa," she said.

From her grandfather's sitting room Josephine was summoned directly to her father's study. He was standing before the desk waiting for her, a younger version of Grandpapa, like a great big smiling, cuddly bear.

He opened his arms to her. "Well, half-pint," he said, "come and be hugged."

Josephine went obediently and was hugged.

"Grandpapa had to be the one to tell you," he said. "And I could not deny him the pleasure since it was he who arranged it all. So my little girl is going to be a duchess and too grand a lady to pass the time of day with her papa, I doubt not." He laughed heartily and tweaked her nose. "What do you have to say, girl?"

"It is what you really want for me, Papa?" she asked, lifting her face to his.

He bent his head and dealt her a smacking kiss to the cheek. "It is a dream come true, half-pint," he said. "You know I have never wanted to take you to London to be ogled by all the fops and dandies who have nothing better to do with their time than eye the ladies. But it is time you had a husband. You are twenty years old already, even though you still seem like Papa's very little girl. I have been concerned about it."

"You did not need to be," she said. "I have been happy at home with you and the others."

"And now you are to be happy for the rest of your life, Jo," he said, beaming happily down at her. "A duchess. My half-pint with forty thousand a year. Are you happy, girl? Tell your papa how happy you are."

"Yes," she said. "It was very kind of Grandpapa to think of me, was it not, Papa, when he met his friend Lord Ainsbury in Bath?"

"He loves you," he said. "As much as I do, though I cannot imagine it can be quite, quite as much."

"Yes, Papa," she said, hugging him. "Thank you, Papa."

And finally she was free to run up to the old schoolroom,

which was no longer a schoolroom since Gussie, the youngest, was now fourteen. But that was where they spent most of their time indoors, Josephine and her brother and three sisters.

The Honorable Bartholomew Middleton looked up from his book and swung the leg that he had draped over one arm of his chair. "Well, Jo," he said, "what was it this time? Left the gate of the pasture open again, did you, and let out all the cows?"

"No," she said, standing so still inside the door that she caught the attention even of her sisters, who had been engrossed in a conversation that had them all for once in perfect agreement. Mr. Porterhouse, who was visiting the Winthrops, was without a doubt the most handsome gentleman on the face of the earth. "Grandpapa has found me a husband and Papa has approved his choice and he is to come within the week to pay his addresses to me."

Bartholomew laughed while Susanna jumped to her feet and Penelope and Augusta gaped.

"Not Phipps?" Bartholomew said. "Oh, poor Jo."

"Not Mr. Porterhouse?" Susanna asked. "Oh, no, Jo."

"The Duke of Mitford?" Josephine said, "whoever he may be."

"Mitford?" Bartholomew frowned. "Can't say I met him when I was in London, Jo."

"The *Duke* of Mitford," Susanna said. "A duke, Jo? A real duke? Are you sure?"

Josephine swallowed. "He is also the Earl of Newman," she said. "And I think a few other things, too. And he is as rich as Croesus."

"Oh, Jo," Sussanna said, her eyes glowing, "how very wonderful for you. How happy I am for you."

Bartholomew chuckled and threw his book at the windowseat close by his chair. "That's famous," he said. "Our Jo a duchess. We had better hope that there are no coronations and no royal weddings and such for the next fifty years or so. Jo would doubtless trip over her ermine robe and pitch her coronet at the feet of the king or the bride or whoever."

"Oh, Bart," Josephine cried, picking up a cushion, which was the best weapon she could lay hands on at that precise moment, and hurling it across the room at him. It missed him by three feet. "Do stop cackling in such an imbecilic way. This is serious!"

"Don't tell me you are on your dignity already," he said. "You'll never keep it up, Jo. Poor Mitford, whoever he might be." He resumed his laughter.

"Oh, Jo," Augusta said, her eyes wide enough to pop from their sockets, "do you suppose he will buy us all gifts when he marries you?"

"Do watch your manners, Gussie," Penelope said. "Grand-papa always says it is vulgar to talk of money."

"But it was Jo who mentioned a fortune," an injured Augusta said.

"Yes," Josephine said gloomily, "and it was Grandpapa who told me. Or was it Papa? I can't remember. They were both so bubbling with happiness. Oh, Bart, what am I to do?"

"Find a tree to swing from in delight at your good fortune, I imagine," her brother said, rising from his chair and stretching. "Just do it far enough from the house so that Grandpapa does not see, Jo, there's a good girl, or we will all be subjected to a lecture on propriety at dinner."

"But what am I to *do*?" Josephine said, her voice taking on a note of hysteria that had her brother pausing in mid-stretch. "I can't marry this duke."

"Can't marry him?" Susanna said. "Can't marry a duke, Jo? But why not?"

"A duke!" Josephine said. "A duke, Sukey. Can you honestly see me marrying a duke? He is bound to be stuffy and toplofty and anything else you may care to name. I hate the very thought of him. I can't marry a duke."

"But, Jo," Susanna said, "you don't know those things about him, do you? Perhaps he is quite the opposite. Perhaps he will be the gentleman of your dreams. Would it not be wise at least to see him before judging?"

Augusta's face lit up. "If you don't want him, Jo," she said, "perhaps I could have him instead. Perhaps he would wait two years for me."

Her brother threw back his head and guffawed with merriment.

"Oh, very sorry, your grace," he said in a tolerable imitation of their father's best hearty social manner, "but Josephine will not have you because you are stuffy and toplofty. You will not mind having Augusta instead, will you? She is fourteen, you know, and will be quite ready for marriage when she is sixteen.''

Penelope glared at Augusta.

''Well,'' Josephine said, thoroughly aggrieved, ''it is very unkind of you to make a joke of it, I must say, Bart, and foolish of you to think of something so nonsensical, Gussie, when I am in such distress. And you need not stand there looking so disapproving, Penny.''

''All you have to do, Jo,'' Penelope said with the greatest good sense, ''is tell Papa immediately that you do not want the duke. If you tell him without delay, he will probably be able to stop his grace from even leaving home, and no harm will be done. I am sure Papa will understand that you would prefer to live out your life as an old maid.''

''I don't want to be an old maid,'' Josephine said crossly. ''I just don't want to be a duchess. But how can I tell Papa or Grandpapa that? They are both so very pleased for me. I could not possibly disappoint them.''

''You have a simple choice, Jo,'' Bartholomew said, completing the stretch that had been interrupted a few moments before. ''Either you disappoint Papa and Grandpapa, or you live out your life as the Duchess of Mitland.''

''Mit*ford*,'' Josephine said, correcting him. ''The Duchess of Mitford. Oh, goodness gracious me, I couldn't possibly. I would sooner die.''

It was a sentiment that she felt even more strongly later that evening after talking to Mr. Porterhouse at the Winthrops'. Mr. Porterhouse was a distant cousin of the Winthrops, who lived most of his life in London, and who was so fashionable a gentleman that he looked rather like someone from a different universe. He was also the most handsome gentleman ever to have set foot in the neighborhood, the proverbial tall, dark, and handsome paragon of manhood.

He had favored Josephine from the moment of his arrival the week before, sitting by her at various assemblies, turning the pages of her music when she played the spinet, taking her on his arm during walks. Susanna was disapproving.

''I don't like him, Jo,'' she had said more than once. ''I don't trust a gentleman who smiles quite so much. Do have a care."

But Josephine had laughed at her. "I like him," she had said. "But you need not fear having him as a brother-in-law, Sukey. I cannot find him attractive. He makes me feel like a veritable child. I don't reach even near to his shoulder."

"Well, he cannot help being so tall," Susanna had said sensibly.

"And I cannot help being so very small," Josephine had said. "But he is and I am, and I cannot feel any attraction to him."

"I am glad of it, then," Susanna had said, much relieved. "For he does single you out for marked attention, Jo. And I know you do not always think wisely before you act. I would not have you fall prey to his charms."

"Besides," Bart had said to Josephine's indignation, "the man is only after Jo's dowry. It's as plain as the nose on your face. Why else would he be rusticating except to find himself a rich and innocent bride?"

"Perhaps to visit his cousins," Josephine had said with as much dignity as she could inject into her voice.

She could not help liking Mr. Porterhouse even if she could not sigh over him. He was very attentive and very kind, and he smiled a great deal. And he knew the Duke of Mitford.

Penelope had mentioned the duke earlier in the evening.

"So you are to marry Mitford," he said, when the two of them were talking late in the evening beyond the earshot of everyone else. "I am cut to the heart."

"How foolish!" Josephine said with no trace of flirtatiousness in her manner. "Yes, it seems that I am to marry him, though it was very wrong of Penny to mention it since he has not paid his addresses yet."

"You do not sound very pleased, ma'am," he said. "Do you know him?"

"No," she said. "And neither does Grandpapa nor Papa, nor anyone else for that matter. But he must be eligible, you see, because he is a duke, and because his grandfather and mine have been friends all their lives."

He sighed.

"Do you know him?" she asked as an afterthought.

"I am afraid so," he said.

He did not want to say more, but Josephine had not had a brother all her life without learning how to wheedle out reluctant information.

"He is excessively handsome," he said. "Blond and blue-eyed, you know. Quite like a Greek god."

Josephine gulped. "And tall?" she asked.

Mr. Porterhouse looked measuringly at the diminutive lady seated beside him. "About my height," he said, "or taller. I am afraid he is very well aware of his looks. He is a great favorite with the ladies."

"Of course," Josephine echoed. "He is very rich, is he not?"

"And squanders his money," he said. He hesitated. "On women, mostly." He took her hand suddenly, the hand that would not be seen by anyone else in the room. "I am so very sorry for you, ma'am. It is a heavy cross you will have to bear. But what am I saying?" He smiled with warm sympathy into her wide eyes. "Of course, he has never been married. When he is, and to you, then of course he will change. Of course he will." He squeezed her hand reassuringly and relinquished his hold on it.

Josephine was summoned the next moment to play a game of spillikins with Augusta and Henrietta Winthrop.

Over the next few days Josephine came to see—with the aid of a kind and sympathetic Mr. Porterhouse—that there was only one solution to her problem. She could certainly not face either Papa or Grandpapa with her reluctance to marry the horrid Duke of Mitford, and Bart was no use at all as an elder brother. Her sisters were all too young. There was only one person in the world who could advise her and help her express her reluctance.

Only one person. And she lived five and twenty miles away. But Aunt Winifred would know what to do. She had herself defied Grandpapa and chosen her own husband. Aunt Winifred would help her. There could be no delaying, of course. The Duke of Mitford might arrive any day and then there would be no way of escaping for what remained of her lifetime.

Mr. Porterhouse was kind enough—he was a very kind gentleman—to offer to escort her to her aunt's house. It was not quite proper to accept, although the journey could be made in one day, and it was rather cowardly to run away from a home where the only complaint she had was that she was smothered in love.

She hesitated, thanked Mr. Porterhouse, told him that he was too kind in saying that he and his carriage were at her disposal at a moment's notice but that she would have no need to inconvenience him, dithered, and finally took fright on the day when the duke's valet and a mountain of baggage arrived.

The valet was so grand that at first everyone mistook him for the duke and flew into a panic. It was a mistake that was quickly put right, and everyone relaxed again when they knew that the duke himself would not arrive for two more days.

Everyone except Josephine, that was. Gracious goodness, if the valet looked and behaved like that, and if all those possessions were merely what his grace traveled with, whatever was she to expect of the man himself?

Her nerve fully broke the day before the duke was to arrive and just after a visit from the younger Winthrops, when she walked alone on the terrace for ten minutes with Mr. Porterhouse. Before luncheon, while everyone was still busy about the house, she stole away to a prearranged rendezvous with Mr. Porterhouse, leaving behind her the message that she would be taking luncheon at the Winthrops', and a note to be delivered later in the day to say that she had gone to Aunt Winifred's.

It was just very unfortunate that Mr. Porterhouse's carriage broke down ten miles from her aunt's. Something to do with the axle, Mr. Porterhouse explained vaguely. He was very apologetic as he settled her into a room at the Crown and Anchor Inn on the Great North Road.

Josephine was frantic. She could imagine just what Papa would say to her if he were there now. And Grandpapa. And Bart. They would say that as usual she had acted without a moment's forethought. And without a thought to ladylike propriety.

But she *had* thought. Very carefully. For several days. She did not want to marry the Duke of Mitford. Aunt Winifred would help her break the news to Papa. It had been a very sensible idea. It was not her fault that the carriage had broken down at such an inauspicious moment.

Poor Mr. Porterhouse. He had been very apologetic about the whole thing.

2

The Duke of Mitford was lying on his bed at the Crown and Anchor Inn wondering if he should do something exciting, like undressing and going to bed. He had come upstairs an hour before, when it had become obvious that the taproom was the local gathering place for a large and somewhat rowdy clientele. He had not felt comfortable in such company.

His coat, with his greatcoat, had been thrown over the foot of the bed. His hands were clasped behind his head. His feet were crossed at the ankles. He had for several minutes past been watching his feet in their white stockings, wiggling his toes to make the occupation more interesting. But his eyes had moved upward and his attention had been caught by a crack in the ceiling, one that extended all the way across one corner of the room.

Perhaps the ceiling was about to collapse on him, he thought, yawning until his jaws cracked. This journey was really not turning into much of an adventure after all. Though why he should have thought that after twenty-eight years of very circumspect living he would be able to find adventure merely by leaving home alone and incognito, he did not know.

He supposed he was incredibly naive. Indeed, he knew it for a fact.

Since the age of six, when he had been precipitated into the title of Earl of Newman by a thunderstorm, he had been groomed for the life of privilege and responsibility that was ahead of him at the time, but that had been his now for the past eleven years. And he had always been an obedient pupil. He had almost never stepped out of line.

He would not necessarily say he had been a willing pupil. The spirit of rebellion that he saw breaking loose in almost every lad who had ever been his companion burned just as brightly in him. But he had never allowed himself to rebel or to do anything that would hurt his mother or in any way tarnish all the illustrious names he bore.

The closest he had come to being as other men were, he supposed, was in making Eveline Cross his mistress four years before. But even Eveline had been a perfectly respectable widow of good *ton*, and their three-year affair—she had broken it off the year before when she had finally admitted to herself that the Duke of Mitford was not likely to do anything as improper as marrying his mistress—had been conducted so discreetly that it was doubtful many people even knew about it.

She was the one and only woman he had ever been intimate with.

Mitford sighed and returned his attention to his feet. He tried to make his big toes stand at right angles to his feet. The left one could achieve only an eighty-degree angle. He tried harder. If he cheated and dug his heel into the mattress, he could do it. Perfect symmetry with both toes.

It seemed that all the world had company and was enjoying it except him. The noise level downstairs was rising in proportion to the amount of ale that must have been imbibed by now. And the female in the next room was talking in a loud, excited voice to her companion. He could not quite catch her words. Not that he would want to eavesdrop anyway, of course.

It was amazing really that he had any friends at all. But he did, even though he knew that most of them saw him as a thoroughly dull dog. Indeed, they were not shy about telling him so. He did not gamble or drink to excess or participate in any of the wild wagers of the clubs or squander money or flirt with the ladies or whore with those females who were not ladies. Such activities were unbecoming to his position in life.

Sometimes, he thought with a twinge of guilt, he felt sick of being a duke—everyone and his dog bowing and scraping to his great superiority; everyone and his cat hanging onto every word that issued from his mouth and roaring with amusement at every suggestion of wit; every mama in the kingdom who happened to have a marriageable daughter between the ages of fifteen and thirty-five gazing at him with tense hope and blatant admiration; all those daughters sighing collective hurricanes and whipping up collective tornadoes with fluttering eyelashes.

Yes, he was sick of being a duke.

He could hear now from the inflection of her voice that the female in the next room was displeased about something. Her poor companion, whoever he or she might be, was being given an earful of wrath. Perhaps after all there was something to be said for being alone.

Except that he would not be alone for long. He was within one day of meeting his future wife. A young lady he had never set eyes on and about whom he knew nothing except her name and the fact that she was the granddaughter of one of his maternal grandfather's friends.

He really did not want to be going there. He really did not want to be getting married, especially to a complete stranger. He did not want to be setting up his nursery yet. He wanted to live a little, as Angie had put it to him. He would have liked just a little adventure in his life before he settled finally into the life he had been brought up to.

What he ought to have done, he realized now when it was altogether too late, was tell Grandpapa that he would meet the girl somewhere—at some carefully organized house party, perhaps—before deciding whether to offer for her. But he had not done so, and so there was no point in teasing his mind with belated wisdom.

That female's voice had moved up a notch in pitch. And it was a poor male who was at the receiving end of the tirade. He had just laughed—unwisely, in Mitford's judgment. The female would not like that.

The duke chuckled without amusement at his big toes. He supposed that his final and very overdue grasp at adventure and independence had been a rather pathetic one. He had decided to make the journey into Northamptonshire a slow one and a lone one. Rather than travel with his valet and his baggage and all the pomp that a ducal journey always involved, he had decided quite on the spur of the moment to send Henry on half a day ahead of himself and to make his own journey by curricle, unaccompanied. And he had dropped those nine cumbersome titles, including the ducal one, and kept only the one he had been born with.

He was traveling as Mr. Paul Villiers.

The Duke of Mitford jumped suddenly and sat bolt upright

on the edge of his bed. A great crashing and smashing had happened in the adjoining room. The pitcher, at a guess, had been hurled with great force against the wall that adjoined his room and smashed in the process. He wondered irrelevantly if it had been filled with water. It had apparently missed that poor unfortunate male's head or the sound would have been dulled.

He had made one interesting discovery, anyway. Mr. Paul Villiers was a far less impressive gentleman than the Duke of Mitford. He had not been treated with utter contempt on his journey. He was, after all, a gentleman and he had money. But he had been treated with the next best thing. There was this room, for example, in which he was fated to spend the night. Whoever had had the idea of covering the walls with wallpaper of such a bilious green? He was quite sure that it must be the smallest and shabbiest room in the inn. Indeed, it could not be much smaller without the bed filling the whole of it.

As the Duke of Mitford he would doubtless have left the inn quite unaware that there was such a chamber within its walls.

Some adventure indeed! The duke smiled ruefully and wiggled his toes again on the floor.

Was he really of so little worth without his titles? It was a sobering thought. His appearance was unimposing, of course. He was not a tall man—and that, he admitted, was a euphemistic way of saying that he was short. And he was slight in build, though years of careful training and exercise had developed that body to its fullest potential. He was not handsome. His hair was brown and curled all over the place, to the despair of every valet he had ever employed. His features were arranged on his face in the most ordinary and unimaginative way. His eyes were gray—just gray, without any interesting adjectives to add to the color name. He was, in fact and altogether, a very ordinary man.

And a dull one too. His friends were right, he thought with a sigh. A dull and ordinary man about to pay his addresses to a dull and ordinary woman. And they would live a dull and ordinary and quite exemplary life for ever after.

Sometimes he could almost envy that beggar in the gutter he had advised Angie to seek.

"I shall scream!" the female from the next room shrieked.

"If you do not leave this instant, sir, I shall scream the roof down."

The walls between rooms were not by any means soundproof.

The male was unwise enough to laugh again. He must be either very young or very silly in the head. Or very brawny.

The noise from the taproom belowstairs was becoming somewhat deafening too. Someone down there must be very witty if the great gusts of laughter were anything to judge by. And someone was singing, though it would be a kindness to everyone in the inn if someone else would just hint to him that he was slightly off-key.

"You will not ravish me!" the female shrieked through his wall. Her voice was a trifle thinner than it had been. "If you try, sir, I shall put my knee where it most hurts."

The Duke of Mitford was on his feet even as the man laughed again. Did the female not have a brain in her head, giving him fair warning like that? And what kind of a female was she to know about such things? But were matters that serious? Was it possible that it was not a simple domestic quarrel he had been listening to?

"Don't!" The female's voice was shaking. There were other words he could not catch. "Stop it! Oh, help, someone. Mmmmm!"

After shooting out through his own door, Mitford tried the handle of the door next to his own, but of course it was locked. The corridor was narrow. He could not take a great run at the door. And doubtless even if he could, he would only shatter his shoulder for his pains. But there was a female in distress inside that room. A voluble and scatter-brained female, it was true, but one in dire straits, nevertheless.

He took his run, hurled his shoulder against the upper panel of the door, and found himself hurtling through it and colliding with a very large and solid object on the other side.

It was a conquest not to be boasted of afterward. Mitford admitted that much to himself in all fairness. The man had been taken totally by surprise. The duke had not even knocked to warn the occupants of the room that there was a concerned citizen outside. There was only a flashing impression of a tall, muscular gentleman with a bewildered expression and a hanging jaw.

And then the duke's fist connected with that jaw, shutting it with a satisfying crunching of teeth. The gentleman swayed on his feet while his assailant's other fist bruised itself against his ribs. Doubtless the gentleman would have recovered and given a good account of himself if the female had not recovered far faster and dealt him a finishing blow to the back of the head with the bowl that no longer had a pitcher to stand up inside it.

The gentleman's eyes rolled in his head and he toppled sideways, hitting the bed and sliding off it to the floor.

Josephine was feeling frantic. It was late in the day already and the carriage was broken. And there were still ten miles to go. And why had Mr. Porterhouse secured her a bedchamber instead of just a private parlor? Was he expecting that they would have to spend the night at the inn?

Oh, dear, what a coil she was in if that happened. Papa would not like it at all. Neither would Aunt Winifred. Or Grandpapa. She had got herself into some scrapes during her twenty years—indeed, she had got herself into a great many scrapes—but none quite as nasty as this one. Why in heaven's name had she not at least brought a maid with her?

The taproom had been full and rather noisy when she came in. It grew noisier as she paced her room, with the result that she was reluctant to go downstairs to investigate the long delay. But it was growing dusk outside, she saw every time her steps took her past the window—every ten seconds, that was.

When there was a knock at the door, she threw it open and only just restrained herself from hurling herself into Mr. Porterhouse's arms, so great was her relief. But his face was as serious as could be, and he stepped inside the room and closed the door behind his back and set her valise against the wall.

"I am afraid the carriage will not be ready for travel until tomorrow, Miss Middleton," he said. "I am most awfully sorry. I feel quite dreadful."

"You feel dreadful!" Josephine could feel only panic. "But what are you going to do about it, sir? There must be another carriage for hire."

"There is not," he said. "And even if there were, I would be loath to endanger your life on dark roads. No, I am very much afraid, ma'am, that we must spend the night here."

"But Papa will kill me!" she said, her squeak sounding very undignified to her own ears. "And Aunt Winifred will turn me off. And Grandpapa will lecture me for a week."

"But perhaps it is for the best after all," he said. "Even if you go to your aunt's, the chances are that you will eventually be forced to marry the lecherous Duke of Mitford. My heart bleeds for you at the very thought, ma'am. I have a better idea."

Hope stilled Josphine.

"You must marry me instead," Mr. Porterhouse said. "You must know I have a regard for you, ma'am. It is the dearest wish of my heart to rescue you from a bleak future."

"Oh, nonsense," Jospehine said, her first panic subsiding. "That is the silliest notion I ever heard. We will just have to be on our way as early as possible in the morning, that is all, and hope that everyone's anger will cool within the next month or so. I suppose it is not the end of the world."

"We are on the road north," he said, possessing himself somehow of her hands. "Come with me to Gretna Green, ma'am. There we may marry and you will be safe both from your lecherous suitor and from the wrath of your family. They will have no more power over you once you are my wife."

"You are serious!" she said in some surprise. "You are indeed a very kind gentleman, but there is no need whatsoever to make such a sacrifice, I do assure you. My papa is not a monster."

"But your reputation will be in ruins after tonight," he said. "Do you not realize that? You *must* marry me. Would it not be better to do so before you have to face your father?"

"Nonsense!" Josephine snatched her hands from his grasp. "We will be spending but one night in the same inn. Papa will understand, though he will scold me for my thoughtlessness and my cowardice in not being able to talk to him instead of fleeing. If you will return to your own room now, sir, I shall settle for the night and be ready to start for my aunt's at the crack of dawn."

"But the inn is full," he said. "I thought you realized that. I took the very last room, ma'am. I am afraid we must share it."

"Share it?" Josephine stared blankly at him for a moment until incredulity and indignation set her tongue to wagging.

Share a bedchamber at an inn with a single gentleman and one whom she scarcely knew? Who did he think she was? Did he think she knew nothing at all about how to go on?

She felt only increased wrath rather than alarm at first when Mr. Porterhouse turned, locked the door, and pocketed the key. Increased wrath and increased eloquence.

And then he laughed.

And moved toward her.

"Perhaps by tomorrow morning, my sweet," he said, "there will be no doubt left in your mind that your only course of action is to elope with me."

Josephine stood her ground. "Your sweet?" she said. "And tell me I have just misunderstood your words. Tell me."

"Little firebrand," he said. "I am glad you have chosen fire rather than water. I dislike vaporish females. Come, sweet, admit that I will be a better bargain than the Duke of Mitford. He is what awaits you if you return home or arrive at your aunt's tomorrow, you know."

Josephine picked up the pitcher of water from the washstand beside her and hurled it at his head. But her aim had never been good. The pitcher missed him by a lamentable margin and dashed its contents against the wall before smashing into smithereens.

Mr. Porterhouse smiled. "Oh, come now," he said, "there is no need for all this drama, is there? You have trusted me for a week. Will you not trust me now? I am offering you the haven of my name and protection. You need not be afraid of me."

Josephine did the most unladylike thing she had ever done. She took aim and spat.

Mr. Porterhouse's smile faded and he took a step forward.

For the first time, Josephine realized her danger. He must be at least twice her size and it was very obvious from the glint in his eye what was on his mind. And the door—the locked door, to which the key was in his pocket—was on the other side of him.

For very dignity's sake she tried to be calm. "I shall scream!" she shrieked. "If you do not leave this instant, sir, I shall scream the roof down."

Mr. Porterhouse took one step closer—there were no more steps to take without walking right over her—and laughed. And he took her upper arms in his powerful hands.

"You will not ravish me!" she shrieked, throwing back her head in defiance. And because it was no longer the time for feminine dignity, she added the most deadly threat of all. "If you try, sir, I shall put my knee where it most hurts."

"Ah, sweet," he said, his eyes dancing with merriment, "naughty, naughty." And his head came down and two wet lips covered her own.

Josephine twisted her head to one side and grimaced. "Don't!" she said. But those lips were at her throat and at her chin. "Stop it! Oh help, someone." His lips were at hers again and one large hand held her head steady. "Mmmmmm!"

She was suffocating. She was straddling one of his legs and off balance so that it was impossible to carry out her earlier threat. And she would surely vomit all over him if he did not stop.

And then there was a great crash and a great deal of commotion and she recovered herself in time to see a great Hercules of a man, eyes burning, hair flying, and fists flashing, and Mr. Porterhouse was tottering on his feet. Josephine picked up the china bowl by the sheer instinct for survival and brought it down on his head.

She watched him topple to the bed and off it to the floor, where he lay still. And she was aware too of the sounds of shattering china and of raucous merriment from belowstairs.

"If you are planning to use your knee on an attacker," the Duke of Mitford said to a flushed, disheveled, and diminutive female, "it is the most cork-brained thing I ever heard of, ma'am, to tell him so. The whole effectiveness of the weapon depends upon the element of surprise."

"You are doubtless right, sir," Josephine said, looking down with some distaste at her fallen foe. "Unfortunately, one does not think quite logically when one is about to be ravished. I shall try to remember next time."

"Next time?" he said, looking severely down at her torn dress, out of which her bosom was perilously close to falling altogether. Was she a barmaid whose price the gentleman had been unwilling to pay? She did not look or speak like a barmaid. "Do you make a habit of this, then, ma'am?"

"Oh, no," she said. "It was just a manner of speaking. Please, what are we going to do with him?"

"Is he your husband?" he asked.

"Oh, no," she said. "He is just Mr. Porterhouse, who was kind enough to offer to accompany me to my Aunt Ermingford's. Except that I realize now he was not being kind at all and had no intention whatsoever of taking me to my aunt's. He wanted to trick me into marriage so that he might have my dowry. He did not say as much, but why else would he want to marry me?"

Mitford could think of a few reasons, a couple of them fair to bursting out the front of her torn dress. He did not say as much, but leaned over the insensible Mr. Porterhouse, took him by the lapels of his coat, and lifted his head and shoulders from the floor.

"He is not dead," he said. "A pity."

"He was so kind," she said regretfully. "And such a gentleman."

"And your mama and papa entrusted you to his care?" the duke asked, removing one of his hands from a lapel in order to slap gently at the unconscious cheeks. He remembered that there was no water left in the room with which to revive the gentleman. He could see it in a dark patch down the wallpaper of the wall adjoining his own.

Suddenly everyone in the taproom below was singing, all off-key.

"Oh, no," she said. "I am running away. Only to my aunt's, you understand. But she is to help me deal with Papa and Grandpapa. She will take my part, I do not doubt."

Mr. Porterhouse groaned and opened his eyes. He stared vacantly at the ceiling. The duke wondered if there was a crack up there, as there was in his room.

He took a firm grip of the lapels again. "Let me help you up, my friend," he said grimly, and kept his hold even when the other climbed slowly and obediently to his feet and the duke's hands were somewhat above the level of his own shoulders. "Does he have any baggage, ma'am?"

"No," she said. "I would not have allowed him in here with a bag, you may be sure."

"Take yourself out of this chamber, then," Mitford said to his half-conscious adversary, "and out of this inn. If I find you anywhere in the vicinity in fifteen minutes' time, I shall pound you into unconsciousness again and you will wake up to find yourself toothless. Do you understand me?"

"Insolent puppy!" the gentleman said with slurred defiance.

"I am not sure he can walk alone," Jospehine said, a note of interest in her voice.

"Then we will crawl," the duke said, not removing his eyes from the pale and handsome face above his own. "He has fifteen minutes in which to do it. Or perhaps fourteen."

"Insolent puppy," the man said again before doubling up in order to retch. The duke swiftly released his hold on the man's lapels. "I shall remember you for this."

"I'm sure you will," Mitford said. "On your way, my friend."

Josephine wrinkled her nose after the man had staggered out. "He might at least have used the chamber pot," she said in disgust. "I shall have to send for a maid to clean up."

"Where does your aunt live?" Mitford asked the girl, ignoring the smell. "And where does your father live? I shall do myself the honor of conveying you to one place or the other tomorrow."

"Oh, would you?" she said, brightening. "I really am stranded here without your help, aren't I? I should have taken a maid and one of Grandpapa's carriages instead of accepting Mr. Porterhouse's kind offer. But I did not know at the time, of course, that it was not really a kind offer at all. My Aunt Ermingford lives ten miles away from here and Papa fifteen. You had better take me to my aunt's, sir. Partly because she is closer and I will be less beholden to you, and partly because Papa would scold and Grandpapa would scold and I would never hear the end of it if I went home."

"And so they should scold, too," the duke said, clasping his hands behind his back and thinking that if she were his daughter, he would take her over his knee and wallop her until his hand was too swollen to allow one more stroke.

"Well, yes." She flashed him a smile and pushed one truant

dark blond curl behind her ear—she would be better occupied tucking her bosom more firmly back inside her dress, he thought. "But he did seem a very kind gentleman, you know, and we were to make the journey all in one day. It was just unfortunate that there was trouble with his carriage."

"It is fortunate that the trouble has now been put suddenly right," the duke said dryly, rocking back on his heels. "That is doubtless it leaving the innyard now."

"Oh," she said, "yes. I suppose it was not broken after all, was it? I did not think of that. But you will take me to my aunt's, sir? How kind of you."

Mitford fixed her with a severe eye. "You had better hope that I do not prove to be quite as kind as Mr. Porterhouse," he said.

"Oh," she said, and laughed. "I can tell that you are not like him. He is so tall and handsome that I daresay he has learned to be selfish and to think a lot of himself. You are not at all like him, sir."

The duke rocked back on his heels again. "I think on the whole it would be as well to return you to your father's house," he said.

"Oh, no." She finally looked down at herself, flushed, and tucked herself back inside her torn garment as best she could. "I won't go back home, sir. Not by any persuasion. Even if it means running away to London and becoming a scullery maid. If I go back home, Papa and Grandpapa will make me marry the Duke of Mitford."

The Duke of Mitford rocked once more. "Ah," he said.

"Any fate would be better than that," she said.

3

"Sometimes," the Viscount Cheamley said to his father, looking up from the note in his hand, "I think perhaps I should have used my hand on that girl when she was growing up. What do you think?"

"I can't see it would have done any good," Lord Rutland said. "Jo is just a high-spirited young girl. She means no harm, and no harm ever comes of her mischief. What does it say?" He nodded toward the note.

The viscount looked down and read it again, as if he could not believe the evidence of his own eyes the first time. "The dratted girl has ridden over to Winnie's," he said. "Just took it into her head that it was time for a visit, and went."

"I told you she was not at the Winthrops', Papa," Penelope said. "When Sukey and I went to call on Anna, both she and Henrietta were in the mopes because Mr. Porterhouse took his leave this morning. But Jo was not there."

"Winnie's is twenty-five miles away," the viscount said with a frown. "What can have possessed the girl? It is a hard day's ride. She will be fortunate to get there before nightfall."

The earl shook his head. "Jo, Jo," he said. "Will she never realize that she is full grown now and must not go jauntering about on her own? Especially not a young lady in her position. I will have to explain to her when she comes home again. The little puss! She took a groom with her, I hope?"

His son was still frowning. "I'll lay a wager she did not," he said. "The last time she rode to Winnie's was four years ago, and that time I told her I would lay my hand to her if she ever did it again. Do you think she remembers? That time, of course, she had us all frantic because she did not think to leave a note or a message of any sort. I don't like to remember that night."

32

"Papa!" Susanna's worried voice broke in on his thoughts. "The Duke of Mitford is arriving tomorrow."

The viscount's jaw dropped while the earl passed a hand over his bald head.

"Heaven help us," Lord Cheamley said slopping his forehead with Jospehine's note. "And so he is, child. Whatever could Jo have been thinking of? Is she planning to ride back here tomorrow and arrive dusty and panting to meet her bridegroom? Jo, Jo."

Bartholomew, who was lolling in a chair, his leg thrown over one arm as usual, appeared to be enjoying the scene. "Do you want me to go and fetch her, Papa?" he asked.

"Eh? What's that?" his father asked, crumpling the note in his hand.

"I could be there before midnight if I left at once," Bartholomew said.

"Break your neck more like," his grandfather said.

The viscount was tapping a knuckle against his teeth. "No," he said. "I must go—with the carriage and with some respectable clothes for Jo to wear. If I leave now, I can get most of the way there before nightfall. I can complete the journey at dawn and be on the way back with Jo before the middle of the morning."

"Scold her gently," the earl said. "You don't want her getting back here all upset."

"I'll set her ears to ringing with what I have to say," the viscount said, looking unusually fierce. "The dratted girl. It is likely his grace will be here before our return. You will all have to hold him off with the story of how Jo insisted on accompanying me visiting the sick."

Bartholomew chuckled and watched his foot swinging.

"Perhaps I'll be able to reach the main road to London tonight," the viscount said. "That's only ten miles from Winnie's. There is a fairly decent inn there. What's it called? The Crown?"

"Crown and Anchor," Bartholomew said.

The viscount nodded. "Sukey," he said, "find a maid who can pick out a decent dress for Jo and all the trappings, there's a good girl. A dress fit for meeting her bridegroom in. Bart, send to the stables and have the traveling carriage ready and before the doors here within the half hour. Drat the girl. I'll lift my hand to her yet."

"Do you think Jo forgot that the duke is expected tomorrow?" Augusta asked her older sister.

Penelope looked at her in some scorn. "I think Jo decided to visit Aunt Winifred just *because* the duke is expected," she said. "I don't know what she wants unless it is to be an old maid. She cannot do much better than a duke, now, can she?"

"But if it were my choice," Augusta said, "I would prefer to marry someone like Mr. Porterhouse, even if he is just a mister. He is so very handsome, Penny. I do wish he had not gone away already. It will be dull visiting the Winthrops now that he has gone."

"I am sure he would not know you if he passed you on an empty street, Gussie," Penelope said. "You are only fourteen years old, after all. Gentlemen like Mr. Porterhouse have an eye for older ladies, and prettier ones."

"Yes, like Jo," her sister said with a sigh. "But perhaps his grace will be handsome too, Penny."

They waved the traveling carriage and their father on the way half an hour later. Poor Papa would miss his dinner, Augusta remarked to Susanna.

"Well," the Duke of Mitford said to the dull, demure country mouse his grandfather had chosen as his bride, "it would never do to be forced into an unwelcome marriage. You have any objection to the Duke of Mitford?"

"More than one," she said, looking up at him with flushed cheeks and large gray eyes. "He is too handsome for his own good; he has all the arrogance one would expect of a man of his position and wealth and looks; and he is a libertine," She counted the points off on her fingers. "I hate him."

The duke pursed his lips and raised his eyebrows. "I take it you have met the gentleman?" he asked.

"No," she said, "and I have no wish to. But I have heard quite enough about him. You should just know the aristocracy as I know them, sir—always more concerned for their own consequences than anything else. Being the daughter of a viscount and the granddaughter of an earl has taught me a great deal. I can just imagine what being the wife of a duke would be like, especially the wife of the Duke of Mitford.'' She spoke the name with great scorn.

''Ah,'' the Duke of Mitford said.

''My Uncle Ermingford is worth every bit as much as any titled gentleman I have ever met,'' she said, ''even though he is a mere mister. Grandpapa did not even want my aunt to marry him at the time.''

''Ah,'' he said. ''I suppose I had better deliver you to Mr. and Mrs. Ermingford's tomorrow, then, instead of into the clutches of your libertine duke.''

''You are very obliging,'' she said. ''I thank you.''

''In the meantime,'' he said, looking about him in some distaste at the sodden wallpaper, two scattered heaps of broken china, and the source of the smell on the floor beside the bed, ''you had better get some sleep, ma'am. And behind locked doors. You must exchange rooms with me, the lock being broken on this door.''

''You must have broken it, mustn't you,'' she said admiringly, ''when you rushed to my rescue? You are quite splendidly brave, sir. I think that punch to the jaw would have killed me.''

The duke thought so too.

''But I hate the think of your having to sleep in here,'' she said, wrinkling her nose again.

''Bring your valise, ma'am,'' he said. ''I shall see you safely into the next room and collect my own bag from there.''

''You are very kind,'' she said, following his directions and preceding him from the room.

A delightful night he was going to spend, the Duke of Mitford thought, following her glumly out into the corridor. The wit downstairs must be in action again. The inn was fairly rocking with raucous laughter. There was the sound of heavy boots on the stairs behind him, denoting the arrival of yet another potentially noisy guest. And he was to sleep amidst broken china and spilled water and vomit, his unlocked door an open invitation to thieves and pick-pockets.

Some adventure, indeed.

And by some unfortunate coincidence he had met his prospective bride, a delightfully demure young lady who had

taken to her heels with a scoundrel rather than stay and listen
to his addresses. It seemed that the day had had nothing but
humiliations to offer.

However, he must try to see the humorous side of it all. He
would arrive back in London in a few days' time a wiser man,
but basically unscathed. He would deliver this untidy, pretty,
and foolish young girl to her aunt's the following day, drive
on to Rutland Park to find her gone—he would greet that news
with the haughtiest surprise—make his excuses for not awaiting
her return, and effect his escape with Henry and his baggage
and his restored consequence.

He would don his titles again for the return journey.
Adventure was not all he had dreamed of its being. Better the
dull world he knew than the far less comfortable one he had
just glimpsed.

Miss Middleton turned to smile up at him—at least she was
smiling *up*, he thought, and not down—as he leaned around her
to open the door into his room. And then she hurtled against
him, wrapped her arms about his neck—her valise crashed
against his spine—and was kissing him with desperate passion
before he could even begin to defend himself from attack.

She backed into the room, dragging him with her, and
slammed the door shut with one foot. For a moment, he thought
she was about to use her knee on him without the fair warning
she had given to Mr. Porterhouse. But it seemed that she had
merely wanted to ensure greater privacy for her passion.

Before he could decide whether to encircle her with his arms
and surrender to the novelty of being ravished by an amorous
female or to wrestle her arms to her sides and hold her firmly
away from him while he lectured her on morality and decorum
and feminine modesty, she released his mouth, though she still
clung to his neck. Her eyes—they were a darker, more
interesting shade of gray than his own, he noticed irrelevantly—
were wide and focused on his.

"Oh, Lord," he said.

"Did you see who that was?" she hissed in a loud stage
whisper. "Did you see?"

"Coming up the stairs?" he asked. "Not having eyes in the
back of my head, I would have to say no, though I thought I
recognized the landlord's voice."

"But you would not have known him anyway," she said. "How could you?" Her eyes widened further, if that were possible. "It was Papa. He has come after me and found me out, though I left a note to say that I was riding to Aunt Winifred's. He would have killed you if he had seen you with me."

"Oh, Lord," the duke said again.

"He didn't see, though," she said. "He was looking back over his shoulder when I spotted him, and then when I put myself right against you, he would not have been able to see me. Oh!" She flushed and released her hold of his neck. She brushed unnecessarily at the creases in his shirt. "I do beg your pardon, sir."

"I hope for your sake that Porterhouse used false names when he took a room here," Mitford said.

"I will wager he did," she said. "But you must not go out there, sir. They must have seen the mess and destruction next door, and Papa will have drawn his own conclusions. If you go out of here and in there, he will kill you. I know he will."

"But I cannot just stay here," the duke said reasonably, turning to the door.

She grabbed his arm. "Yes, you can," she said. "You can stay here where it is safe and keep me safe. For if you go in there and he kills you, he will then come looking for me. And he will scold dreadfully."

"Perhaps you deserve a scolding," he said. "And at least you will be safe with your father. All will be proper again. I should go and speak with him, ma'am."

"Don't," she said, her eyes large and anxious and pleading. "He will take me back home, and I will have to marry the Duke of Mitford. He is coming tomorrow to ask me."

The Duke of Mitford hesitated. "Oh, Lord, yes, there was that. Sometimes propriety did not seem so very wise. He glanced down at the bare planks of the floor and at the one pillow and two blankets on the bed. He sighed.

"It is most dreadfully improper for us to stay here together," he said, his words sounding to his ears like the understatement of the decade.

But she recognized her victory immediately. Her face bright-

ened and she whisked herself over to the washstand, where she
deposited her valise.

"I shall sleep on the floor," she said. "This is your bed, sir.
You have paid for it. I shall not disturb you. I beg you to lie
down if you are ready for sleep. I shall just wash my hands
and face, if I may."

Mitford gave the back of her head a speaking glance and did
not deign to reply. He picked up his bag, lumpy with his shaving
gear and a clean shirt, and tossed it against the wall beside the
bed. He eyed the blankets again, noted their thinness, and
reached regretfully for his greatcoat.

By the time Josephine had turned away from the washstand,
he was lying down on the floor and covered up. "Good night,
ma'am," he said, resisting the impulse to groan. Hardness was
one thing. Unevenness was going to be something else again
to contend with.

"Oh," she said, "you really should not, you know. I would
not mind the floor in the least. You are very kind. Are you sure
you will not have the pillow? But you really must have one of
the blankets. Your coat does not cover you completely, and it
will doubtless get cold later in the night. It usually does in
October."

Her face appeared over the edge of the bed, looking rosy again
from the washcloth, and she dropped a blanket in a heap onto
his stomach.

Mitford almost forgot his physical discomfort in the mental
one. As he spread the blanket over his coat, he could hear
shufflings and rustlings from the bed above him—the sounds
of a young lady settling for sleep.

Good Lord, he had an unmarried young lady in his room at
the inn, about to fall asleep on his bed. And he was still inside
the room himself. And her father was also at the inn, doubtless
breathing fire and brimstone and contemplating the murder of
her abductor.

Good Lord! Had she said the night would be cold? He pushed
back the coat and blanket to his waist. He was sweating just
as if he were running in a tropical jungle.

And his temperature did not abate by even one degree when
he remembered the recent sensation of warm and generous
breasts pressed to his chest and a tiny waist beneath his hands,

with the suggestion of very feminine hips below. And warm and soft lips. And an enticing feminine fragrance.

The duke pushed his blankets lower. He was not at all accustomed to dallying with females. The only woman he had ever touched was Eveline. And though he had learned a great deal under her tutorship and had taught himself and her a great deal more over the course of three years, nevertheless he had only ever practiced it all on one female. And she had been considerably larger boned than this girl. Besides, it was more than a year since he had touched anyone.

It seemed as if months or even years had passed since he had been lamenting the very tame nature of his great adventure, since he had been able to find nothing more exciting to do than contemplate the angle of his big toes.

So much for adventures. He would never, never again crave anything beyond the ordinary. The ordinary was blessedly safe and familiar. How long would it take him to cover ten miles tomorrow morning, he wondered, if he sprang his horses?

He could feel beads of perspiration on his forehead. He wondered if it would be worth trying to turn onto one side. Probably not. He stayed on his back.

And then a flushed and anxious little face was leaning over him from the bed again and the duke found himself wishing that he could drop through the uneven floor to the room below.

"By the way," she said, "I am Josephine Middleton, sir. My family and friends call me Jo."

"Pleased to make your acquaintance, Miss Middleton," he said with all the formality he would have used if she were being presented to him at court. "Paul Villiers at your service, ma'am."

She smiled at him. "Good night, Mr. Villiers," she said. "You are a very kind man. Shall I blow out the candle?"

"The candle?" he said. "Oh, the candle. Yes, do so, ma'am, if you do not need it any longer."

And then the room was plunged into darkness and the shufflings and rustlings from the bed began again.

The duke pushed the blanket to his knees.

There was a riotous burst of laughter from the taproom below, and the company gathered there swung into collective song.

* * *

Bartholomew Middleton was up very early the following morning, as was his frequent habit, in order to go riding. He walked through the stables, whistling, as a groom saddled his horse for him. It was something he could just as easily do himself, but as his grandfather had explained to him on one occasion, servants did not like to be made to feel useless. It was their task to wait upon the gentry. It was the task of the gentry to have the courtesy to be waited upon.

It was not a long wait. Bartholomew strode out into the stable-yard, eager to be on his way. He always liked the autumn air more than the air at any other season. He set one booted foot in the stirrup and prepared to mount.

And then he paused in his action and frowned. He returned his foot to the ground and strode back into the stables again. Yes, it was as he had thought. He looked deliberately down one row of stalls and back along the other.

A minute later he was striding back toward the house, having instructed the groom to walk his horse for him until he came back.

"Sukey." He was shaking his sister by the shoulder just a few minutes after that. She was fast asleep at such an early hour. The bed at the other side of the room—Josephine's bed—had not been slept in. "Wake up."

"Mmmm," she protested irritably and burrowed her face into her pillow. "Go away, Bart. Ask Jo."

"Sukey, wake up," he said, shaking her by the shoulder again. "There is something wrong."

"Go away," she said.

"Listen," he said, "do I have to shake you good and proper? There's something wrong. Jo rode to Aunt Winifred's yesterday, yet the only horses missing from the stables are the ones Papa took."

Susanna groaned. "Perhaps she is back," she said, opening one eye and peering at the very empty bed at the other side of the room.

"No, she is not," Bartholomew said. "And what is more, Sukey, if she went to Aunt Winifred's, she must have walked."

Susanna rolled over onto her back and opened her eyes.

"Look," he said, "Jo left here yesterday, saying she was going to Aunt Winifred's. But she made very sure Papa would not get her note until late in the day. How else could she have got there if she did not take her horse or anyone else's and if she did not walk?''

Susanna thought a moment and regarded her brother fearfully.

"She went with someone else, that's what," her brother said. "Look, Sukey, was Porterhouse planning to leave the Winthrops' yesterday? I mean, did you hear of it in advance?"

"No," she said. "He had to leave in a hurry. His sister is very sick."

"Devil take it," Bartholomew said, "I'll wager Jo went with him. I'll wring her neck off her shoulders."

Susanna was sitting up suddenly, blue eyes wide, golden hair in a halo about her face. "She has eloped with Mr. Porterhouse?" she cried. "Oh, surely not, Bart. Jo would not do such a thing. She is frequently thoughtless and impulsive, but she would not elope. Certainly not with Mr. Porterhouse."

"Isn't he the one who told her all those things about Mitford?" Bartholomew said. "And got her into the royal jitters?"

"Do you think they were untrue?" she asked. "Has he got Jo so frightened that she has run off with him? Oh, surely not, Bart. Not Jo. But whatever are we going to do?"

"Just let me think for one minute," her brother said, his brows knit together in a deep frown. "Jo would not elope. She isn't that lost to all conduct. But she is the most brainless little female it has ever been my misfortune to be related to. She probably went off with him to Aunt Winifred's. *He* is probably the one who is eloping. It is just sheer lunacy for someone like Jo to have such a huge dowry, you know. Men like Porterhouse can spot women like Jo from five miles away without spectacles."

Susanna kneeled up on the bed. "You think he has abducted her, then?" she asked.

Bartholomew slammed one fist into the other palm. "He'll do it, too," he said. "Even if he doesn't get her to Gretna, she will be ruined. She already will be, in fact. Devil take it, but I'll kill him with my bare hands. And then I'll throttle Jo. I have to go and get her back, Sukey. This will kill Papa and Grandpapa."

"You are going after them?" she said, catching at his sleeve. "But what if it is already too late? Oh, Jo. Poor Jo. She would not even have realized what a trap she was being led into."

"Get dressed," he said, "and fast. You can see me on my way and think of some story to tell Grandpapa and the girls when they get up. Not the truth—definitely not that. Tell them it was such a lovely day that I decided to ride over to Aunt Winifred's too."

"You are not going without me," Susanna said. "Poor Jo. I am coming too."

"Don't be ridiculous," Bartholomew said. "You know you can't travel, Sukey. You would be bilious after two miles."

"I'm coming," she announced resolutely, throwing the blankets from her, both cheeks flushing. "It will look far more the thing if we all return together, the three of us. I will help smooth things over, Bart. Oh, poor Jo."

"Poor Jo!" Bartholomew said in exasperation. "Wait until I get my hands about her neck, that's all. I'll poor Jo her, all right. Get dressed then, Sukey. I'll give you fifteen minutes. And not a word of complaint, mind, when we are on our way. I'll write a quick note to Grandpapa."

"We will ride?" Susanna asked, gazing valiantly at her brother's back. "Will you choose a horse for me that will not rear up, Bart?"

He looked up at the ceiling and clucked his tongue. "We will have to take that old traveling carriage of Grandpapa's," he said. "There's no other choice. I wish you would stay, Suke. I could travel much faster without you."

"I'm coming," she said, jumping out of bed even before her brother had closed the door behind him.

4

Josephine yawned widely and stretched. Where was Betty this morning? Betty always had a suble way of waking her. Nothing as obvious as taking her by the shoulders and shaking her, as Bart sometimes did if he wanted a riding companion; or peeling off the blankets and leaving her to freeze as Sukey did when she wanted someone to pay morning calls with her; or yelling peevishly in her ear and tapping none too gently at her cheeks as Penny and Gussie did when they wanted her to go bird watching or picking wild flowers with them.

Betty was her maid. She had to be subtle. She merely threw back the heavy velvet curtains from the window each morning, bathing Josephine's face in instant sunshine. Not that the sun was always shining, of course. But even instant daylight usually had the effect of waking her.

She often felt envy for those fabled ladies in London who were allowed to sleep until noon and occupy half the afternoon with making themselves beautiful. What a delightful life they must lead. It would drive her crazy within a week!

Morning at Rutland Park had always been considered a valuable commodity. Everyone was always up for breakfast by nine o'clock, and anyone who was not at least ten minutes early was frowned upon by Grandpapa and called a lazy sleepyhead by Papa. It was a myth that breakfast began at nine. It would be more accurate to say that it ended at nine.

Where was Betty? Josephine wrinkled her nose but could detect no noticeable aroma of chocolate.

Her pillow was hard. The blankets on her were so light that they might as well not be there at all. She was feeling chilly.

Her eyes snapped open.

Oh, goodness gracious. There had been all that silliness over the Duke of Mitford, and Papa and Grandpapa trying to marry her off to a man she had never set eyes on. And a man who, it seemed, was tall and blond and blue-eyed—all the things she dreaded in a husband because she was so small and insignificant herself. And toplofty. And a rake.

And there had been all her reluctance at the proposed match and all her inability to disappoint either Papa or Grandpapa. And her stupid, stupid decision to flee to Aunt Winifred's with Mr. Porterhouse. Would she never learn?

Mr. Porterhouse! Josephine closed her eyes again. Oh, dear!

There was a rustling from beside the bed and a muffled groan. Josephine's eyes opened once more and came to rest on the crack across the corner of the ceiling. Oh dear. There was Mr. Villiers, too, that great Hercules of a gentleman who was also very kind. And Papa still at the inn, as like as not, contemplating murder and searching the place for the couple who had occupied that wrecked and reeking room next door.

Oh, goodness. What had she got herself into now? Bart always said, and Gussie and Penny always agreed with him, that she was quite incapable of using her head.

"Of course," Bart added as often as not, "Jo doesn't have a brain, so she starts off with a disadvantage."

She always hotly denied the charges—usually with some weapon hurled at her brother's head.

"It is a good thing Jo can't throw straight either," Bart always said with that imbecilic grin.

But sometimes—oh, just sometimes in the strict privacy of her own mind—she had to agree with the judgment of her brother and sisters. However had she got into this dreadful coil? It surely would not have happened if she had just used her head from the start.

Poor Mr. Villiers. He was going to have to delay his journey to wherever he was going in order to accompany her to Aunt Winifred's. He would doubtless be dreadfully inconvenienced. Yet she would have to accept his escort. Ladies just did not travel about the country alone. She was not always a stickler for proper conduct, but even she knew that much. Of course, it was equally improper to travel about with gentlemen who were not one's father or brother.

But she had no choice. Even if she wanted to travel alone,

she had nothing to travel in, and ten miles sounded rather a long way to walk, especially with a valise.

Mr. Villiers was a very kind man. She must remember to tell him so when he woke up. And so strong. Mr. Porterhouse's knees had buckled under those two punches. And his teeth had snapped together so loudly that she would not have been at all surprised to find them showering down about her head. And Mr. Villiers had come through the door without opening it.

She wondered where Mr. Porterhouse was. She hoped he had had to stop his carriage every mile along the road to retch again. Horrid man. She had been totally deceived by him. The memory of his words and his face and his touch the evening before after he had locked the door to her room was quite sufficient to give her the shudders.

Josephine turned onto her side and leaned cautiously over the edge of the bed. Mr. Villiers was lying facing her, asleep by some miracle. He certainly did not look comfortable. His bag looked as if it were a far more lumpy pillow than her own. His greatcoat and the blanket were bunched around him, leaving him largely uncovered. He must be cold, poor man.

But she was surprised as she continued to gaze downward. In the light of day he did not look so very large after all, certainly not the Hercules he had appeared to be when he flew into the room next door. Indeed, he was not at all as she remembered him.

She propped herself on one elbow and regarded her savior critically. He looked—nice. Oh dear, what a weak choice of word. But it was better than any other she could think of. He did look nice. He had a rather thin face. He needed a shave. He had a good-humored mouth. It seemed to be curved into a smile even in sleep. There was nothing else remarkable about his face. It was just nice.

She liked his curls. They were rather long and riotous. The sort of curls a mother's fingers would itch to smooth back from his face. She wondered if they would look less attractive when he combed them.

Well, perhaps he was not a giant of a man after all, but she liked him. He was a very kind man, and she must remember to tell him so. Anyway, he really was a strong man. She could not have imagined what he had done to Mr. Porterhouse. Besides, she had done more than merely see his strength in action. Oh dear, there had been that episode when she had seen Papa at the top of the stairs and he would have seen her just one second after. She had thrown herself against Mr. Villiers. And kissed him. Oh, gracious.

Grandpapa would look very sorrowful while scolding her for that one. She had never been kissed before. And finally it had happened twice in one day. First Mr. Porterhouse and his wet lips—surprising really. One would have thought that such a very handsome man would kiss beautifully. But then perhaps he did—perhaps other, more experienced ladies would enjoy being kissed like that. Her opinion had been rather clouded, too, by the fact that she had known he had ravishment in mind.

And then Mr. Villiers. It was rather unfair, of course, to say that he had kissed her, when it was perfectly obvious that it was she who had kissed him. But that was an academic point. She could make no judgment on the kiss since all her thoughts had been on Papa and preventing him from seeing her and killing Mr. Villiers, which would have been very unfair under the circumstances.

But she could remember—she could distinctly remember now that she thought about it—that his body was very firm and well muscled.

Mr. Villiers might be no Hercules, but for all that he was still her hero. She gazed down admiringly at his rumpled curls and nice face. And he stirred even as she did so.

She smiled down at him, the side of her head still propped on one hand. "Good morning," she said. "I am relieved to see that you slept, though I will not ask if you slept well, for I am sure you did not. It was very kind of you to put yourself to so much discomfort when you paid for the room and therefore the bed. You are a true gentleman, sir."

And then she remembered, as his eyes looked up to her, first blank and then startled and then with full consciousness, that she had pushed her blanket down to her waist and that the previous night after she had lain down she had wriggled out of her torn dress. She was lying in bed inside a small room with a strange gentleman, dressed in her shift.

How unspeakably mortifying!

"Oh, dear," she said, sitting up and bringing the blanket up to her neck even as he sat up hastily and turned away from her.

"Good morning, Miss Middleton," he said. "I trust you had a comfortable night."

"It would be ungrateful of me to complain," she said. "Quite comfortable, I thank you, sir."

Oh, yes, she could see through his wrinkled shirt that he did indeed have well developed muscles in his shoulders and arms even though his back tapered to a slender waist and hips. His fair hair curled down over the collar of his shirt. She blushed and pulled the blanket to her chin.

And then she realized that she was facing a nasty predicament. How was she going to get her dress on—the untorn one that was in her valise? The room suddenly seemed very small indeed. She should have made herself busy while he still slept, instead of lying gazing at him and dreaming of heroes. Would she never use her head?

He was on his feet and plucking at his coat, which was draped over the foot of the bed. "I shall leave you for half an hour, ma'am," he said, not once turning to look at her.

"Is it safe?" she asked. "I mean, are you sure Mr. Porterhouse really did leave last night? And what about Papa? He will kill you if he gets his hands on you."

"Mr. Porterhouse will have left if he knows what is good for him," he said, his hand on the doorknob. "Your father will hardly set upon a stranger. Besides, if he really is in pursuit of you, the chances are that he either did not stay here at all last night or else left again at the crack of dawn. The crack of dawn is when I finally fell asleep, I believe."

"Oh, dear," she said as he let himself out of the room, "I knew you could not have had a comfortable night, sir. And it is all my fault."

But she had no time to indulge in remorse. She leaped off the bed, splashed water into the basin, washed herself as thoroughly as she could at such great speed, gasping at the coldness of the water, and pulled out her clean dress from her valise. Oh, dear, she should have thought to take it out the night before so that some of the wrinkles might have fallen out.

Betty had a gift for packing garments in such a way that they
did not wrinkle at all. Unfortunately, she had not been able to
ask Betty to pack for her.

She pulled the dress on and slapped and shook ineffectually
at the wrinkles. Well, it would have to do until she reached her
aunt's. Aunt Winifred would send a servant for a trunk of her
clothes—if they did not run into Papa on the way there, of
course. But she would not think of that. She would not think
of that at all. Time enough to give it thought if it happened.
The chances were that Papa would have gone rushing back home
already.

She tackled her hair next. Unfortunately, whenever it grew
to her shoulders or below, it came to bear a disturbing
resemblance to a bush. But she had insisted on growing it long,
even though Bart had come back from Cambridge and a vacation
in London to say that short hair was all the crack. Who cared
about being all the crack?

She had never had to worry before. Betty had a way with
her hair as she seemed to have a way with everything else.
Unfortunately, Josephine did not share that way.

She was staring rather gloomily into a cracked and tarnished
mirror at what looked woefully like a crow's nest when there
was a tap at the door and Mr. Villiers appeared again. He had
his bag with him. He must have found somewhere to change
his shirt and shave himself. He looked quite respectably neat
and tidy, and not at all as if he had just spend the night sleeping
in his clothes on a bare floor. Even his curls had been brushed
to look soft and orderly. Josephine preferred them tousled, and
blushed as she caught herself in the thought.

"I am afraid I look rather rumpled," she said, smiling at him
in the mirror.

His eyes passed over her. "You look quite pretty enough to
me," he said. "Your father passed the night here, Miss
Middleton, but left very early. I still think I should take you
back to Rutland Park."

"You know where I live?" she asked, turning from the
mirror.

He rocked on his heels in that habit she had noticed the night
before. "You mentioned it last night," he said.

"Did I?" She flashed him a smile. "I daresay I did, and a

great deal more besides. I am afraid my mind was considerably addled.''

"Understandably so," he said. "I shall bring a breakfast tray up to you, ma'am, and then take you home. Doubtless your father will be there before you, having not found you at your aunt's.''

"No," she said, "you cannot do that, you see, because Papa would want to know where I spent the night and when I met you. And even if Papa is still from home, Grandpapa will be there. And Grandpapa would kill you. I should hate that.''

"Yes," he said. "So should I.''

"You must take me to my Aunt Ermingford's if you will be so kind," she said. "There is a long and winding driveway leading to the house. If you set me down halfway up it, you will not be seen either by my aunt and uncle or by Papa if he is still there. I can walk the rest of the way and think of some convincing story by the time I arrive. And Aunt Winifred will take my part if Papa is out of sorts.''

The duke sighed. "I shall fetch the tray," he said. "We will decide after breakfast what it is best to do.''

"You know," she said kindly, "the servants will bring it up for you if you ring, sir. You do not have to do everything for yourself when you travel. You must assert yourself, as Papa would say. Servants will respect you the more for it.''

"I registered here as a single gentleman," he said. "What would the servants think if they were to find you here?''

"Oh," she said, "I had not thought of that. You are quite right. You are trying to protect my reputation. How kind of you.''

He pursed his lips and left the room.

"You know, Suke," Bartholomew was saying at precisely that moment, a note of impatience in his voice, "if you did not think of it, it would not happen. You should think of something else.''

Susanna was standing outside the open carriage door, facing a hedge. "I have thought about Mr. Porterhouse being even more of a villain than I suspected," she said wanly. "I have thought about Grandpapa's face when he reads your note. I have thought about Papa's face when he arrives at Aunt Winifred's and finds Jo not there. I have thought about a thousand and one different things, Bart, and it makes no difference.''

"Devil take it," he said, "you did not even have breakfast before we left. How can you feel bilious?''

"I don't know how," she said apologetically, "but I do.''

"Come on," he said, as she gulped in an attempt to control her queasiness, "get in again. We will stop at the Crown and Anchor for something to eat. You can rest there a while.''

"For something to eat," Susanna said faintly. "Oh, Bart, can't we wait here just a little longer?''

He clucked his tongue in exasperation. "Get in," he said. "I'll take you back and drop you off a mile from home. I ought not to have brought you in the first place.''

"I shall be all right," she said, squaring her shoulders and looking up at her brother with resolute eyes and green cheeks. "Jo needs me. I shall think of Penny and Gussie all alone at home, and Grandpapa making excuses to the Duke of Mitford for Jo's absence. I shall think of . . . other things.''

"Think of the duke or marquess or prince or whoever that Grandpapa is likely to pick for your husband," Bartholomew said, handing her back into the carriage. "He has done so wonderfully well for Jo.''

"I don't want a duke or marquess," she said, "just someone I can have a regard for. But if Grandpapa did pick out someone good for me, Bart, I would at least meet him and get to know him. It would be unfair to condemn a man out of hand just because one expected him to be toplofty.''

But she had to cut short her reflections as her brother shut the door.

Josephine turned her attention back to her bird's nest. But there was nothing to be done. If she tried to make the coiffure smoother, like as not the hair would all come cascading down and she would have to start all over again.

She liked Mr. Villiers. He was not near as tall as Mr. Porterhouse or Papa or Grandpapa or Bart. She did not know how she could have got the impression the night before that he was. She remembered now that when she put her arms about his neck the night before—oh, dear, had she really?—she had not had to reach up very far. She would wager that her head must reach at least to his shoulder and perhaps even a little higher. How pleasant it would be to walk beside him. She might even feel that she was a woman and not a child.

She would like to walk beside him into Aunt Winifred's drawing room. She would like to tell her aunt all about his heroic rescue of her the night before. But she had better not. For she would also have to tell about sleeping in his room, even though she had slept on the bed and he on the floor. And then someone—Uncle Clive, probably, and certainly Papa if he was there—would get some ridiculous notion about how she had been compromised and how Mr. Villiers should marry her. If Papa did not kill him first, that was.

Poor Mr. Villiers. She was quite sure she would prefer him to the Duke of Mitford any day of the year, but it would be a mean trick to play on him after his extreme kindness. Besides, perhaps he was married already or betrothed or promised. Now there was a lowering thought. And a slightly depressing one.

She rushed across the room to open the door, at which someone was kicking gently. She smiled at Mr. Villiers.

"Only one egg and one cup of coffee, I'm afraid," he said. "But I could hardly say there were two of us up here."

"You may have both," she said magnanimously, "provided I can have one piece of toast, sir. But will they not know there are two of us when we go downstairs to leave?"

"I shall go down first," he said, "to see to the harnessing of my horses to my curricle. You must stroll down after ten minutes, ma'am, and hope that no one notices you were the lady who occupied the wrecked room last night."

"I really shall not care if they do know," she said. "Are you sure I am not inconveniencing you dreadfully, sir? Were you planning a very important journey for today?"

"Nothing that cannot wait," he said. "It is to be to your aunt's then, ma'am?"

"Yes, please," she said, jumping to her feet in order to stuff her town dress and her hairbrush into her valise. "I am ready whenver you are."

She watched him drain the coffee cup and get to his feet. And then she felt the blood drain from her head, just as the coffee had done from the cup. The next moment her valise was open on the bed, all its uncarefully packed belongings flying out of it again.

"It's gone!" she said, her voice shaking almost out of her control. "It really has gone. I suddenly realized that when I put my dress in it was not in there. Oh, whatever am I to do?"

"What is gone?" he asked.

"I know I brought it," she said. "I distinctly remember putting it into the bottom of my valise. I remember thinking perhaps I was foolish since I was only going to Aunt Winifred's. But I was afraid that Papa would try to drag me back to marry the Duke of Mitford even with Aunt Winifred to plead for me and I would never be able to go home again. So I know I brought it with me."

Mr. Villiers's voice sounded reassuringly calm—except that there could be no reassurance. She knew she had brought it with her. "What did you bring with you?" he asked.

"My jewelry case," she said. "I brought it with me because I thought I might be destitute without it. I have spent all my pin money for this month, you see, and my purse is quite, quite empty. So I thought of bringing my jewels."

"And you are quite sure it is missing?" he asked, looking about at her few scattered belongings and into the empty valise.

"It's gone!" she said, sitting with a plop on the bed and staring at him with blank eyes.

"Were there any valuable pieces?" he asked.

"There were Mother's garnets," she said, "which Papa used to keep for me because he said I was such a scatterbrain. But he let me keep them for myself after my eighteenth birthday because I really am careful with things of value. Though I appear not to have been careful now, do I not? Oh, dear."

"What else?" he asked. He was leaning over her, a look of concern on his face.

"There were my pearls," she said, "which Grandpapa gave me also on my eighteenth birthday. Oh, and the diamond ring that used to be Grandmama's and is now mine, though I do not have a finger big enough for it to fit on."

"Anything else?" he asked.

She stared at him and thought. "The little emerald earbobs that Bart brought from London," she said. "He brought ruby ones for Sukey and sapphire pins for Penny and Gussie.''

His hands were on her shoulders. They felt very comforting, except that there was no comfort to be had. ''You are quite, quite sure you brought the box?'' he asked. ''You did not leave it on a table somewhere, thinking you had packed it when you had not?''

''No,'' she said. ''I remember that the edges were sharp against the bottom of the valise, and I warned Mr. Porterhouse about bruising his leg with it.''

''Saying that it was your jewel case, I suppose,'' he said.

''Yes.'' Her eyes kindled suddenly and her nostrils flared. ''The villain!'' she cried, leaping to her feet and almost colliding with the duke's chest. ''The black-hearted, conscienceless villain! He is a thief as well as a . . . as well as a . . . an abductor. He has stolen my jewels.''

''I'm afraid it appears to be so,'' the duke said.

''Well.'' She began to pace the room, no mean accomplishment in such confined space. ''I was prepared to let him off lightly. I was prepared to consider your fisticuffs punishment enough even though he deserved worse. But he has gone too far. If he thinks I am going to ignore the loss of my jewels, then he will be sadly disappointed. Oh, just wait until I get my hands on him. He will be sorry he was ever born.''

''It is likely that he will head for London if he is carrying stolen property,'' the duke said, ''a two-day journey at the very least. I shall convey you with all speed to your aunt's house, ma'am, since it is closer than your home, and inform your uncle of your loss.''

''What?'' she said, turning to frown at him with such ferocious incredulity that any stranger would have thought he was the one who had mortally offended her. ''You think I would sit quietly at my Aunt Ermingford's while a villain for whom a noose is too good makes off with my jewels? You do not know me, sir. I thank you for your assistance. Now, if you will excuse me, I have to inquire after the hiring of a carriage and horses.''

The duke rocked on his heels and scratched his head. ''And doubtless tear off all alone to London,'' he said. ''It is madness, ma'am. I cannot allow it.''

He had once watched a hot air balloon filling with air in preparation for taking its owners up into the sky. Miss Middleton bore a distinct resemblance to that balloon for a few moments as she inhaled audibly through her nose. "*You* cannot allow it?" she said. "I must remind you, sir, that you have no responsibility whatsoever for my actions."

"But having rescued you from one decidedly perilous situation," he said, "I feel a certain vested interest in keeping you rescued."

She was stuffing her belongings back inside the valise with even less care than before. "I am not going to my aunt's," she said, "and I am not going back home. I am going in pursuit of Mr. Porterhouse and my jewels. And I shall find them, too, even if I have to circle the globe in order to do so."

The duke was standing beside the bed, blowing out his cheeks. "Tell me," he said, after watching her struggle with the clasp of her valise for a few silent moments, "do you know anyone in London?"

She looked up at him and thought for a moment. "Grandmama," she said. "Mama's mother, that is. And Aunt Elsie."

"Very well," he said with sudden decision. "Highly improper as it is, I shall convey you that far, ma'am, since you seem determined to go anyway. And I don't believe you will find a faster vehicle here than my curricle or a faster set of horses than my own."

She looked full into his eyes, not very far above the level of her own, and favored him with a wide smile. "You are going to take me?" she said. "Oh, I knew you would. You are a very kind gentleman."

He rocked on his heels. His hair, she was pleased to notice, had already escaped from the taming he had given it earlier. It was looking nicely unruly again. He looked very pleasant and dependable. But it was a comfort to know that the coat covering his slender frame hid some very impressive muscles.

"I think," the Duke of Mitford said mildly, "I am a very mad gentleman, ma'am."

5

He was even more convinced of the truth of his judgment on himself before they drove out of the innyard. It was a sad and sudden insanity. He had always led a proper and exemplary life. He was known as a dull dog—certainly as no one who would be likely to involve himself in any activity that was remotely daring or improper.

What was he doing, then at nine o'clock in the morning, tooling out to the king's highway in his curricle, a flushed and rumpled young lady at his side, and nary a maid or groom or maiden aunt in sight?

He was turning north with her, that was what he was doing. Turning north toward an unknown destination, not south in the direction of London and her grandmother and aunt as he had planned to do.

He had left the inn room ahead of her. "Give me ten minutes," he had said. "By that time the curricle will be ready and we can be off with the minimum of fuss."

"Yes, sir," she had said, still flushed and agitated from her discovery of the loss of her jewels. "Ten minutes it is. But please make them a fast ten minutes."

He had gone downstairs, puzzling over that last sentence and wondering if the bride his grandfather had chosen as so suitable to his position had any brains at all. It was rather disconcerting to think he had almost married a girl who had no brains.

At least she was shorter than he. The top of her head reached barely to his chin. That was some consolation, at least, though totally irrelevant to the present situation.

She had waited seven minutes. He could have forgiven her the three since all was ready for departure by that time, anyway. Unfortunately he had forgotten when he left the room that she was brainless. The only strict instruction he had given was that

55

she must wait ten minutes. He had not thought it necessary to
spell out for her again the importance of slipping quietly from
the inn, stepping up quietly into the curricle with his assistance,
and sitting quietly beside him until they were out in open country
so that only a few grooms would witness the impropriety of
a young lady making off alone with a young gentleman. A young
lady and gentleman who had not registered at the inn as husband
and wife.

He had forgotten to give those instructions. Or rather, he had
not thought it necessary to give them. Any properly brought
up young lady with half a brain would have known for herself.
She would have kept her head lowered and her chin tucked
against her chest.

Lord, why had he not traveled in his closed carriage? And
with Henry and his baggage and numerous coachmen and
footmen? And by a different route?

When she came, she paused in the doorway of the inn, looked
all about her with bright and curious eyes, picked out the head
ostler, and hailed him in a voice that was accustomed to be both
heard and obeyed.

The Duke of Mitford closed his eyes and offered up a brief
prayer that no one he knew would ever hear of this scene.

"I arrived here last night with a gentleman," Josephine
Middleton announced to the head ostler, every other ostler in
the innyard, every servant and guest at the inn, and every
inhabitant of the village beyond. "A tall, handsome dark-haired
gentleman. Did you by any chance see him leave?"

The ostler lifted his cap and scratched his head. He shifted
his weight from one leg to the other. "That be the gruff and
grim gent what was in such a hurry to get on his way at first
light?" he said.

"Oh," the girl sang out for all the world to enjoy, "that would
have been Papa, who was in pursuit of me. No, this was a young
man, who left last night."

The head ostler had not been on duty last night after nine
o'clock. He would have to go and consult with someone called
Sam.

The Duke of Mitford did not grab her by the scruff of the
neck and deposit her in his curricle. He did not make off alone
and leave her to her fate. He did not do any of the things he

might and should have done. He waited meekly beside the horses, waiting for the world to take note that he was about to abscond with a very young lady with whom he had not arrived the night before.

He knew of no other way of dealing with the matter. He had no experience in handling embarrassing and improper situations.

Sam—a totally bald giant whom one would certainly not want to meet in a dark alley at night—emerged from the inn with the innkeeper and two unidentified maids in tow. And Sam was quite insistent that the handsome gent had traveled north, not south.

Josephine Middleton was skeptical. The Duke of Mitford was skeptical too, though he did not open his mouth to say so, or anything else for that matter. But Sam was adamant. And ultimately convincing. He was the gent who had the bright blue and yellow carriage, was he not?

"Yes, indeed," Miss Middleton answered. "A very bright blue and yellow."

"And 'e was the gent who looked dazed in 'is eyes and what chucked up 'is vittles in the corner there where there is now a pile of straw?" The huge bald head nodded in the direction of one corner of the innyard.

"Yes," Miss Middleton said, eyes kindling, "he was the gentleman."

Sam spat and ground his heel into the foaming patch. " 'e went north," he said.

And who was to argue with someone of Sam's conviction and physique?

"Actually," Miss Middleton said, settling herself into the seat beside the duke as he took his horses through the gateway of the inn into the street beyond, "it makes sense. I don't believe Mr. Porterhouse is a stupid man, and it would be rather stupid to head for London, where pursuit was bound to follow him. It makes sense for him to turn north." She turned to wave to the innkeeper and Sam and the head ostler and the unidentified maids and anyone else who cared to raise a hand in farewell. They were all smiling in sympathy—she had told them about the stolen jewels.

"That rascal will never spend another night in this hostelry, mum," the innkeeper had assured her.

"Not unless 'e wants 'is ears to meet in the middle of 'is 'ead, mum," Sam had added with menace in his voice.

The head ostler had winked and grinned at the Duke of Mitford, and identical grins had been painted on the faces of all the other grooms, every one of whom had lost interest in the task at hand; they were all leaning on their pitchforks to witness the indecorous departure.

They might as well have had flags attached to the curricle and strings of bells to pull behind, the duke reflected.

So here they were, headed north instead of south, for all the world as if they were making a dash for Gretna Green. He supposed that he should keep a wary eye over his shoulder for ferocious looking older gentlemen brandishing pistols.

"Perhaps it would have been as well," he suggested, "if we had left quietly, drawing as little attention to ourselves as we possibly could."

"But then," she said reasonably, "we would not have known, would we, that Mr. Porterhouse came north instead of going south. We would have been going in entirely the wrong direction. Had you made any inquiries of your own, sir?"

"No, I'm afraid not," he had to admit. "I assumed he must be heading in the direction of London."

"And there," she said. "You would have taken me all that way and doubtless spent days there searching for him with me, and it would all have been in vain. I would have wasted all that time for you."

"And so you would," he said.

"And now," she said, "if he decides to play a trick and turn back again and we do not see him, that Sam will have an eye out for him and do nasty things to him, no doubt. And his carriage is very distinctive. I secretly thought it rather tasteless, to be honest with you. Though I would not have said so for worlds while I thought Mr. Porterhouse to be a kind man. But now I do not mind speaking my mind on the subject."

"I suppose you realize, do you," he said, "that you have now blazed a very clear trail for your father to follow if he returns to that inn?"

"Perhaps it is just as well," she said. "For Papa will be very severe with Mr. Porterhouse. Papa cannot abide thieves. Of course, he will insist that I go back home again and marry that obnoxious Duke of Mitford, but perhaps by that time his grace will be tired of waiting for me and will have taken himself off home again. You should just see his valet, sir."

"Should I?" the duke asked, noting that she was clinging to a fistful of his coat sleeve with one hand and the rail on the outside of the seat with the other. "Am I driving too fast for you?"

"Oh, no," she said. "I wish you would spring the horses, for Mr. Porterhouse has a great start on us. It is just that I have never ridden in a curricle, and I feel as if I am suspended over space. It is rather exciting actually. Oh. Do you mind my holding on to you?"

"Not at all," he said. "You may link your arm through mine if you wish. Why should I have seen Mitford's valet?"

"Oh," she said with the greatest scorn, "he is just what one would expect of the servant of a duke, sir. His nose sniffs at the air as if it is not clean enough to be breathed by such an exalted personage."

Mitford repressed a chuckle. Yes, the description did rather fit Henry.

"You can just imagine what his grace must be like," the girl beside him said, her scorn intensified.

"Yes," he said. "Earth is doubtless far too lowly a planet for him."

"Exactly," she said with enthusiasm. "And Papa and Grandpapa think I should marry him! I would rather marry a toad."

"An admirable sentiment," he said. They were passing a southbound stagecoach, on top of which a merry band of dandies were grinning and whooping and raising their hats in greeting. The duke waited for her response and was not disapppointed. His companion smiled and raised one hand.

One of these times they were going to pass someone he knew. Oh, Lord.

"What I should have done," he said, "was gone out and talked to your father last night, Miss Middleton. I cannot now imagine why I did not. Perhaps he would have been angry with you, but at least no major impropriety had been committed at that point."

"But," she said, "he would have killed you."

"I think not," he said, "once I had explained. Then he would have been with you when you discovered the loss of your jewels, and he would have been able to make this journey with you.''

"Oh," she said, her voice crestfallen. Her face matched it, he saw when he looked. "You did not wish to come with me, did you?''

"It is not that," he said. "It is just that this is all so very improper, ma'am."

"But I would have had to marry the Duke of Mitford," she said, gazing at him with soulful eyes.

"Your father could not have forced you," he said. "Besides, perhaps the duke would not want to marry you when he saw you and knew you reluctant. Have you thought of that?''

"Oh yes, he would," she said. "He has any number of women for his plasure, you see. All he would need me for is respectability. And to breed his heirs.''

The duke flushed and gave up that particular line of conversation.

A couple of hours later he spotted a large inn ahead on the road. He must stop there and change horses, however reluctant he might be to do so. So far he had traveled by slow stages from home so that he might keep his own horses with him for the whole distance.

"I am going to stop at that inn," he told Josephine Middleton. "I need to change horses. And I will make inquiries there. I will make inquiries, do you understand? It would be advisable for you to stay as quiet as possible, ma'am. It is really not the thing for you to be traveling alone with me in an open curricle, you know. It would be better that no one we pass remembers your face.''

"You are kind to worry about me," she said. "But it would not be improper if you were my husband, would it? I shall borrow the title of Mrs. Villiers for the rest of our journey, if I may, and then no one will think my being with you strange at all.''

The Duke of Mitford would have rocked on his heels if he had been standing up.

"Is there a real Mrs. Villiers, by the way?" she asked. "She is going to be very cross with me for keeping you from her if there is.''

"No," he said hastily, "there is no Mrs. Villiers. Don't,''

he added on an afterthought while he lifted her to the ground at the inn and led her inside to request a private parlor for his wife, "mention your jewels. It would not be wise to turn this into a treasure hunt for all the sundry."

"That makes sense," she said. "Yes, that is a good idea, sir."

"I shall order tea for you," he said. "It will take about ten minutes to change the horses."

"Will it?" she said, removing her gloves and bonnet and looking about the small parlor with interest. "Please will you make them a short ten minutes, sir?"

The duke raised his eyebrows and shook his head slightly as he left the room.

Mr. Porterhouse had left an almost insolently blazing trail. Not only had he stopped at the inn to change horses, but he had also put up there for a few hours. He had stopped at all the most predictable places along the highway throughout the day. It seemed that by the time it was almost too dark to see the horses' heads ahead of them and a convenient inn loomed in sight, they were only four hours behind their man.

"It is almost as if he thinks I was glad to relinquish my jewels to him in exchange for my virtue," Josephine Middleton said indignantly. "As if he thinks I would not pursue him, or could not. He would not have realized, of course, that you are a kind gentleman and would have agreed to put yourself and your conveyance at my disposal. I am sure he did not see you as a kind man." She giggled a little. "Where did you learn to punch like that, sir?"

"To be fair," he said modestly, "I did take the gentleman by surprise. And you lent a hand."

"Oh, yes," she said admiringly, "but I think you would have done quite splendidly well without me, sir."

"It would not be wise to continue on our way," the duke said, turning his horses into the yard of the inn. "We will have to put up here for the night."

"Oh, but I trust your driving," she said, "and I am no longer afraid of being perched up here. I would far prefer to continue and catch up with the villain."

He might have caught a touch of insanity, Mitford reflected as he drew his horses to a halt and vaulted down from his high seat, but he was not reckless. He never had been.

"We will stay here," he said, reaching up his arms to lift her to the ground.

And she might be basically a brainless female, but she had had one sensible idea in the course of the day. It would be far less embarrassing and conspicuous to register at the inn as husband and wife than as Mr. Villiers or the Duke of Mitford and Miss Middleton. The only trouble was, of course, that although it was a perfectly clean and decent inn, it was not a large one. There was no such thing as a suite of rooms within its walls. And it would have been very peculiar for Mr. and Mrs. Villiers to rent two rooms.

After an almost sleepless night and a long day on the road, the very last place he felt like sleeping was on the floor again. But that was where he seemed destined to sleep, nonetheless.

The next time his grandfather took it into his head to go taking the waters in Bath, perhaps he should suggest a brief holiday in America or Brazil. Or China. Perhaps they had hot springs there.

"It is as I thought," Bartholomew said, slamming one fist into the other palm. "The villain headed north instead of toward Aunt Winifred's. He is eloping with Jo. Just wait till I get my hands on him. He must have had her tied up or she would have given him what for."

"The gent left 'ere alone," the bald giant at the Crown and Anchor said. " 'e left with the lady's jewels. She went after 'im with that other gent."

Bartholomew looked blank. "What other gentleman?" he said. And then he brightened. "Oh, my father. Papa caught up with her, did he?"

"No, sir," Sam said. "That was the gent what went east this morning, according to Walter, what was on dooty then."

"Oh, Bart, may I sit down?" Susanna asked weakly. She was leaning heavily on his arm.

"Carriage sickness, ma'am?" Sam asked sympathetically. "Wot you needs is a good breakfast so there's some'at to chuck up when you continues on your way."

Susanna grimaced.

"Go inside," Bartholomew said, "and order tea at least."

Susanna went.

"Now," he said turning back to the huge groom, "who was this gentleman my sister went north with?"

Sam shrugged. "Little bit of a fellow," he said. "In a curricle. Not quite the conveyance for the lady, if you was to arsk me, sir. But she was that anxious about 'er jewels."

"She was fool enough to entrust her jewels to that scoundrel?" Bartholomew asked, his brows drawing together in a frown. "But what was this gentleman's name?"

Sam shrugged again. "Arsk inside," he said. "Was you driving careful with that little lady wot is sick, sir?"

"Well, of course I was driving carefully," Bartholomew said with some indignation. "Can I help it if English roads have more holes than road? If she did not expect to get sick every time she drives farther than two miles, she wouldn't be."

"Ah," Sam said, "but ladies is delicate creatures, sir. And 'o is to tend 'er inside the carriage?"

"No one," Bartholomew said. "She sticks her head out of the window and yells at me when it is time to stop. Every mortal mile of the way."

"Wot you need is a skilled coachman," Sam said.

Bartholomew was visibly irritated. "Do you have any idea where I might find such a paragon in this part of the country?" he asked.

"That I do, sir," Sam said. "I did not like the look of that 'andsome creature last night, not by 'alf, I didn't. I wouldn't mind getting my 'ands on 'im, I wouldn't, sir, and protecting the little ladies. And if there is 'oles in the road, sir, why I drives around them, like. And the little lady would not be so sick and you could tend 'er if she was."

"You are offering to come?" Bartholomew asked.

"That I am, sir," Sam said.

"Done," Bartholomew said. "Can you be ready in ten minutes? And who the devil was that man with Jo?"

"Arsk the innkeeper," Sam advised.

She should not be enjoying herself. Josephine had smoothed out the creases of her only decent dress and washed herself with care and done the best she could with her hair and was sitting in the public room of the Peacock Inn with Mr. Villiers, waiting for dinner to be served.

She should not be enjoying herself. She had shown great want of conduct in leaving home with a strange young gentleman, and had been robbed and almost ravished by him. Papa and Grandpapa would be severely disappointed with her behavior. And goodness only knew how they had explained her absence to the Duke of Mitford, who must have arrived by now. And were they worrying about her? Oh dear, of course they would be worrying about her.

And now she was chasing after the first strange young man with a second and had spent all day on the road with him, in an open curricle. She had been seen by dozens of different people and had waved to some of them in passing until she had recalled that it was not genteel for a twenty-year-old young lady to do so. Indeed, she was obliged to Mr. Villiers for not scolding. Papa and Bart would have scolded. Grandpapa would have explained that the daughter of a viscount and granddaughter of an earl was not expected to comport herself with public vulgarity.

And now she was sharing a room at an inn with the second young man for the second night in a row, and she was traveling incognito, under the name of Mrs. Villiers.

And perhaps they would not catch up to Mr. Porterhouse for several days. She had not thought of that in the morning when she had been so anxious to pursue him and recover her jewels.

She could cetainly not be enjoying herself. But she was.

"Did you say your name was Paul?" she asked quietly after looking guardedly about her.

Mr. Villiers looked surprised. He also looked very nice indeed, with his curls all about his face and down over the collar of his coat. He had brushed them upstairs in their room, but really he was wasting his time doing so. His hair, thank goodness, did what it wanted to do. "I did," he said.

She felt herself flushing. "Will you mind if I call you that in public?" she asked. "I know that some wives call their husbands Mr. So-and-so, but I always think it silly. It will be more convincing, don't you think, if I call you Paul?"

It was true too. She really believed her own words. But mainly she wanted to hear herself call him Paul.

"I suppose so," he said, looking up as a maid brought their soup.

"It is oxtail soup, Paul," she said, smiling at him and at the maid with delight. "My favorite."

"Then I am happy for you, ma'am," he said.

"Oh." She leaned forward toward him as the maid withdrew, and lowered her voice. "You must do it too, you know. You must call me Jo. Just in public, you understand. I would not presume to be so familiar in private."

He leveled at her a look that she took to be one of assent.

She had learned a few things about him in the course of the day. He had a mother and two sisters, two nephews, and a niece. His younger sister was in expectation of a happy event. His maternal grandfather was still alive. He had attended Eton School and Oxford University. He had been to Scotland and Wales, but not to the Continent because of the wars. He spent part of each year in London and most in the country. He liked vigorous outdoor activities, and he liked reading. He liked music, though he was not himself an accomplished performer.

She felt she knew him very well indeed even after one day. There was only one important thing about him that she did not know. And it worried her.

"I told you this morning," she said, plucking up her courage, "that my purse is quite, quite empty, sir."

"Yes," he said, "you did."

It had not been easy to get all that information out of him during the day. Only persistent questioning had drawn it all out.

She flushed. "I do not have even a single farthing."

"Perhaps it is just as well," he said. "There is less for someone else to steal."

She swallowed. "I will have to repay you at some furture date," she said.

He looked at her in some surprise and put down his spoon in his empty soup bowl. "There is no need, I do assure you, ma'am," he siad.

"Do you have enough with you?" she asked, and could feel the blush heating her neck. "I mean . . ."

"Oh." He covered her hand on the table with his for a brief moment. "You are not to worry, ma'am. I have quite sufficient to cover all our needs for some time to come. It is to be hoped that we will recover your jewels tomorrow. Then I shall be returning you to Rutland Park."

Her mouth formed an O, though she did not say it. Yes, it would have to be that way, of course. There would be no going to Aunt Winifred's now. There would be too many explanations to make. Yes, she would have to go home and face the music as soon as she had her jewels safely back in her possession. But her silence was caused not so much by that realization as by the fact that Mr. Villiers had stated it as a quite immutable fact.

She wondered what he would do the next day if she argued with him and insisted on being taken somewhere else. She looked at the slim, fairly ordinary young man across the table from her—except that the curls made him extraordinary—and had a strange feeling that perhaps, just perhaps, she would not get her own way.

It was an interesting idea. She almost always got her own way. She would wager that she would even have had her way over the Duke of Mitford if she had only had the courage to face Papa's and Grandpapa's disappointment.

That was the moment when the unthinkable happened. There was a great to-do and hustle and bustle as four other guests took their places in the dining room, and Josephine, staring with idle curiosity across the room at them, suddenly found herself gazing into the brightening and smiling face of another young lady.

"Jo!" she exclaimed, and almost tipped over her chair in her rush to cross the room. "Jo Middleton! I have not seen you forever. Whatever are you doing here?"

6

"Caroline!" Josephine cried, smiling brightly at the bosom friend of her school days. And, looking beyond her friend to the other occupants of the table, who were all getting to their feet and smiling at her, "Mr. and Mrs. Hennessy. Warren."

She had spent two months of one summer at the Hennessy home.

"My dear, Jo," Mrs. Hennessy said, taking both her hands and kissing her on the cheek, "you have quite grown up. What a pleasant surprise, my dear."

Mr. Hennessy pumped her hand and Warren Hennessy made his bow. He was growing past the awkward, pimply boy stage, Josephine was interested to note.

Mr. Villiers was standing.

"Oh," she said, feeling her blush return in full force. "May I present Mr. Paul Villiers?" She swallowed awkwardly and wondered if any more words would find their way past her throat. But two did. "My husband."

"Your husband?" Mrs. Hennessy clasped her hands to an ample bosom.

Caroline shrieked. "You are married, Jo? Oh, but you did not write and tell me so, you horrid, horrid creature."

"It was all done rather hastily," Mr. Villiers was saying, smiling fondly at her. "Special license and all that. We fell in love and there was no waiting. Was there, Josephine?"

"No," she said. Now, had she put her hand in his or had he taken it? But there it was, resting in his. And she thought she was smiling at him. At least, it felt as if there was a smile on her face. "We were married yesterday, actually."

"Just yesterday!" someone squeaked—Caroline probably.

And Mr. Hennessy was roaring for a bottle of champagne or the next best thing the house could provide. Noisy

introductions were being made on all sides, and they were all
seated at the same table.

And her hand was still clasped in Mr. Villiers's.

Oh, dear.

"Would that be one of the Sussex Villiers?" Mr. Hennessy
was asking.

Mr. Villiers hesitated. "Just a very junior branch," he said.
"Do you live hereabouts, sir?"

It seemed that the Hennessys were on their way home from
London—a long and weary journey, but only one day longer.

And it seemed that they, the newlywed Villierses, were on
their wedding trip to Scotland. At least, that was what Mr.
Villiers was explaining in a very amiable manner and smiling
at her for confirmation. One of them had dropped the other's
hand by that time.

The Hennessys had been on the road for all of four days, yet
all looked immaculate, as if they were dining in their own
drawing room at home. Josephine became conscious of the
creases in her dress and the crow's nest balanced on her head.

"Oh," she said, "the most amusing thing has happened. My
maid, and, ah, um, Paul's valet left home with all our baggage
several hours before we did. They were supposed to be waiting
for us at the inn last night and again tonight. But somehow the
wrong directions must have been given. We have not set eyes
on them since they left. Have we, Paul?" She giggled a trifle
hysterically.

He grinned. Oh goodness, he had a lopsided grin. It
transformed his face from nice to definitely attractive. "I am
afraid I am reduced to one small bag and Josephine to one
valise," he said.

Josephine pushed at her hair. "I am afraid I am quite lost
without Betty," she said.

"But Jo," Caroline said, "I will lend you Lucy tomorrow
morning. You remember Lucy. And I have trunkfuls of clothes.
You must come to my room and choose a clean dress for
tomorrow. I am not a great deal larger than you."

"Indeed," Mrs. Hennessy said, looking to her husband for
confirmation, "we would be quite honored and delighted if the
two of you would come with us to Hawthorn House to spend
a few days. Jo will tell you, Mr. Villiers, that the house affords

a very pleasant prospect of the countryside around. You may walk and ride to your heart's content."

"And in the meantime we will send out to find your missing servants and belongings," Mr. Hennessy said with a rumbling laugh. "That is quite a thing to happen on your wedding trip."

Mr. Villiers somehow turned aside the invitation, Josephine was relieved to hear. The explanation involved him in picking up her hand again and kissing her fingers and smiling deep into her eyes. And Mr. Hennessy was laughing again and asking his wife if she remembered what young lovers were like and how they liked to be off on their own.

"Yes, Harvey," his wife agreed, "but off on their own with no baggage is another thing altogether."

It was decided, before they all settled to their meal and chattered away on numerous other topics, that the invitation should be considered an open one and that the newlyweds would accept it if they changed their minds during the following few days or if they found their baggage coach hopelessly lost.

But Josephine had noticed something else while Mr. Villiers was kissing her hand, and she felt constrained to explain to the Hennessys that when Paul had put her wedding ring on her finger the previous day, it had promptly fallen off again.

"The silly man," she said, smiling fondly into his gray, interested eyes, "was in such a hurry to marry me that he bought the ring without measuring my finger. And it is too large. So it has to be carried around in his pocket until we can find a jeweler to make it smaller."

"Whoever would have thought that anyone could have such very slim fingers," Mr. Villiers said, grinning at her again in such a way that she almost lost the thread of her story. And he set three fingers and a thumb around the finger, where the ring would have been if there had been any ring, and slid them down to the end of her finger.

She did lose the trend of the story, but it did not matter. Mr. Hennessy laughed and Caroline sighed and Warren took snuff and sneezed rather more loudly than he ought.

And then just when Mr. Hennessy and Mr. Villiers were discussing the political situation and she and Caroline were reminiscing about school and she was feeling almost comfortable, the most dreadful thing of all happened.

"Eleven o'clock," Mr. Hennessy announced, consulting a large pocket watch. "Time for bed, everyone. Especially for these two. They have doubtless been ready for it this hour and more and have been cursing this chance meeting." He laughed heartily.

"Harvey!" Mrs. Hennessy said, laughing too.

Even Mr. Villiers was blushing, Josephine saw in one swift peep as he took her hand in his and placed it on his sleeve.

And their room, when they reached it a few minutes later, seemed very, very quiet indeed. And very much dominated by the large bed.

"I think," said the Duke of Mitford, dragging off his coat and throwing it over the edge of the bed before raking one hand through his hair, "I have told more lies in one evening than I have in my whole lifetime before. It's downright frightening."

"I am so very sorry, sir," Josephine Middleton said, clasping her hands before her and gazing up at him with wide, remorseful eyes. "But whoever would have thought I would run into people I know? I know hardly anyone—Papa and Grandpapa having this gothic notion that young persons are better brought up in the country than exposed to all the evils of town. But I did go to school, you see, and I suppose I do have acquaintances scattered all over the kingdom.'''

"Well," he said, "I suppose no real harm has been done, except that the Hennessy family are going to find next time they hear from you that matters are somewhat different from what they thought."

"Yes," she said, and her hands fell to her sides and brushed ineffectually at the wrinkles in her dress.

It was probably as well that she had told the story about the lost baggage and servants, Mitford thought. Otherwise the Hennessys, believing they had been married just the day before, would doubtless have put quite another interpretation on her decidedly tumbled looking appearance. It quite put him to the blush to think of it.

And he really had told some bouncers. Most of the details of their marriage would, of course, come true, he had been coming to realize throughout the course of the day, although they should have been told in the future tense instead of in the past. Even down to the detail about the special license. By the time he got Miss Josephine Middleton back to Rutland Park, he would have to rush her into marriage just as fast as he possibly could before dreadful scandal broke for both her and him—at least, he hoped it would be before. She had been hopelessly compromised over the course of twenty-four hours.

But he would be sure to measure her finger. And he would be very sure that Henry and her maid knew where to take their baggage for the first night of their wedding journey. The very idea that he could be such a careless fellow as to lose his own servants!

The only real inaccuracy even in the future tense was the detail about their having fallen deeply in love. In love with this brainless little lady who could lie like a Drury Lane actress? Oh, Lord! He had never in his life met anyone so lacking in conduct and a sense of proper decorum.

She was blushing and smiling and removing the pins from her hair. "I will sleep on the floor tonight, sir," she said. "It is only fair, and really I do not mind at all."

"You will sleep on the bed, Miss Middleton," he said, watching, fascinated, as heavy curly hair cascaded almost to her waist. It must weigh as much as she did. It was really rather magnificent. She should always leave it loose. He repressed the thought, though, when he suddenly had a mental image of her sitting beside him in his curricle, waving to the dandies on the roofs of the stages, her curly locks blowing in the wind.

Oh, Lord.

"Really," she said, and she flushed a deeper shade of red, "there is no need for either of us to sleep on the floor. It is rather a large bed, and we could both keep over to our side. I think it would be silly for you to sleep on the floor."

Mitford did not think it would be silly, but he knew it would be deuced uncomfortable.

"I will leave you for ten minutes," he said, watching her hands go to the neck of her dress and then fall to her sides again. He picked up his recently discarded coat. "Sleep well, ma'am, and don't worry about me. Tomorrow is likely to be a long and busy day again."

He wandered down to the taproom and ordered a pint of ale. He hoped none of the Hennessys would decide to come down for a nightcap. It would look strange indeed that he had abandoned his bride after eleven o'clock on the second night of their marriage.

What a coil! All he would need now was to run into someone he knew.

It really was quite shocking how easy it was to lie down when one felt the necessity of doing so. And it had been necessary. He did not care to imagine the looks on the faces of Miss Middleton's friends if they had known that she was traveling alone with a man who was not her husband, and had discovered that she was sharing a room at the inn with him.

Good Lord, was that what was really happening? Could it possibly be that he, Paul Villiers, Duke of Mitford, not to mention his string of lesser titles, was really involved in such an indiscretion? And the word *indiscretion* was such an understatement that it was laughable.

He was never indiscreet. Or improper. Or impulsive. Or reckless. He could go on and on. He was never anything but perfectly respectable. How could he be otherwise? He had held all those titles since he was seventeen years old, and one for much longer than that, and all the responsibilities that went with them.

A junior branch of the Sussex Villiers, indeed. Good Lord, he was head of the family and had been for eleven years. It had been a sticky moment when Mr. Hennessy had asked that. And now that he was thinking on the subject, did Miss Middleton not know that the Duke of Mitford's family name was Villiers? Apparently not.

Half an hour passed before he returned to their room. It was not one of his traveling companion's quick ten minutes. Perhaps he should not have left the room at all, he thought as he dawdled his way up the stairs. Going back in there was probably the most difficult thing he had done in more than twenty-four hours. Even entering her room, shoulder first, the evening before had not been so difficult because he had had no time to think about the matter.

But he had had half an hour to think about this one. He was about to share a room with an unmarried young lady. It was a hair-raising prospect. He had never even spent a whole night in Eveline's room. And that had been different, anyway. Eveline had been a widow, and one year older than he, and a woman of the world. And she had been his mistress.

Good Lord, what was he about? He really should have returned her to her father the night before. He could not now imagine why he had not done so. And that morning, when she had discovered the loss of her jewels, he should have taken her home without further ado and enlisted help—her brother's perhaps—to go after the thief.

He should never—never!—have consented to take to the open road alone with her.

And what he ought to do now, since he could not go back to amend the past, was rise with the dawn and convey her home with all speed. It was disastrously late to take such a course, but nevertheless it was the only course to take.

He would do it.

In the meantime, he would have to pluck up the courage to enter their shared bedchamber. Well, he thought, turning the key in the door resolutely, there was no help for it. And at least she had the modesty to be pretending to sleep. He had half expected to find her sitting up in bed in that shift or whatever else it was she had been wearing—or almost not wearing—when she had smiled down at him that morning, waiting to chatter his head off about something. The girl could certainly chatter. She had scarce stopped all day long.

But she was curled up so far to one side of the bed that she looked as if she were in danger of falling off. And the blankets covered her decently to the chin. She had her eyes closed, but she was breathing too quietly and too quickly to be sleeping. She had left a second pillow balanced at the opposite edge of the bed from where she lay.

Mitford looked at it longingly and at the floor with some distaste. It did not look quite as uneven as last night's floor, but he realized suddenly that he was all over aches and pains. What he would really like more than anything in the world was to throw off all his clothes and step into a bathtub overflowing with hot soapy water.

He took off his coat again and pulled off his boots. The rest of his clothes would have to stay where they were, he thought regretfully. And he did not even have a clean shirt to put on the next day. He picked up the pillow and hurled it vengefully at the floor. At least it would be an improvement on his bag.

But every muscle screamed at him when he lowered himself to the floor and tried to cover himself with his greatcoat. It seemed that either his shoulders or his feet would have to be exposed to the night air.

But dammit, he thought with unaccustomed vehemence as he realized finally that there was no such thing as a comfortable way to lie on such a surface, there were three quarters of a soft looking bed and warm blankets waiting just above him. And perhaps she really was asleep. It had been a long and tiring day for her too.

He got quietly to his feet, rolled his greatcoat and set it carefully down the center of the bed, and climbed gratefully between the blankets on his side, balancing himself on the edge of the bed. He did not think he had ever in his life lain on a softer, warmer, more inviting surface.

But he did not have long to rhapsodize. He was sleeping within minutes.

All good things must come to an end, of course—sometimes sooner than necessary. He awoke with a jump when a bolt from heaven landed on his left eye. Except that it was not a real bolt, he realized as soon as he shook himself free of his dream, but a feminine fist.

The owner of the fist was not, apparently, awake. She turned over onto her side facing him—and when had he moved to the center of the bed facing her?—with a great deal of wriggling and rustling and sighing, had discovered that his shoulder was warmer and more comfortable than her pillow, and burrowed her head against it. There was some muttering, and the arm and hand that had smacked him curved around his waist. She settled back into deep sleep again. The rolled coat was still between them.

Oh, Lord! Oh, good Lord! Her hair was tickling his nose. And during the extended ten minutes of his absence at bedtime, she must have washed and put something on herself. Something with a soft feminine fragrance. Something good.

The Duke of Mitford was no expert on feminine fragrances. Eveline had always worn a strong, sweet perfume. He had never liked it, though he had never been impolite enough to tell her so.

Miss Middleton smelled good. And her breath was warm at

his neck. And where the deuce was he supposed to put his arm? It was dangling rather awkwardly over hers, down along his side. He set it at her waist—a soft and small and warm waist. And good Lord, there was nothing except a very thin shift between his hand and her.

"I won't marry the duke, Papa," she said in a voice of firm determination, making the Duke of Mitford jump and then lie very still, holding his breath. The words were followed by mutterings and grumblings and more head burrowing against his shoulder.

"The ring fell off," she muttered, and she was still and quiet again.

What a coil! If he tried to move away, she would doubtless wake up and think he was trying to ravish her. If he did not move away, she might wake up before he did and think that he was responsible for this cozy arrangement of bodies.

Oh, Lord, what was he to do? The Duke of Mitford wished fervently that he had had more experience with the worldier side of life. Of course, there was no chance whatsoever that he would sleep another wink that night anyway. Perhaps after a while, when he was quite sure she was fast asleep, he could ease his way over to the side of the bed and down onto the floor again.

"Nice," she muttered against his neck. She sighed deeply, sending tickles right down to his toes. "Nice."

The Duke of Mitford, who would not have a wink of sleep for the rest of the night, had a deep sleep instead.

It was far more comfortable to ride inside the old coach than up on the box, Bartholomew discovered. And the riding was smoother too. Not that it was the driver who made the difference, of course. It was a fact that the road north was kept in far better repair than the one they had traveled early that morning.

However it was, Sukey was not sick any more. Sam said it was because she had eaten some breakfast. She said it was because the ride was smoother. Bartholomew said it was because she had grown accustomed to the motion of the carriage.

And Sam had turned out to be something of a tyrant. He had

stopped to change horses long before Bartholomew thought it was necessary.

"The little lady needs a rest and some tea and vittles," the new coachman said quite firmly when his new master voiced his objections.

And so Susanna had her tea and some cakes while her brother fumed at the delay.

And Sam stopped for the night long before it was quite dark.

"The road is still quite clear to me," Bartholomew protested. "And it is going to be a clear night, doubtless with moon and plenty of stars."

"The little lady needs 'er dinner and 'er rest," Sam said. And who was to argue with such a giant? Certainly not Susanna, who looked quite exhausted although she had valiantly withheld all complaints. "The gent won't escape with the jewels," he added with a reassuring grin. "Nor the other gent with the lady. The trail is clear enough."

And it was too. There was no lack of people who had seen the gaudy blue and yellow carriage with the handsome gentleman, and the gentleman's curricle with the lady passenger. They would catch up to them the next day or the day after, Sam said with the greatest confidence.

But who the devil was Paul Villiers? And what the deuce was Jo doing with him?

Josephine was awake a full five minutes before the knock sounded on the door. She woke feeling warm and drowsy and quite unwilling to be roused. She simply must remember to ask Betty what new soap the sheets were being washed in. A musky smell. Nice.

"Nice," she heard herself mutter, and then felt remarkably foolish and remarkably something else too, for she was not, of course, lying in her bed at home but in the bed at the inn that Mr. Villiers had paid for. And she was snuggled up warmly against Mr. Villiers's person, her head against his shoulder, her nose against his neck, her arm about his waist and her leg pushed up against his—except that the blankets or something had got bunched up between them.

She opened her eyes and closed them again, afraid that her eyelashes would tickle his neck and waken him. She was afraid to breathe for the same reason until she discovered that doing so was necessary for survival. His own arm was over hers and clasping her shoulder.

Over hers. That meant that her arm had gone into place first. She was responsible for this most embarrassing situation. Embarrassing? Mortifying in the extreme. Papa would kill them both. Grandpapa would read her a week-long lecture. Even Bart would be shocked.

Oh, goodness gracious, and oh, dear. However had she got herself into such a dreadful state of affairs? She was quite beyond redemption. If she had sat down at home and dreamed up the very worst predicament she could possibly get herself into, she could not have imagined something quite as bad as this. She would have thought of something like having to marry that toplofty duke.

It was a good thing, a very good thing, that Mr. Villiers was a nice man and such a kind one. She would be in a very nasty case indeed if he were not. In definite peril of a fate worse than death.

Fortunately, she did not feel in great peril at all. Indeed, if she calmed down and stopped thinking of Papa and Grandpapa and Bart, she did not feel in any peril at all. She felt decidedly safe. She had known before that Mr. Villiers's shoulders and arms were well muscled. She could feel some of those muscles beneath her head now. And yet his shoulder was comfortable too. She did not think she would be afraid if a whole army of Mr. Porterhouses were to come storming into the room. She felt quite safe and warm and comfortable.

Paul. It was a nice name. If someone had asked her the day before to say what her favorite men's names were, she would have said Justin or Nicholas or Christopher or Robert. Never Paul. That would have been low on her list. But only because she would not have thought of it. If she had thought of it, surely she would have put it quite at the top of the list.

She liked his smile. Oh, not just the social smile, though that was nice too, but the one he used when he was really amused, the one that dragged the right side of his mouth higher than the left and set his eyes to dancing. It was quite the most attractive smile she had ever seen.

Paul.

Josephine's eyes snapped open when she realized that she was on the verge of dozing off again. Oh, goodness gracious, she must not sleep. She had a very important job to do. She had to extricate herself from an embrace that would surely have him thinking her a brazen hussy at the very least if he were to wake up. She edged her head away from his shoulder and tried to slide her arm from beneath his.

"Mm," he complained, and she stopped moving.

He moved his hand up from her shoulder to the back of her neck and rubbed lightly over the smooth skin beneath her hair. Josephine felt shivers twirl down to her stomach and cause it to perform a complete somersault. She swallowed hard.

But he was not awake. And there was one thing she must do before edging farther away from him. There was one thing she could not resist doing any more than she had been able to stop breathing a few minutes before. She lifted her head and touched one of his curls very lightly. She was smoothing the hair over one finger when the knock sounded at the door.

A gentle tap, not a loud pounding.

But Josephine rolled toward the edge of the bed with such speed that she teetered at the edge for a moment. And Mr. Villiers leapt straight up in the air—she would swear until her dying day that he did—and came down on his feet beside the bed.

At least he would never know, she thought, what he would have discovered if he had woken of his own accord at that particular moment. He glanced at her—looking quite adorably rumpled—and answered the door.

A few minutes later Mr. Villiers had been borne off to see if any of Warren Hennessy's shirts would fit him—was it going to be very obvious that he had slept in the one he was wearing? Josephine wondered—and she was in the blessedly competent hands of Caroline's maid. And Lucy, glancing a little consciously at the untidy bed, congratulated her on her marriage two days before.

Oh, dear.

7

"What I should have done," the Duke of Mitford was saying, "was take Mr. Hennessy to one side last night and explain the whole to him. He could have taken you home with his family and I could have continued in pursuit of your jewels."

"But what would he have thought about the fact that we were together and had been all day?" she said.

"I could have explained," he said, "that I met you yesterday morning after you discovered your loss and had agreed to chase after the thief with you. It would have seemed unwise, but not too, too improper. I wish I had thought of it."

"But he would have sent me back home," she said. She clung to her usual fistful of his coat sleeve as the curricle swayed around a bend in the road. "And perhaps I would have arrived back before the Duke of Mitford, and I would have had to marry him."

"And what is so bad about that?" he asked. "You have never met him. Perhaps he is not near as bad as you think. Perhaps he is a very personable man.'

"How could he be?" she asked reasonably. "There is his man."

"Ah, yes," he said. "There is his man. Incontrovertible evidence against the master. I had forgotten about him."

"Besides," she said, "I would rather be with you than with the Hennessys."

"But good Lord," he said, aghast, "you should not, ma'am. My mind is quite plagued with the thought of the past two days and all the terrible impropriety of them. And the lies!"

She looked at him in that way he wished she did not have—all large and soulful gray eyes. "I have inconvenienced you terribly, have I not?" she said. "You have no wish to be wasting your time with me any longer. Perhaps I should after all throw myself on the mercy of Mr. Hennessy. I have been very selfish.''

Mitford passed a hand over his brow. "It's not that at all,'' he said. "If you are mad enough to travel about England with a strange gentleman, ma'am, then I would as soon it was with me. And it is too late by far to be telling the Hennessys the truth. They would collapse with a collective apoplexy.''

"Yes,'' she said, still clinging to his sleeve, "I suppose they would. You are willing to continue with me, then, sir? You are very kind.''

"Kindness has nothing to do with the matter,'' he said fervently. "Insanity has everything to do with it.''

She smiled at him, but he deliberately did not look down to see the smile. He kept his eyes on the road ahead. Good Lord, Mama would go into a permanent decline when she discovered just what sort of bride her own father had picked out for him.

They had had breakfast with the Hennessys and repeated their promise to consider accepting the invitation to stay at Hawthorn House if they did not find their baggage coach that day. And they had laughed and blushed a great deal at Mr. Hennessy's insistence that they both looked as if they could do with another few hours of sleep.

"Or perhaps I should not use the word *another*,'' he had added, so that everyone at the table had blushed except Mr. Hennessy and his good lady.

They were far later setting out than Mitford had intended. But it seemed that a bride and her groom did not rush anywhere, except perhaps to bed at night, and they had been forced to play the part to the end. And of course, there had been some delay while Caroline Hennessy's maid sewed up the hem of the borrowed dress a good three inches.

And then when they had set out, it had been in quite the opposite direction from the one he had planned so very sensibly the night before. For the Hennessys turned out in force to wave them on their way, and it would have looked peculiar indeed if they had turned south in order to continue their wedding trip to Scotland.

Though, of course, they could have turned south in search of their missing baggage coach. Now, why had he not thought of that at the time? Oh, Lord, if he only had had some practice at intrigue!

The trail was still very easy to follow until they lost it abruptly and completely late in the afternoon. At one inn the blue and yellow carriage and the tall, dark, and handsome gentleman were clearly remembered. He had changed horses there during the morning. At the next inn, no one recalled seeing anyone fitting the description, though there had been a black and yellow carriage carrying an elderly couple south, one groom had informed them helpfully.

At the next inn it was the same story, except that no one mentioned the southbound carriage.

"But we would have passed him if he had turned back," Josephine said, frowning and contorting her lips to one side so that she might bite at the inside of her cheek. "He is not getting away with my jewels, that is for certain. If he thinks I will abandon the search so easily, he is sadly mistaken."

They were brave words. But what did one do when the man one was pursuing seemed to have dropped off the face of the earth together with the carriage he was traveling in?

"We will have to go back to the inn where he was last seen," the duke said. "There is no point in going any farther north. By the time we get back there, it will be nightfall and we will have to spend the night." He spoke with sudden decision. "And tomorrow, Miss Middleton, I am going to start on the way back home with you. I should never have brought you this far. It was sheer madness. I'll take you back to your father."

"Oh, no, you will not!" she said vehemently. "I am not going back without my jewels, sir. And if you will not search farther with me, then I will search alone. I don't need you."

"Yes, you do," he said. "I hold the purse strings, remember?"

"Oh!" she said. "How horrid of you to remind me of that. As if I did not know it. And I have already told you that I will repay every farthing that you have spent on my behalf. You need not fear eing out of pocket, sir."

"I do not fear it," he said. "I am more afraid of swinging from a noose for kidnapping."

"Oh, rubbish and nonsense," she said. "Do you think I have

no tongue in my head to speak up for you? We must continue with the search for my jewels. Not that they are of very great value, you understand, Grandpapa being very insistent that all the really valuable family jewels be kept under lock and key—his key. But it is the principle of the thing. I cannot bear to think of that horrid man handling Mama's garnets and gloating over Grandmama's ring and turning up his nose in disgust at the smallness of the emeralds in Bart's earbobs.''

"I will find Porterhouse and your jewels eventually," he said. "But we cannot pluck him out of thin air, Miss Middleton. And the longer you and I travel about together and keep up this charade of being man and wife, the more your reputation will suffer. I shall take you back home. And it seems to me that that is a good place to start my search again. Perhaps the people he was staying with there will have some idea of where he may be found.''

"The Winthrops?" she said. "But I don't want to go home. You won't force me to go, will you?"

"Yes. I will," he said.

"Oh," she said accusingly, "and I thought you were nice."

She sat beside him with slumped shoulders and lowered head for all of three miles as they headed south again. And why was he feeling so very guilty about finally deciding to do what was right and proper? He felt like putting one arm about her and cradling her head against his shoulder—where it had rested last night, now that he came to think about last night—and murmuring soothing words into her ear.

Was he mad? He never put his arms about young ladies or murmured into their ears. Either in public or in private. It was a most improper thing to do. And was he thinking of doing both now perched on the high seat of a curricle on the open highway for all the world to see? It did not bear thinking of. The Duke of Mitford kept his hands on the ribbons and his eyes on the road ahead of him.

He had miscalculated. Darkness—and a very thick and heavy darkness—was already falling when they reached the first inn where there had been no news of Portherhouse. They were forced to put up for the night there.

Josephine ate her dinner in stony and unhappy silence, and Mitford kept glancing at her, uneasy and guilt-ridden. Though whether he felt more guilty over having begun this charade in the first place or over finally trying to end it before she was completely ruined, he would have been hard put to it to say.

He felt like a monster and a tyrant.

But good Lord. Good Lord! He could scarce believe in the reality of the past two days. He would not have believed himself capable of such behavior. He had rescued a maiden in distress, and ten minutes or less later he had had the chance to turn her over, unharmed, to her father.

And what had he done instead? Well, he did not care to think of what he had done.

An he had wanted adventure in his life before settling to a dull and proper marriage. Oh, Lord.

He would suffer the effects of this adventure to his dying day. He would have to marry this mad little creature, who preferred to be with a strange male than with the respectable Hennessys. He looked gloomily across the table at her unhappy face. And shook off the memory of her head on his shoulder the night before and the thin shift that had been all that separated his hand from her warm woman's body. And the thought of her clinging trustingly to his sleeve through most of the day.

She would suffer the effects of her indiscretion. It had all started when she had run from the unwanted marriage. Poor Miss Middleton. He could almost feel sorry for her. The moment she had begged him not to go out to her father was the moment she had sealed her own doom. For now she was bound to marry the duke she had fled.

A fine marriage they were going to have, indeed! He doubted he would ever be able to train her to fit into the life he had been raised to from childhood. A more unlikely candidate for a duchess—and *his* duchess—he had never in his life met.

She yawned suddenly across the table from him and made no attempt, as a genteel young lady would do, to disguise the fact. Her eyes were on her fork, which was pushing a piece of potato aimlessly around.

Mitford found himself smiling despite himself. Good Lord, had not Grandpapa said she was twenty years old? She seemed like a very child, one quite innocent of the ways of the world. Except that she did not feel at all like a child.

"Come," he said, "I shall take you up to our room. You are tired."

She did not argue but waited for him to come around the table and pull out her chair, and rose listlessly to her feet. She moved ahead of him to the doorway, one of his hands at the small of her back.

And of course, Mitford thought, a trying day must have the perfect ending. And if it had happened the night before, why not this night too? He was hardly even surprised.

There was a young and fashionable gentleman sitting in the shadow at a table close to the door. A gentleman who looked in amusement and appreciation at Miss Middleton and in greater amusement at him. A gentleman who raised his wine glass in a mock toast and winked at the Duke of Mitford as he passed.

A gentleman who just happened to be Sir Thomas Burgess, one of his closest friends.

Mitford walked past without acknowledging either the toast or the wink or the familiarity of the gentleman who offered both. He led Josephine up the stairs in silence, opened the door into their room, and stepped inside with her.

"You are very tired," he said. "It has been a long and a distressing day for you. Go to sleep now, and everything will appear a little better in the morning."

"No, it will not," she said, looking down at her hands. "Everyone is quite right about me. Everyone says I am an utter shatterbrain. I would not talk to Papa, though I know he would have listened to me. And I trusted Mr. Porterhouse when I should not have. And I brought my jewels with me instead of leaving them at home where they were safe. And I interfered with your journey and dragged you north with me when you were too kind to say no. And it has all been in vain. We have not found either Mr. Porterhouse or my jewels."

"But I will find both," he said. "I promise you that I will sooner or later."

She raised miserable eyes to his. "Why should you?" she said. "What concern are my problems of yours?"

It was a good question, the duke thought. He smiled down at her and set one hand on her shoulder, patting it reassuringly. "I don't like to waste two days either," he said. "Go to bed now. You need sleep more than anything. I shall go downstairs again for a while.''

"Mr. Villiers?" she said, as he turned away to the door. He turned back and looked inquiringly at her.

"I am sorry I was cross with you," she said. "I had no right. You have been very kind to me."

He smiled in some amusement. He wished he had kept count of the number of times she had said that since he had met her.

Sir Thomas Burgess was still sitting in the dining room. He was just cutting into a plateful of roast beef and vegetables. The Duke of Mitford took the seat opposite him.

"Your summer in Scotland has extended well into the autumn, Tom," he said. "Are you finally on the way home?"

His friend finished cutting into his beef and put a forkful into his mouth. He ate it unhurriedly, regarding the duke the while with the same amusement as had been on his face earlier.

"And it would seem that it is about time," he said at last. "The world must be coming to an end if my eyes did not deceive me ten minutes ago. Paul, you old dog, you. I never thought to see you squiring around a little ladybird on the king's highway."

The duke sat back in his chair and blew out his breath from puffed cheeks. "She isn't a ladybird," he said.

"Ah." Sir Thomas laughed. "Sorry, old boy. This dim light was deceiving my eyes. Your octogenarian aunt, was she, Paul?"

"No," the duke said. "She is not my aunt either, Tom. I suppose I could not persuade you to forget that you have seen me here, could I?"

His friend held up his right hand. "My lips are sealed," he said. "Am I keeping you from the lady's arms, Mitford? And does she treat you well when you are in them? I am mortally jealous. Nights spent alone at inns are deuced long and tedious, are they not?"

"Look, Tom." Mitford shifted uncomfortably on his chair. "It's not what you think. She's a lady."

Sir Thomas seemed to forget about his food. He leaned back in his chair and grinned. "Mitford, you old dog," he said, "I

knew you had it in you. I knew you would have to break loose
one of these days. But a lady? Are you serious?"

"Yes, I'm serious," the duke said. "And I would prefer it
if you weren't so loud and free with the 'Mitfords,' Burgess.
Could you make that Villiers?"

His friend stared at him, and a slow grin spread across his
face again. "I'm a bit of a slowtop, aren't I?" he said. "But
I get there eventually, Mit—ah, Villiers. You are traveling on
the north road incognito with a young thing whom you claim
to be a lady. You are heading north, I suppose?"

The duke nodded.

"Gretna, by any chance?" his friend asked.

"Oh, good Lord," Mitford said.

"Ha!" Sir Thomas cut into his food again. "Guessed it, have
I, my boy? Though I can't imagine why you would have to elope
with any young lady when any number of them have been trying
for years to trap you and I know at least a dozen baronets and
earls and such who would kill to acquire you for a son-in-law.
She must be promised to someone else, is she?"

"Oh, Lord," the duke said. "You always were hopeless at
charades and guessing games, Tom. Look, just forget you have
seen me, will you? I'll see you in London when I get back there.
You shall tell me all about Scotland."

"And you shall tell me all about the one part of it I missed,"
Sir Thomas said, raising his wine glass and winking at his friend
again. "Gretna Green. I can tell you this, Mit—Villiers, no one
will ever call you a dull dog again after this escapade. You will
be the *on-dit* for a year or more. Go and enjoy the little lady,
then. I admire your choice, by the way. She is quite exquisitely
pretty."

The duke rose to his feet. "Good night, Tom," he said. "I
would rather my . . . um, I would rather Miss . . . I would
rather she did not know there is someone here I am acquainted
with. She may find it rather distressing."

His friend winked once more. "If we meet at breakfast,"
he said, "I shall look straight through you, Paul. Never saw
you in my life. I suppose you are registered here as Mr. and
Mrs. Villiers?"

"Yes," the duke said, flushing.

"Mitford," Sir Thomas said, lifting his wine glass to his lips, "welcome to the human race. Go. Don't worry about leaving me to enjoy a solitary meal. And don't worry about the fact that I broke an axle of my carriage this afternoon and am doubtless stranded at this godforsaken inn for the next fortnight. Do not worry about me at all. Mrs. Villiers awaits you."

The Duke of Mitford scratched his head and left.

But as he passed the taproom, the landlord called to him and asked if he was still interested in a blue and yellow carriage.

"Yes, indeed," the duke said, stepping inside and up to the counter.

"That gent"—the landlord nodded in the direction of a burly farmer who was in the process of tipping back a large tankard of ale—"says that a dark gentleman in a carriage of that description lost a wheel earlier today when he collided with a herd of cows being led across the road. Came near to killing one of the cows, he did, too."

Mitford looked to the farmer in question. "And which direction was he headed in?" he asked the landlord.

The man pointed off in an easterly direction. "Probably on his way to the baron's," he said. "That's where all the other nobs have been going today, if you will pardon me, sir."

"The baron's?" The duke raised his eyebrows.

"Lord Parleigh that would be, sir," the landlord said. "Deerview Park is seven miles away. Always having guests, he is, sir."

"Thank you." The duke set a coin in the landlord's hand.

Josephine laid the borrowed dress carefully over the back of a chair. It would do for the next day too. It would have to do. She washed herself carefully and brushed out her hair. She knew she did not have to hurry. Mr. Villiers would not return soon.

And she was going to have to do some deep and fast thinking. Mr. Villiers was going to take her home the next day. And she had known earlier that afternoon, looking at his profile as he drove his curricle, that he had meant what he said and would not be shifted easily.

Men! They were all the same. Stuffy and immutable when it came to doing what they thought was right for a lady's well-being. They never thought to consult the lady in question and consider her wishes. Oh no, they simply decided and that was that. Just as if women were children or featherbrains.

Mr. Villiers was as bad as any of them. Even though he was no great hulking gentleman who would intimidate females by his size, and even though he was mild mannered and amiable and had that good-humored mouth and those soft, unruly curls, nevertheless he was a gentleman through and through. And that meant that he was an oppressor of ladies.

He knew what was right for a lady, and he would impose his will on her.

Josephine tossed her brush back into her valise after dragging it through her hair twenty times—Betty always said that fifty was the minimum allowable, but who had the time to be brushing hair half the night? She was feeling thoroughly and satisfyingly aggrieved.

And a little guilty. Mr. Villiers had, after all, just given up two days of his life to cater to her whims and was about to give up two more in order to take her back home again—where he would doubtless be killed by Papa and lectured by Grandpapa.

Josephine yawned suddenly and hugely. If they went back home, she would never see her jewels again. And that villain would escape scot-free. It was not good enough. Oh, it would just not do at all.

She yawned again at great and noisy length. She would have to sleep. There was no choice in the matter. She would think in the morning. She would come up with some plan then. She was not quite defeated yet, despite her earlier depression. Oh, not by any means.

But lying on her bed, her arms crossed over her waist, staring upward, did not after all bring the expected oblivion. And where was Mr. Villiers going to sleep? Probably on the floor again if he had any inkling of how well their experiment at sharing a bed had turned out the night before.

He should not have to sleep on the floor, she thought with a rush of contrition for all the uncharitable thoughts she had had of him in the past half hour. Indeed, he should not be inconvenienced at all. She should be the one to face all the discomfort. And if she was doomed to a sleepless night anyway, then it might as well be on the floor so that Mr. Villiers could sleep on the bed.

Five minutes later, she was lying on the floor beside the bed, her cloak under her, one pillow beneath her head, and one blanket covering her. It was not even remotely comfortable. But she would not utter one sound of complaint. When Mr. Villiers came back to the room, she would pretend to be sleeping, and she would lie quiet all night long.

After a few minutes the floor no longer seemed quite so uncomfortable. And she really was very tired. She turned onto her side and curled up warmly beneath the blanket.

And then suddenly she was a little child again and had been naughty and had hidden in the long cupboard in the schoolroom. And Papa had found her there and was not after all cross but only relieved that he had found her safe and sound when he had thought her lost. And she was telling him that she had broken a priceless vase in the morning room, a vase that could never be replaced. But instead of scolding and punishing, he scooped her up in his arms and called her his half-pint and told her that she was more precious to him than any vase.

She felt like crying because he was always so loving and kind to her while she was often thoughtless and disobedient. But those safe arms were not to be resisted and she curled into them and reached up in protest to cling to his neck when he set her down.

"Paul," she said, "I was quite comfortable there. I don't want you to sleep there. You should have the bed."

His face was very close to hers because of the hold she still had of his neck. And his one arm was still beneath her shoulders and the other beneath her knees.

"Sh," he said softly. "Go back to sleep."

"Don't sleep on the floor," she said. "I feel guilty. Sleep on the bed, Paul. There is lots of room."

"Hush," he murmurd, his nice gray eyes smiling at her. "Just go to sleep and don't worry about me." And he leaned down and kissed her on the forehead.

Josephine released her hold of him and closed her eyes. And she curled over onto her side when he slid his arm from beneath her and covered her with the blanket. He was Mr. Villiers, not Papa. And she had called him Paul. Oh, dear. He had lifted her to the bed and covered her up. And he had kissed her on the forehead.

She knew the difference between her dream and reality, but she would not allow the reality to be more than a dream. She kept breathing slowly and deeply and kept her eyes closed. And she listened to the comforting sounds of Mr. Villiers moving quietly about the room before settling to rest in the bed on the floor that she had made for herself.

She would not let herself wake up. If she was sleeping, she could still feel free to enjoy being with him more than she would enjoy being with the Hennessys.

The duke awoke from a drea... torturously considered a dozen cou... the last couple of days that would... times more decorous than the one ... actually taken. Unfortunately, even in the moment of ...aking, he could not think of even one of the dozen. He had a headache instead.

Josephine Middleton was kneeling on the floor beside him, her hair wild and quite glorious about her face and down over her shoulders and bosom. Her face was alight and her mouth in motion.

" . . . silly," she was saying. "There was plenty of room for us both."

"Thank you, ma'am," he said, "but the floor was quite comfortable." Why was it, he thought, that sleepless nights always ended in the most delightful slumber after dawn? And why was there always someone to wake one on such mornings?

"I have had the most splendid idea," she said. "I cannot think why neither of us thought of it yesterday."

Mitford closed his eyes and tried to pretend that he was still dreaming. The floor felt almost cozy.

"Somewhere between here and the last inn Mr. Porterhouse disappeared," she said. "Right?"

"Right," he muttered.

"And he cannot really have disappeared into thin air, can he?" she said.

"No." He tried to catch onto that thin and fast disappearing thread of sleep.

"We know he did not turn back or we would have seen him," she said. "Right?"

"Right."

"Then he must have turned off along another road," she said,

nd looking down at him in triumph.
e said.

e said, "it is simple. All we have to do is
ry single road and laneway between here and
and drive along it until we find someone we may
. We must remember to look on both sides of this road,
ourse."

The duke, admitting regretfully to himself that he was doomed to awaken and begin a new day, was suddenly profoundly grateful for the thirst of a certain burly farmer that had brought him to the inn the night before. Good Lord, they could spend weeks exploring every cart track over the previous five miles of highway. He opened his eyes.

"I haven't woken you, have I?" Josephine Middleton asked him with a wide and apologetic smile.

"Not at all," he said. "I would have been up long ago if I had not been afraid of waking you."

"Oh," she said, "you need not be afraid of that. I am always up early."

The duke's mental eye peered gloomily along the years ahead of them. Instead of Henry and his discreet cough as he brought the shaving water, he could look forward to his duchess kneeling on his bed beside him, prattling about some harebrained idea that no one but she would ever even dream of.

"And if we do not find him after this search," she said magnanimously, "then I shall allow you to take me back home. Is that fair?"

"I know where he is," he said, shifting position, and finding from the reaction of all his bones and muscles that the floor had not, after all, been a comfortable bed. He ran a hand through his hair and reminded himself that he must have it cut the very next time he was in some civilized part of the world.

For once she was silent. She knelt beside him, her eyes wide, her hands clasped together. He found her nearness quite disconcerting and immediately shut his mind to the memory of the night before when he had lifted her to the bed and almost been mad enough to join her there when she had looked up at him with such sleepy invitation and clung to his neck. Good Lord!

"He has gone to a house party at Lord Parleigh's," he said.

"Seven miles away. He was seen by a farmer in the middle of an altercation with some cows. And since Lord Parleigh's is along the same road, and he is apparently always organizing large house parties, it is well nigh certain that that is where our man was going."

"Then we have him," she said, her eyes shining. "At last. Oh, I can hardly wait to see his face when I confront him."

"Not a good plan at all," Mitford said hastily. "He would crush you up and eat you for breakfast."

"Well," she said, "if you are suggesting that I return home now out of fear, sir, you do not know me at all, I do assure you."

"I think I am getting to know you, Miss Middleton," he said, gazing gloomily down at his borrowed shirt. Now if he had had any sense at all, he would have changed for the night into one of his own wrinkled shirts. He could have done so while she was sleeping. Unfortunately, he and his good sense seemed to have parted company more than two days before.

"You shall take me to him, if you please," she said, "and I shall get my jewels and tell him exactly what I think of him and then you shall take me home as I know you are longing to do and can be on your way with my thanks to wherever you were going."

"That is not at all a good idea, ma'am," Mitford said. "It would be far better for me to take you home and tell your father where Porterhouse may be found. If it is a house party he is attending, doubtless he will be there for a week or more."

"You are suggesting that I go home now when I am within a few miles of Mr. Porterhouse?" Josephine asked, all wide-eyed incredulity. "What utter nonsense."

Mitford closed his eyes briefly. Now what he ought to have done was said nothing about knowing where Porterhouse was until he saw her father. Oh, Lord, he was totally out of his depth in this sort of situation.

"I have a better idea," Josephine Middleton was saying, and he had no doubt for a moment that she was right. It was bound to be a suitably insane idea. "We must accept the Hennessys' invitation and go to Hawthorn House. It is not very far from here. Then we can pay a call on Mr. Porterhouse. Will he not be surprised?"

The Duke of Mitford mentally groaned. He sat up—what had he been doing lying all this while with a young and single lady kneeling over him, anyway?''

"Lord," he said, one hand to his brow. "How can we go to the Hennessys' still pretending to be man and wife?" And what was he doing even considering going there instead of putting his ducal foot down very firmly and tooling off with her in the direction of Rutland Park?

"We seemed to do quite nicely the night before last," she said, having the grace at least to blush.

"Well," he said, grabbing his coat and his bag, "having once given up my sanity, I suppose it would be madness to try to reclaim it now."

"I knew you would agree," she said, jumping to her feet and clapping her hands. "You are such a kind gentleman. I know that I will be quite safe with you and that I will recover my jewels too. And if Mr. Porterhouse has other ideas, well then, you will knock him down again." She smiled.

The Duke of Mitford paused, his hand on the knob of the door, and looked back at her, a rumpled, diminutive little fiend surrounded by a large halo of fair hair. A young little brainless innocent who had just spent the third night in a row with him and was smiling and gazing at him as if he were a mighty Hercules.

He would probably be a pile of mashed bones on the floor if Porterhouse ever got his hands on him without being taken by surprise and without an angry young lady with a large china bowl standing directly behind him.

He let himself out of the room and blew out his breath from puffed cheeks. Could life possibly get any more complicated? If he ever got back to London in one piece, he was going to be a candidate for Bedlam. Instead of which, of course, he was going to have to lead to the altar yet another candidate for the same institution. Well, it was as well to keep insanity all within one family, he supposed. They were almost certain to have very interesting children.

Sir Thomas Burgess slept late. It did not matter since he would not be going far that day, and indeed would be going nowhere at all until his carriage was repaired. But he did regret the fact that he had missed his friend Mitford that morning. He would have enjoyed sitting through breakfast in the dining room, no glimmering of recognition on his face while he took a closer look at Paul's intended bride.

Mitford traveling incognito and alone with a young lady! The two of them eloping and on their way to Gretna Green. Sir Thomas stood in the innyard watching his horses being groomed, his coat collar turned up against the chill of the morning, and grinned to himself. He would not have believed it if he had not seen it with his own eyes. Mitford had never done anything daring or indiscreet in his life. Never. Even that mistress he had had for a few years had been highly respectable.

Who could the little chit be? He would give a great deal to know. But then he would know eventually, he supposed. But why the deuce did the Duke of Mitford have to elope with anyone? It made no sense.

He wondered with another grin if there were an irate father in hot pursuit, a pistol clutched in each hand, a cutlass between his teeth.

He watched idly and with renewed amusement the old-fashioned carriage that pulled in from the road under the care of the unlikeliest coachman he had clapped eyes on for a long while. He looked more as if he belonged in a boxing ring than at the ribbons of a private coach.

Sir Thomas pursed his lips in appreciation at the golden-haired beauty who stepped down into the yard with the coachman's assistance. A slim and pale creature, she was, with hair as golden as the summer sun peeping from beneath her bonnet.

"You go inside and 'ave some tea and vittles," the bald giant said to her in such tender tones that Sir Thomas wondered hilariously if perhaps he was her father.

"But we have scarce begun our journey," a tall, fair-haired young man protested impatiently, vaulting out of the coach after the lady. "We will never catch up to them at this rate, Sam."

Sir Thomas watched as the young lady crossed the cobbles toward him, glancing at him with candid blue eyes before her lashes lowered over them, and disappeared into the inn. Ah, delectable. But his reverie was disturbed by the fair young man, who stopped to address him.

"Pardon me, sir," he said, "but are you traveling south?"

"I have been for a few days," Sir Thomas said. "Not today, though."

"Have you by any chance in the past day or so set eyes on a curricle driven by a gentleman with a young lady passenger?" the young man asked.

Sir Thomas thought for a moment and shook his head. "One does not see many curricles on this road," he said. "Certainly not with lady passengers."

The young man looked disappointed.

"Anyone you know?" Sir Thomas asked politely.

"My sister," the young man said. "And a Mr. Paul Villiers."

Sir Thomas pursed his lips and looked keenly at the young man. "Describe them," he said.

"I cannot describe Villiers," the other said. "And nobody else seems able to do so either. Everyone seems agreed that he is a very ordinary looking man. My sister is very small, with hair the color of mine. It is imperative that I find her as soon as possible."

Sir Thomas raised his eyebrows. "An abduction?" he asked.

The young man flushed. "Not exactly," he said warily. "I do not care to give details, sir. Have you seen them? If not, I must ask inside."

Sir Thomas Burgess was really quite a close friend of the Duke of Mitford. He continued to look keenly for a moment at the anxious young man beside him.

"I did not see the curricle," he said. "That was why I said no at first. But I have seen the couple you describe. They stayed here last night. The lady was small and fair. And I overheard part of their conversation at dinner. I was not eavesdropping, you understand, but I was seated at the next table, and I was alone. She called him, er, what you said. Vil—?"

"Villiers," Bartholomew said, his face lighting up. "They are still here?"

"No," Sir Thomas said. "They were planning to leave early. I noted their destination because it was the same as my own. I suppose that hearing that, I should have introduced myself to them, especially as my carriage has met with an accident, but it seemed forward to do so."

"And the destination?" Bartholomew asked eagerly.

"Lord Parleigh's," Sir Thomas said. "Deerview Park. East of here several miles. There is a house party gathering there. He invited me several weeks ago when I was passing through on my way to Scotland. I have decided to spend a few days there."

"And you are sure that is where my sister and Villiers are going?" Bartholomew asked.

Sir Thomas shrugged. "That is what they decided last night," he said. "They seemed quite certain of their plans at that time."

"How do I get there?" Bartholomew asked.

"Very easily," Sir Thomas said, "if you are willing to take me up with you. I have a broken axle. I would be delighted to show you the way and at the same time avoid having to spend a tedious day here."

"Then we may be of service to each other," the young man said with some eagerness. "Will you be ready to be on your way, sir, as soon as my sister has breakfasted? I wish it might be sooner, but our coachman insists that Susanna eat frequently. She suffers from travel sickness, you see." He grinned apologetically. "And Sam is a tyrant one does not care to argue with."

Sir Thomas pulled on his leather gloves and flexed his fingers after the young man had rushed eagerly into the inn. He was not at all sure he was proud of his lie. The brother of Paul's lady seemed a decent sort, and he would be taking the travel-sick little beauty miles out of her way. But his friendship for Mitford must come first. At least the pursuit would be delayed and Mitford, if he was not a dreadful slowtop, would be married right and tight to his lady before the brother had recovered from his error and caught up to her.

He would just have to hope that the brother would not think to check the story with some employee at the inn who might have seen Mitford leave along the road north that morning.

But Bartholomew and Susanna joined him in the innyard before ten minutes had passed, all eagerness to resume their journey. Sir Thomas presented himself and discovered at least one piece of information about Mitford's intended bride in the ensuing courtesies. She was a Miss Middleton.

And if he had thought Mitford's Miss Middleton pretty the evening before, he considered this other Miss Middleton—her sister—quite the most beautiful creature he had clapped eyes on in many a day. She smiled full at him with shy gratitude as he settled himself in the seat opposite hers. And he felt uncomfortably villainous.

Bartholomew listened to Sir Thomas's directions to Sam without feeling even a qualm of uneasiness. The landlord of the inn had confirmed the gentleman's information that Mr. and Mrs. Villiers had indeed turned east with the intention of calling upon Lord Parleigh.

Mr. and Mrs. Villiers! He had kept that detail from Susanna. He was going to kill a certain very ordinary looking gentleman when he caught up to him. Not to mention what he was going to do to Jo.

The Hennessys lived in the same direction as Lord Parleigh, by some happy coincidence. Hawthorn House was a bare four miles from Deerview Park.

Josephine was very relieved. It would be good to stay in a house again for one night and to eat regular food at a regular table. And she liked the Hennessys for all that Mr. Hennessy had a disconcerting habit of saying embarrassing things and roaring with laughter at his own rather risqué jokes. Grandpapa would call him vulgar. But his heart was in the right place. It would certainly be good to see Caroline again and to have the services of Caroline's maid. And perhaps to borrow some more clothes and have her own washed and mended and ironed.

What she wanted more than anything else in this world was a bath and a hair wash. It was three days since she had had all her clothes off.

She sat atop Mr. Villiers's curricle, clinging to her usual fistful of his coat sleeve as they swayed alarmingly along narrower, more curving roads than the one they had traveled in the previous two days. She felt almost happy again and guilty for doing so.

"Do you suppose Mr. Hennessy really will send out in search of our missing coach?" she asked. "But they will be glad to see us again, will they not, sir? And perhaps we will be given two adjoining rooms instead of just one and you will not feel obliged to sleep on the floor again as you did last night, though there was no reason to do so. And I was quite comfortable there before you picked me up." But she blushed as she remembered that particular incident.

"What we will do," he said, "is get you established at the Hennessys', where you will be safe while I call upon Lord Parleigh. I imagine our man will have something of a nasty shock to see me there. And doubtless he will relinquish the jewels to avoid a public scene, and then I can bring them to you."

"But they are my jewels," she said. "I am the one who must get them back."

"You will get them back," he said. "From me. Do you think I am going to make off with them too?"

"No," she said. "I would trust you with my life, sir." She did not stop to look into his surprised face. She was too busy clinging to his arm with both hands—somehow his arm seemed far steadier and safer than the rail at her other side—while they negotiated a corner that had the road almost doubling back upon itself. "But your plan will not do, anyway. We have been married for only three days."

"Eh?" he said.

"The Hennessys think we have been married for only three days," she said. "How can I descend on them for a visit while you go off alone to a house party? We would have to invent a dreadful quarrel, and I would feel obliged to weep oceans and have the vapors all over the place and refuse my food."

"Would you?" he asked with a frown.

"Certainly," she said. "We are very deep in love, remember? I could not quarrel with you and separate from you after three days of marriage without suffering dreadful dismals."

"Separate from me?" he said with a frown. "I will be gone from you for but a few hours in order to visit a—ah—former acquaintance. You will stay with your former schoolfriend. What could be more natural?"

"Except that we are in love and newly married," she said. "I could not be separated from you for a single hour without going into the mopes. I am coming with you."

"You are not going to be difficult, are you?" Mitford asked, looking down at her with suspicion. And he wondered immediately why he was wasting breath on such a redundant question. Of course she was being difficult.

And then he was hauling back suddenly on the ribbons and with consummate skill avoiding a collision with a herd of cows that were ambling along the road ahead of them—perhaps the same herd as the one Mr. Porterhouse had come to grief with the day before.

Josephine clung harder and hid her face against one cape of his greatcoat, expecting every moment to be tossed into oblivion and choosing to be tossed with her companion.

"I do beg your pardon," he said. "I was driving carelessly. Are you all right?"

Josephine peeped up at him. "Yes, I am," she said, "and feel foolish for being so frightened. I might have known that you would keep me safe. It is just that I am not used to traveling in a curricle, you see. Though I should be used to it after two whole days, should I not?"

She smiled, though her face felt suddenly colder than a late October breeze would account for, and the buzz in her ears was not caused by the wind, either.

"You are really quite safe now," he said as the world darkened rather pleasantly around the edges of her vision.

And she believed him, even though what she was experiencing was remarkably like the faint her friends had described to her— she had never fainted before. And she was safe, quite perfectly so, for was not the curricle now still and the cows still ambling onward, quite unperturbed by the near disaster that had happened behind their waving tails? And was not Mr. Villiers at the ribbons and would not have allowed the accident anyway? And was not his arm about her and her head comfortably on his shoulder?

"I am fainting," she announced in some surprise, and her voice sounded rather far away. "I have never fainted in my life. What a goose you must think me."

"Not at all," he said, and his hand was loosening the strings of her bonnet. "I was driving carelessly. I never drive carelessly."

Well, Josephine thought as consciousness began to return without ever completely disappearing, perhaps three nights ago she could not have said in all honesty that Mr. Villiers had kissed her since she had been the one to do all the kissing, and anyway it had not really been a kiss but merely a way of avoiding being seen by Papa. And last night's kiss had not really been a kiss. It had been on the forehead. But now she would be able to say in all truth that he had kissed her, for she had not initiated it at all. She had been in a strange faraway land, her head on his shoulder.

But he had definitely kissed her. Or rather, he was definitely kissing her. For his head was bent to hers and he was murmuring things that were so soothing that she did not bother to listen to the actual words, and his lips were at her temple and then— oh, yes, definitely; she was not so far gone into the faint that she could not be sure—on her lips. As warm and comforting as the words he was murmuring.

Perhaps it was not a kiss in the strict sense of the word, but then she had never been kissed in the strict sense of the word and so would not for sure recognize it if she had had it. That is, he seemed less concerned with depressing her lips with his own than with murmuring those soothing sounds against them.

But she called it a kiss to herself. She had been kissed. By Mr. Villiers. And she would dearly like him to do it again, but she would have to faint again if she was to expect him to do so, and it was too mortifying to know she had fainted even once in her life.

"Are you all right?" he asked.

"Oh, quite perfectly so," she said, pushing herself upright and knocking her bonnet to the road with one careless elbow. "I did not really faint, you know. That is, the world did not go completely black and silent as I am told it does when you really faint. I just came over strange for a moment and all on account of being unfamiliar with curricles, you see. I feel remarkably foolish."

"But we will remember that you did not quite faint," he said, vaulting down into the roadway to retrieve her bonnet. "And that I was not quite reckless."

He looked up at her and smiled—that all-over grin that ruined the balance of his features and made him quite adorably attractive. Oh, dear, Josephine thought, taking the bonnet from his outstretched arm and beginning to tie the ribbons beneath her chin again, he was not a tall man or a large man or a very, very handsome man. Some girls she knew—indeed, many girls she knew—would not afford him a second glance.

But he was nice. Very nice.

She could not for the moment imagine why so many other young ladies she knew sighed for tall and dark and handsome men. Like Mr. Porterhouse, for example. Mr. Porterhouse gave her the shudders, for all he was a paragon of masculine beauty.

She would take Mr. Villiers any day of the year.

Except that she must not think so, or even let him know that she was thinking so. For he had already done her a great kindness and she had been a great nuisance to him and he would doubtless be very glad to be rid of her within the next few days.

But she would look for someone like Mr. Villiers. If Papa would ever countenance her marrying anyone else after the scandalous loss of that horrid duke, she would choose someone like Mr. Villiers.

Except, she thought with a flash of insight into her own future, there could not be anyone *like* Mr. Villiers. There could only *be* Mr. Villiers.

Oh, dear. She had better not pursue that line of thought. It made no great sense, anyway.

"You were quite right, you know," he said, "we are too deep in love and have been married far too short a time to separate for any length of time. Not that a visit of a few hours is a very long time. But it is true that the Hennessys may wonder at the fact that you do not accompany me if Parleigh is supposed to be an acquaintance of mine. You will just have to make some convincing excuse for not coming."

"But I intend to go," she said firmly. "They are my jewels, and Mr. Porterhouse is my enemy."

He sighed. "Miss Middleton," he said, "there is a house party in progress at Parleigh's. All sorts of people might see us there together, and your name would be forever ruined. You must let me do this alone. I do not doubt your courage, ma'am, but this is a time for discretion, not courage."

"Oh," she said. She thought for a moment. "That is just what Grandpapa would say."

"You can pretend tiredness after our journey," he said.

"But you know the sort of comment Mr. Hennessy would make to that," she said.

Their eyes met briefly, and they both flushed deeply.

"Perhaps I can be increasing and feel very bilious," she said hastily.

He looked at her, aghast. "After three days?" he said. "I think it would take a little longer, wouldn't it?"

"I don't know," she said, thinking. "Yes, I suppose the sickness would take a little longer. Besides, I do not want to make any excuse, you know. I still intend to go with you."

"Well, you can't," he said firmly. "I won't allow it."

Josephine did not argue the point further, though she would when the time came. She was not feeling nearly as tired and cross as she had done the evening before. It was true that men were tyrants and forever bullying the ladies in their charge. But then ladies had the wits to set against the dullness of men's brains. She had never suffered particularly much from being female. She generally had her way when she wanted it badly enough.

"Are you going to remember to call me Jo when we reach Hawthorn House?" she asked brightly.

"Joe is a man's name," he said firmly. "A man servant's name. I will call you Josephine."

"Oh," she said. "Well, it is a good thing that Paul can not be changed in any way. We cannot argue about that."

She had always hated being called Josephine. It was what Papa and Grandpapa called her when she had disappointed them in some way and puss and half-pint seemed inappropriate names. And her grandmother in London always called her Josephine, always in a somewhat impatient and irritated tone.

But Mr. Villiers made the name sound feminine and dignified and adult. Perhaps she would not argue the point. And it would be as well not to do so when there was a much larger point to argue.

She smiled ahead of her and resumed her comforting hold of his sleeve.

9

Someone must have alerted the Hennessys to the fact that visitors were arriving, for the head of the house and his good lady emerged from the front doors of Hawthorn House as the Duke of Mitford was lifting his companion down from the seat of the curricle. He spotted them out of the corner of his eye.

And if this farce must be played out to its conclusion, he thought with a desperation bordering on hilarity, he might as well play the part well. He smiled fondly up at Josephine, bent his elbows, and slid her down along his length. And he bent his head and kissed her very briefly on the lips. Nothing totally beyond the bounds of decorum, of course, but merely what a fond husband might be expected to do with his bride of three days when he thought himself unobserved.

Unless, of course, the fond husband were the Duke of Mitford. That paragon of correct behavior would surely do no more than touch the fingertips of his bride beyond the privacy of their own apartments. And the Duke of Mitford would certainly not slide any young lady down his body and kiss her square on the lips. Not ever. Such a possibility would not even enter his head.

But where was the Duke of Mitford? Paul Villiers seemed to have lost him back at a certain inn at approximately the time when his grace had been forming angles with his big toes.

And what did he know of fond husbands and brides of three days anyway? Mitford asked himself as Miss Middleton colored up prettily. But she must be as accomplished a little actress as he was becoming an actor if she had blushes so ready to her command. She was going to lead him a merry dance all right when they really were married.

He smiled and touched his nose to hers briefly before turning in some confusion to his beaming host and hostess, who had descended the steps to the cobbles of the courtyard.

"Ah," he said, extending a hand, "do please forgive me. I did not know we were observed." It really was frightening to discover at the age of eight and twenty that lying came so easily. He could not recall any untruth he had told prior to two days before. And when had his fingers come to be laced with Miss Middleton's?

Mr. Hennessy laughed and shook his hand with equal heartiness. "I could have wished you had thought yourself unobserved for a while longer," he said.

"What?" Mrs. Hennessy said, enfolding Josephine in a hug and looking back along the driveway. "No baggage coach? Never tell me that you have still not caught up to your servants."

"Paul thinks that he sent them to London by mistake," Josephine said with a smile. "Don't you, Paul?"

Did he really? And how might that highly unlikely possibility be explained? He waited with interest. But she was regarding him with raised eyebrows and parted lips. She was waiting for him to deliver the explanation.

"Yes," he said, laughing. "Did you have to say that out loud to complete my mortification, Josephine? It was the original plan, you see, ma'am, my wife having a grandmother in London, not to mention other relatives, that we go there after our wedding. But at the last moment I decided that I could not possibly share her on our wedding trip. I decided to bear her off to Scotland. Unfortunately, I forgot to inform the servants of the change in plans. I am afraid love has muddled my brain."

And if they were convinced by such utter nonsense, then they would be convinced by anything at all.

And how had he got himself into this mess, anyway? What on earth had happened to his life? He had been staying at that inn, the only difference from usual being the fact that he was traveling incognito and without his ducal train. He had been quite blamelessly minding his own business. He had even removed himself from the taproom because life there was becoming somewhat too raucous for his taste. All quite exemplary. All he had been looking for was a little adventure. A very little.

And yet here he was three days later, smiling like an imbecile at an insane and brainless little creature and lying his head off to a pair of perfectly decent gentlefolk. He could be back in London by now, looking about him for a bride worthy of his own upbringing.

"Paul," Miss Middleton was saying, lowering her voice as if she thought she would not be overhead, and tilting her head to one side, so that any normal unsuspecting mortal would think her the innocent and sweet bride of three days that she affected to be, "I am glad you did not take me to Grandmama's even if I am without my maid and my trunks."

Mrs. Hennessy clasped her hands to her bosom. "And so am I," she said. "How wonderful it will be to have two lovebirds staying at Hawthorn House, will it not, Harvey?"

"But we will not impose on your hospitality above a day or two, ma'am," Mitford said hastily. "It is just that I remembered that I have a particular acquaintance living not four miles away—Parleigh, you know, sir. I feel I must pay my respects. And it seemed the perfect opportunity for Josephine to have female companions to take her shopping for new clothes. I hope I may impose upon you to lend her your assistance tomorrow, ma'am, while I pay my call."

He bowed and smiled to Mrs. Hennessy and avoided noticing Josephine's look of reproach.

She was not given a chance to voice her disapproval. Miss Caroline Hennessy chose that moment to come hurtling through the door and down the steps, shrieking, and Josephine started squealing, and Mrs. Hennessy started talking, and Mr. Hennessy started bellowing with laughter.

And the duke stood on the cobbles, rocking on his heels and wondering if it was his former dull and decorous life that he had dreamed up or whether it was this present mad one that was the unreality. Whatever the truth of the matter, he found himself now laughing as heartily as his host, though he would not for the life of him have been able to say what it was he laughed at.

Sam had given what sounded like good advice the first time he had been forced to stop the carriage. Look off to the horizon, he had told Susanna, so that she would be unaware of the motion and the swayings of the carriage.

Sam was so very kind, and far more understanding of her problem than Bart was. Susanna tried very hard not to be a nuisance to anyone, and of course she knew, even without Bart's telling her a dozen times a day that time was of great importance, that if they were to catch up to Jo before she was utterly and irrevocably ruined—if she were not so already—then they must not delay by even one unnecessary minute.

But there was nothing she could do about her weak stomach. She had almost died of mortification the first time they had stopped that morning because the auburn-haired and handsome gentleman who was taking them to Jo had looked at her with concern and asked if there were any way in which he could be of service to her. She had been unable to answer but had only grabbed gratefully for his hand when he had vaulted to the roadway to help her out. She had had to rush on past him. It had been very humiliating indeed.

And now it was happening again. "Bart," she said weakly, looking at him with wide and pleading eyes and clamping a hand to her mouth as soon as the word was spoken.

"Deuce take it, Suke," he said, exasperated, before poking his head through the window and bellowing to Sam.

Sam, the dear giant, stopped immediately and had the door open and blessed fresh air rushing in only one moment later.

"Out you come, little lady," he said gently, his huge hands spanning her waist and lifting her gently to the roadway before Sir Thomas could jump out himself.

She was gulping air and touching the backs of her hands to cold and clammy cheeks when he descended.

"Deerview Park is but a mile off," Sir Thomas said gently, "if that is of any consolation to you, ma'am."

Susanna threw him a grateful look. "I am very foolish," she said. "But if we catch up to my sister, all this will have been worthwhile. You are very kind to show us the way, sir."

He looked somewhat uncomfortable and bowed slightly. Susanna remembered that some gentlemen did not like to be praised.

"I hope you will not be disappointed," he said. "It is possible that I misunderstood, you know, or that they changed their minds."

"Villiers," Bartholomew said, jumping into the roadway to

join them. "Who the devil is Villiers, do you suppose?"

Sir Thomas said nothing.

"I think I am well enough to go on," Susanna said, looking ahead of Sam, who was doing something with the horses.

"Allow me, ma'am," Sir Thomas said, and he picked her up by the waist and lifted her back inside the carriage again.

Susanna forgot about her biliousness for the remaining mile of the journey. She was concentrating on not blushing and revealing to either Bart or the handsome gentleman across from her how discomposed she was feeling. Bart would make fun of her.

And she completely forgot about both her health and her embarrassment when they arrived at Deerview Park and were shown into a salon to await the arrival of Lord Parleigh. She was eager to see Jo. She did not care what Jo had done or who Mr. Villiers was or why Jo was traveling with him as Mrs. Villiers. Once she saw Jo and they were together again, everything would be all right.

But Lord Parleigh, when he came, though he was kind and amiable and quite delighted to see all three of them, did not have comforting news. He had not set eyes on either Mr. Villiers or Jo.

"I am most dreadfully sorry," Sir Thomas Burgess said, glancing uneasily at Bart and crossing to Susanna's side to raise her hand to his lips. "I have taken you seven miles out of your way and all for nothing, it seems."

"It was not your fault, sir," Susanna said. She knew just exactly how dreadful he must feel, but he ought not. He had tried to help.

"Confound it," Bartholomew said. He was pacing about the room. "They must have continued traveling north after all. I might have guessed it."

"Villiers," Lord Parleigh was saying, rubbing a hand over his chin. "Villiers. Sounds familiar. Can't think I invited him here or I would surely remember. You heard them say they were coming here, Burgess?"

"They must have changed their minds," Sir Thomas said. "I most sincerely beg your pardon."

Susanna smiled at him, though her mind was feeling almost numb with dismay. Would they never find Jo? And who was the dreadful man she was with?

"But the landlord at the Swan Inn said the same thing," Bartholomew said with a frown, tapping one finger against his teeth. "He said Villiers was coming here, too."

Susanna noticed Sir Thomas's eyebrows shoot up. She was glad for him. He was not the only one who had been deceived.

"Well," Lord Parleigh said heartily. "I would suggest, Middleton, that you and your sister stay here for a few days before returning home. Always glad to have guests, you know. I have some now. Good company, I do assure you."

Susanna looked at Bartholomew. How very good it would be to rest in a real house for a few days, to get up in the morning and not have to face a journey in the carriage.

"We must go, Bart," she said. And she felt the tears spring to her eyes as she tried to swallow them. "We must find poor Jo."

"Lady Hedgeton is here," Lord Parleigh said as if he had not been interrupted at all, "Sir Crawley Fabian and Miss Fabian—an acclaimed beauty—Mr. Seymour, Lady Dorothy Brough, Mr. Porterhouse, Mrs. Hope and her two daughters . . ."

"Porterhouse?" Bartholomew said sharply as Susanna felt the blood drain from her head.

"Handsome devil," Lord Parleigh said. "You know him?"

Susanna's eyes locked with her brother's. "He is here?" she asked.

"*Was* here," Lord Parleigh corrected. "He went off today to visit an aunt. Should be back tomorrow. Now, ma'am, do allow me to persuade you and your brother to honor me with your company for a few days."

"Yes," Susanna said hastily, looking across at her brother. "May we, Bart?"

"Perhaps we ought," he said, frowning. He turned to Lord Parleigh to make their acceptance.

But where was Jo? Had something dreadful happened to her? Oh, dear, where was Jo?

She met the serious and searching eyes of Sir Thomas Burgess and smiled as brightly as she was able.

"Splendid!" Lord Parleigh was saying heartily.

"What I should have done," the Duke of Mitford said later

that same night, plunging his hands into the pockets of his borrowed dressing gown, "was pretend to have had a dreadful cold so that I might have asked for a separate room. I am so deep in love with you, after all, that I certainly would not wish to pass the germs on to you."

"But you would have had to sneeze and blow constantly and talk nasally and develop a very red nose and watery eyes," she said. She did not move about their very single bedchamber a great deal, he noticed, because her nightgown was at least three inches longer than her person. "Besides, I have been married to you for only three days and I promised to love you in sickness and in health and I would want to nurse you if you had such a dreadful cold, would I not?"

"I am merely saying what I ought to have done," he said, exasperated. He was gazing out of the window into blackness. Except that his eyes could not help but focus on the reflection of the little figure behind him in her voluminous nightgown. Her hair was quite tame, having been braided into a circlet all about her head by a maid after her bath. He far preferred it in its wild and natural state, but she did look neat and pretty, he had had to confess to himself all evening. Her eyes looked larger without all the wild hair, and her face rather like a pixie's.

"It was very sly of you to arrange that I go shopping tomorrow while you go after Mr. Porterhouse," she said now. He could see her standing in the middle of the room, close to the foot of the bed. "You know that I had every intention of coming with you."

"And you know I had every intention of preventing you from doing so," he said.

"But you are not my father or my brother." Her head was thrown back in defiance.

"No," he said, "but I am your husband for a few days, am I not?"

"How foolish," she said. "Besides, how can I go shopping? I do not have even a farthing in my purse."

"You will have the bills sent to me, of course," he said.

"But I don't need any new clothes," she said, gathering the borrowed nightgown in folds about her thighs so that she might take one step closer to the bed. "And Papa has already given me an advance on my next pin money. And Sukey gave me hers this month because she said she did not need it. But of course I will have to repay it. It will take me a year or more to repay you, sir."

"If you are to pretend to be my wife," he said, "you will have to pretend all the way. I will pay your bills. It would be very strange if I did not."

"It is all very well to talk of pretense," she said. "But money is a very real thing. Perhaps you do not have a great deal of it, sir. Perhaps you will be a beggar by the time I have rescued my jewels and returned home." She had seated herself on the side of the bed and looked unaccustomedly disconsolate.

"I will not be a beggar," he said, turning from the window to look at her. "And you need new clothes. I cannot have people saying that I do not know how to dress my wife."

"Oh, dear," she said, "you are very kind. But even aside from the shopping, I really do not like the thought of your confronting Mr. Porterhouse alone. Perhaps you will be hurt, and I shall be sorry for it all my life. And what if he kills you?"

He smiled and stepped closer to her. "Then I will have died in a good cause," he said, "and you may mourn for me and tell your grandchildren about the brave gentleman who gave his life to recover your jewels."

"Oh," she said, jumping to her feet and stumbling over the hem of her nightgown so that she lurched against his chest. "I really don't want you to die. And I do beg your pardon."

"Don't you?" he said. "And do you?" She had not a stitch on beneath the nightgown. The garment looked perfectly decent, provided one merely looked at it. But when one was obliged to hold it and—more to the point—the little lady who was inside it, one's thoughts and one's bodily responses soon became woefully indecent.

The Duke of Mitford found himself smiling foolishly and for no reason at all except that he could not think of anything else to do or anything else to say unless it were to ask her to please remove herself from him or else to remove her himself with his hands, and either course of action seemed unmannerly, or would have seemed so if he had thought of either with any coherence.

"Don't get hurt," she said, her hands spreading themselves over his shoulders. "Not for me. And not for my jewels. They are only old jewels, after all. We will forget them. I will learn to live without them. Don't let yourself get hurt.''

"I don't intend to," he said. His hands were at her waist, but his thumbs, for lack of anything else to be, were pushing up under her breasts. And his temperature, for lack of anything else to do, was soaring. And somehow he felt obliged to follow up the words by dipping his head and laying his lips against her throat. "I can look after myself, ma'am, I do assure you.'' And one of his hands moved quite of its own volition behind her back and below her waist in order that he might arrange her more fully and more comfortably against his person.

"Promise?" she said. Her fingertips were light in his hair. They felt good. She was holding his head and gazing into his eyes, her own huge and troubled. "Promise you won't get hurt. Promise you will forget about my jewels and Mr. Porterhouse.''

The Duke of Mitford forgot—yet again—that he was the Duke of Mitford. He forgot completely about his very proper upbringing, about the years of training and discipline that had developed in him a stern self-discipline and a strong sense of propriety and responsibility. He forgot that his dealings with the female gender had been confined to one affair with a widowed lady and that his dealings with young unmarried ladies were nonexistent.

He forgot that the very idea of being alone in a bedchamber with such a young lady would have been well nigh enough to have sent him into a fit of the vapors a mere week before. He forgot that a week before he would hardly have even been able to imagine a soft and warm and feminine body pressed to his own, with only a nightgown and his own nightshirt and dressing gown separating their bodies.

He forgot everything except a hitherto unsuspected male instinct to possess what was feminine and sweet-smelling and yielding. He lowered his head and opened his mouth over Josephine Middleton's.

She tasted as good as she looked and smelled. He tasted her lightly with his lips, discovered that his thirst for her ran deeper than lips could satisfy, and reached into her mouth with his tongue.

She was warm and moist. She tasted of the sweet wine she had drunk with her dinner. And she felt warm and soft in his arms. And very small. He felt large and male and protective.

With every surge of blood that pulsed through his temples he was aware of the large and soft bed behind her.

And the heat of her, and the supple way she arched herself to him and made her mouth available to his invasion told him that she was equally aware. And available. And desirable. And she was, after all, his bride.

Was she? Good Lord!

Fortunately, or unfortunately, depending upon whether one were on the side of decorum or irresponsible romance, Mitford became suddenly aware that blood was not the only essential of life occupying his head. Somewhere, in a not very active part of his brain, for sure, but somewhere nonetheless, there were rationality and intelligence. And guilt and embarrassment and incredulity. And truth.

Oh, Lord, what on this good earth was he about now? Was it really—could it really be—he, the dull and very proper Duke of Mitford, who just happened to be alone in a bedchamber with a single young lady, every curve of her body fitting itself very nicely indeed against his body, her hands in his hair, her mouth opened beneath his? And both of them in their night clothes? Could it really be?

Yes, indeed, it could. And was.

What on earth was he to say to her when he had finally put between them the space that should be between them? His inability to answer his own question made him prolong the embrace.

"We really do not have to be doing this, you know," he said eventually, "since the Hennessys are not in the room to be convinced of our undying love for each other. I am afraid that living this lie is just getting to be something of a habit."

"Oh, yes," she said, looking somewhat dazed and clasping her hands in front of her. "I do beg your pardon, sir. My mind got a little addled over the thought of your getting hurt on my behalf when it really is not necessary at all. And if I had not been such a green girl and believed that Mr. Porterhouse was a kind gentleman just because of his soft words and his serious and sincere looks, I would not have left home with him and given him the chance to steal the jewels. Though as for that, if I had stayed, I would have been forced to receive the Duke

of Mitford's addresses and to accept them too, no doubt, since
I would have had no good reason to say no and would have
disappointed Papa and Grandpapa if I had. Though as for that,
I suppose I have disappointed them even more by disappearing
off the face of the earth when I wrote that I was merely going
to Aunt Winifred's, haven't I?''

Her color was high, her voice quite breathless.

The Duke of Mitford set his hands behind his back and rocked
on his heels. ''It is late,'' he said, ''and time we were in
bed.'' And then he wished feverently he could have recalled
the words. ''I shall sleep on the floor.''

''Oh,'' she said, ''but you do not need to do so. Really you
do not. It is a very wide bed. And if someone must sleep on
the floor, then I absolutely insist that it be me this time. It is
the least I can do to thank you for all your kindness.''

The Duke of Mitford found his night on the floor somewhat
more comfortable than he had done on the two previous
occasions, partly because it was carpeted, he supposed, and
partly, perhaps, because his body was becoming hardened to
privation.

Besides, a bed of nails would have been preferable to the one
in their bedchamber, occupied as it was by a small lady whose
proximity could do disturbing and totally unfamiliar things to
his sanity.

10

The village dressmaker did not have racks and racks of delightful fashions to choose among. In fact, she did not have even a single rack of fashions. Or any fashions at all, for that matter. Josephine purchased a plain wool dress for day wear and an even plainer silk for evenings, though both dresses needed to be shortened considerably before she could wear either.

But the very plainness of the garments, for which Mrs. Hennessy apologized profusely, eased Josephine's mind. She would have felt vastly more guilty over sending the bills for pretty clothes to Mr. Villiers.

The spending did not end there, of course. Mrs. Hennessy happily rummaged through undergarments and nightgowns, while Caroline fingered ribbons and lace and fans. Josephine stared out of the window into the street.

He would be at Lord Parleigh's by now. He would be confronting Mr. Porterhouse, taking him firmly by the lapels of his coat and demanding her jewels. And he would be using those powerful fists on Mr. Porterhouse's face. Right now. At this very moment.

What if Mr. Porterhouse did not go down as easily as he had done at the inn? Mr. Villiers had had the advantage of surprise on that occasion, and she had helped a little bit by smashing the china bowl over the man's head. Though, of course, Mr. Villiers would have managed perfectly well without her assistance.

But would he manage perfectly well now? What if Mr. Porterhouse had a chance to punch back? He might break Mr. Villiers's nose. He might kill him. Right now at this very moment. Mr. Villiers might be stretched out dead in Lord Parleigh's drawing room or on Lord Parleigh's lawn. And all because of her jewels. Worse than that—all because of her stupidity in going off with Mr. Porterhouse when all she had had to do was have a private word with Papa.

Of course, he would partly deserve his fate. She was very vexed over the sly way he had maneuvered events so that he could go alone to Deerview Park to fight her battles and to recover her jewels. Very vexed indeed.

But for all that, he did not deserve to die. And she would feel very guilty for the rest of her life if he really were hurt in any way.

"This silk nightgown, do you think, dear?" Mrs. Hennessy asked her with a smile. "It is so very fine. Do you think dear Mr. Villiers would approve?"

Caroline flushed and concentrated her attention on the ribbons.

"Oh." Josephine gulped. "Yes, but it is almost winter, ma'am. Perhaps I had better buy the flannel."

"You are afraid of being cold at night, dear?" Mrs. Hennessy exchanged a knowing smile with the dressmaker.

No. No, she was not at all afraid of being cold. She had felt as if someone had lit a roaring blaze inside her the night before when she had got all silly about Mr. Villiers's safety and almost thrown herself at him. She had quite forced him to kiss her. And then she had lost her head completely and behaved in a manner that would have Grandpapa lecturing her for a month without once pausing for breath if he ever found out.

She had never ever realized that gentlemen kissed ladies like that. Or that ladies kissed them back like that, either. Mr. Villiers must be very experienced to know about those things. But he would think her a dreadful hussy for having allowed him to do them to her. She had opened her mouth without any coaxing at all on his part.

Oh, dear. What on earth was she doing? Less than a week before, she had been at home with Papa and Grandpapa and Bart and the girls, waiting for the Duke of Mitford to come and pay her his addresses. And it was all his fault, horrid man. Why could he not be satisfied with all his women instead of wanting her as his bride? She hated him. She hated him now more than ever.

Would he be waiting for her? Would Papa have found some convincing way to explain her absence so that the man would still be expecting her to be his bride? Oh, surely not. Surely she had not gone all through this for nothing.

Josephine's attention was suddenly diverted from her uncomfortable reveries. She was gazing sightlessly out of the window when suddenly her eyes focused and widened. And she shot out of the door even as Mrs. Hennessy turned to her with a pair of silk stockings draped over her arm.

"Stop, you villain!" she commanded, striding along the pavement in the wake of a tall and handsome gentleman.

He turned in some surprise and regarded her with raised eyebrows before turning fully toward her and sweeping her an elegant bow.

"Miss Middleton," Mr. Porterhouse said, smiling his most charming smile. "To what happy coincidence do I owe this welcome surprise?"

"Welcome nothing," she said, setting her clenched fists on her hips. "Where are my jewels?"

He raised his eyebrows again and regarded her with polite interest. "Your jewels?" he asked.

"My jewels," she repeated. "Where are my jewels, sir?"

"Really, ma'am," he said, smiling apologetically down into her indignant face, "unless this is some riddle, I do not see how I can be expected to know the whereabouts of your valuables. Have you misplaced some?" He looked beyond her shoulder and inclined his head gravely. "Well met, indeed, Miss Middleton. Are you staying in the neighborhood?"

Josephine turned to find a smiling Mrs. Hennessy and a blushing Caroline behind her. What could she do but smile and make the introductions?

"But have you not heard, sir?" Mrs. Hennessy said when all the explanations and curtsying and bowing and simpering were over. Josephine closed her eyes briefly. "It must have happened since you last stayed with your relatives, the Winthrops. Dear Jo has married Mr. Villiers and is on her wedding journey."

Mr. Porterhouse's brows shot up and he reached for Josephine's hand and raised it to his lips. "Wedding journey?" he said. "You are recently married then, Miss Midd—, I mean Mrs. Villiers?"

"Four days," she said firmly, looking back defiantly into his eyes and seeing a flicker of amusement there.

"Four days," he repeated, covering the hand he still held with his other hand. "Ah, the fortunate gentleman. This lady would have none of me, you know, Mrs. Hennessy, ma'am."

Mrs. Hennessy tittered and Caroline blushed an even deeper shade.

"I shall look forward to meeting you again," Mr. Porterhouse said, finally releasing Josephine's hand and making his bows to all three ladies once more. "I am staying at Lord Parleigh's, you know. I shall look forward to meeting my rival and seeing what he has that I do not."

His eyes had the gall to twinkle at her, Josephine thought, watching helplessly as he turned to make his way unhurriedly along the street.

The only consolation in the whole frustrating situation—the only one—was that she could finally release the mental image of Mr. Villiers lying bleeding and dying somewhere on the Parleigh estate.

No, there was another consolation. She would have the satisfaction of informing Mr. Villiers—that amiable gentleman and male tyrant—that she had been the one to make the first communication with Mr. Porterhouse. Not that she had seriously discomposed him, it was true. But if Mrs. Hennessy and Caroline had not come out of the shop when they had, she would have given him a piece of her mind indeed. She would have had him quaking in his boots.

Oh, the handsome, slimy villain!

"What an extraordinarily amiable and charming young man," Mrs. Hennessy was saying.

"Did you really refuse him, Jo?" Caroline was asking her. "How could you possibly? I would simply die if he were to ask me."

Tom Burgess looked rather as if he had seen a ghost and been shot between the eyes with a pistol all at the same moment, the Duke of Mitford thought. And indeed, he was somewhat surprised to see Tom at Lord Parleigh's when he had assumed two evenings before that he was on his way home to London.

Though Tom had said, when he came to think of it, that he had had trouble with his carriage.

The morning room at Deerview Park was not entirely filled with guests, the duke saw at a glance when the butler ushered him into the room. But it was not empty, either. There were Tom and a slim dark-haired lady, a fair-haired young man, and a golden-haired beauty. The genial looking and rather portly young man who got to his feet and came toward him, hand extended, must be Lord Parleigh himself.

"Ah," he said, taking the duke's hand in a firm and warm clasp, "pleased you could come. You must be . . . ?" The butler had made no public announcement of his identity.

"Mitford!" Sir Thomas Burgess cried, leaping to his feet and bounding across the room as if he had long thought his friend dead and was only now discovering his error. "By all that's wonderful, what are you doing here?"

The duke frowned. Drat the man! So much for his plan to keep his real identity hidden. Had Tom forgotten so soon?

"Ah, yes, Mitford," Lord Parleigh said, smiling broadly and frowning only very briefly. "Met you at the races, did I? So glad you saw fit to accept my invitation, old chap. Come for a week or two, have you? Splendid, splendid."

The *Duke* of Mitford," Sir Thomas said very pointedly, widening his eyes at the duke's in a message that was totally indecipherable.

"Ah, the duke." Lord Parleigh clapped him on the shoulder and turned back into the room. "Splendid, old fellow. Come and meet Lady Dorothy Brough, Miss Susanna Middleton, and her brother, Mr. Bartholomew Middleton."

Lady Dorothy swept into a deep curtsy and favored Mitford with the type of speculative glance he was used to seeing in unmarried ladies of all ages. The golden beauty and her brother stood like pale statues, staring at him.

And Mitford feared that he gazed back at them in like manner. Oh, good Lord!

"Your grace," the fair girl said eventually, dipping into an awkward curtsy.

The brother found his voice. "You are Mitford?" he asked foolishly. "You are not at Rutland Park?"

The duke inclined his head in a half-bow. And he slipped into his old self again almost as if it were a long forgotten stage part.

"I was," he said stiffly. "I, er, spoke with your grandfather. Your father and Miss Middleton were from home. I shall do myself the honor of calling again at some future date."

The sister was regarding him with wide blue eyes and pale cheeks. "What did Grandpapa say?" she asked.

Mitford bowed again. "He mentioned something about, er, your aunt being unwell and your father and sister going to tend her," he said.

He watched in some fascination as both brother and sister jumped into the comfortable lie he had presented them with and assured him quite vociferously that their aunt was indeed feared to be at death's door. The sister's eyes looked rather as if they were about to pop from their sockets.

"You have some acquaintance with one another, then?" Lord Parleigh said, rubbing his hands together with some satisfaction. "Splendid, splendid!"

Oh, good Lord, Mitford thought, taking the seat his host offered him and settling into cozy and meaningless chatter with the occupants of the room. What a coil. All those present now knew him as the Duke of Mitford, whereas the occupants of the house four miles away knew him as Mr. Villiers; Miss Middleton's brother and sister were in hot pursuit of her, apparently unaware that she was staying a mere few miles away, and doubtless not knowing that she was staying anywhere under the name of Mrs. Villiers; Tom was frowning and looking alternately between him and the Middletons, and seemed to be in imminent danger of letting his jaw hang; and Porterhouse was nowhere in sight.

And of course, the Middletons would know Porterhouse. Did they know of his part in absconding with their sister? Did they know about the jewels?

And was the father about to put in an appearance too, brandishing a hatchet in each fist?

Maybe the grandfather, too?

Lady Dorothy was sending out lures his way, using that trick ladies had with their eyelashes. He wondered idly if she would even have afforded a second glance at Mr. Paul Villiers.

"Jo is devoted to our aunt," Miss Susanna Middleton said,

her blue eyes fixed on his face, her pale cheeks flushing. "She is very tender-hearted."

"And quite devoted to duty," Bartholomew Middleton said. He had the grace to look rather as if his cravat were strangling him.

Mitford had a sudden, unbidden memory of Miss Josephine Middleton as she had felt in his arms the night before.

Oh, Lord.

"I will see you to the door," Lord Parleigh said genially when Mitford rose to bring his visit to an end. It had already been established that the duke was staying at the Swan Inn and for reasons of his own preferred to remain there than remove to Deerview Park. Something to do with ducal eccentricity, it seemed. Or that was what Tom had said.

"I will walk with you to the stables," Tom Burgess said, leaping to his feet once more.

"Porterhouse?" Lord Parleigh said when the three of them were standing on the steps outside the main doors. "Yes, indeed. He has been to visit an aunt, but he is supposed to be back later today. Handsome fellow. All the ladies go wild over him, lucky devil. You know him, Mitford? A well-known fellow. The Middletons are of his acquaintance, too. You must call again. Come to my ball the evening after tomorrow. The ladies will be delighted to have a duke to fight over." He laughed heartily.

Mitford made his bow. "I shall certainly call again," he said. "I regret to say that I do not plan to stay for another two days, though, Parleigh."

"Paul," Sir Thomas almost hissed at him as they walked beyond earshot of their host. "Are you mad? I only just prevented the Middletons from knowing that you are the Villiers who has abducted their sister. Where is the little bride, by the way? And why are you not making in all haste for Gretna?"

"Simply beccause I am not going there at all," the duke said.

"Oh, Lord, what a coil. How did her brother and sister end up here, of all places?"

"I brought them," Sir Thomas said, exasperated, "to keep them off your trail. Where is she, Paul?"

Mitford stroked his chin. "At Hawthorn House, four miles away," he said. "With her friends, the Hennessys. Oh, Lord, what the devil am I doing? What I should have done was call the brother aside as soon as I knew who he was. I should have explained the whole thing to him.''

''Are you looking to have your nose broken and your eyes blackened and your ribs all poking out your backbone?'' his friend asked incredulously. ''You have been riding all over the country with the little lady by day and tumbling her by night, and you want to explain to her brother? My boy, it is time you stepped into the real world and learned how to look after your own skin.''

''Tumbling her.'' The Duke of Mitford, who had stopped walking when they were still a discreet distance from the stables, passed a hand over the back of his neck and rocked back on his heels. ''Oh, I say Tom, that is not what I have been doing, you know. I have been merely trying to help her recover her jewels. If I had not, she would have been mad enough to tear over the whole country doing it herself.''

''Her jewels.'' Sir Thomas looked blank.

''Porterhouse has them,'' the duke said.

''Porterhouse.'' His friend frowned. ''It was when they heard his name that Miss Middleton and her brother decided to stay here. Why is it that I have the feeling I am seeing the tip of an iceberg here?''

''Lord,'' Mitford said. ''Is my head still facing forward, Tom, or is it turned backward? I am no longer capable of telling. She is the most pestilential female it has ever been my misfortune to meet. I was supposed to be paying my addresses to her.''

Sir Thomas Burgess stared at him. ''Past tense?'' he said. ''Do you mean to say you think there is going to be any way of avoiding doing so in the future?''

''Lord,'' Mitford said. ''No.'' He reached up a hand and scratched the curls at his temples. ''I just don't know where I am going to begin teaching her how to be a duchess though, Tom. She doesn't have even the glimmering of an idea how to go on.''

Sir Thomas grinned suddenly. ''Strangely,'' he said, ''considering the fact that I have not understood one thing that has happened in the last hour, I begin to see the faintest trace of a hope for you, Paul, my lad. And not before time, either. You are coming back here, you say?''

''Tomorrow,'' the duke said. ''I still have to confront

Porterhouse—if he has not got wind of the reception committee awaiting him, that is, and taken to his heels.''

"I shall see you tomorrow, then," his friend said. "But listen, Paul. There had better be a good explanation for all these goings-on, you know. I never would have suspected you could be such a mad dog. But there are likely to be sufferers. I don't know the little lady herself, but her sister is beside herself with worry."

"Oh Lord," the Duke of Mitford said, "I don't need you to lecture me, Tom. If I could see an honorable way out of this tangle, I would take it. But I cannot find it in me to abandon that brainless little chit. She would probably tackle Porterhouse alone and have herself ground to powder. Then what would happen to the sister? And what is your interest in the girl, anyway? I thought you cared for only one kind of female."

"When they have golden hair and great big blue eyes and tender hearts," Sir Thomas said, "I can force an interest, Mitford, believe me. Perhaps we will end up brothers-in-law yet, my lad."

He wouldn't worry about such a possibility, the Duke of Mitford thought as he hurried into the stableyard. It was becoming more and more of a probability that he would not emerge live and intact from the new few days. Porterhouse and the various male members of the Middleton family would doubtless end up having to put their names on a waiting list to get their fists at him.

And while he waited for them all to take their turn, he was going to have to spend another night at the Hennessys'. On the floor. With Josephine Middleton in the bed. Their fifth night together.

The very thought was enough to make him break into a cold sweat. Or perhaps not so cold, either.

"Paul." Josephine had been leaning forward in her carriage seat since they had turned through the gates and onto the long driveway leading to Hawthorn House. She appeared quite unaware of the amused, affectionate glances of Mrs. Hennessy and the somewhat envious ones of Caroline. She had spotted Mitford standing in the courtyard with Mr. Hennessy. "Paul."

She waited only as long as it took a footman to lower the steps,

and she was out and tripping across the cobblestones in quite
undignified haste, her face lit up with eagerness. It did not
appear at all strange that the duke opened his arms to her, and
not at all improper that she ran straight into them and raised
her face for his kiss. Truth to tell, the proprieties had never
been farther from her mind.

"Paul," she said, her words all in a rush to escape at once.
She was clinging to his neck. "You would never guess. Not
in a million Sundays."

"Wouldn't I?" he said, his hands fitting themselves
comfortably to her waist. "Did you do all your shopping?"

Mr. Hennessy was laughing heartily. "Well, Livy," he said
to his wife, who was only then descending from the carriage,
"do you not have such a wifely greeting for me?"

"Oh, Harvey!" she said, laughing and viewing the newly
married pair with complacence. "What nonsense."

"We ran into Mr. Porterhouse in Ammanford," Josephine
said, her hands busy at the lapels of Mitford's coat. "And he
was quite perfectly polite and charming, and he had never in
his life heard of jewels."

"A most amiable young man," Mrs. Hennessy said. "And
staying with Lord Parleigh, Harvey. Doubtless you will meet
him at the ball. Did you send to the Park?"

"I did not," he said, "having decided to ride over there my-
self, Livy, now that I have completed my morning's business.
But I shall certainly mention the fact that we have visitors, and
Parleigh will doubtless extend the invitation to them too."

"Oh, Jo." Caroline clapped her hands. "You are to come
to the ball at Deerview Park with us. Lord Parleigh's balls are
always splendid occasions, I do assure you. There are always
visitors staying there. Mr. Porterhouse is surely the most
handsome gentleman I have ever seen, Papa."

Her father chuckled and set an arm about her shoulders. "I
believe our presence here is *de trop*," he said. "Come along,
chicken, you shall show me what you bought and tell me what
bills I am to expect."

"Oh, I say," the Duke of Mitford said, removing his hands
from Josephine's waist.

"Oh, I do beg your pardon," Josephine said, simultaneously
dropping her hands from the duke's lapels.

But the Hennessys seemed only too delighted to leave them alone together.

"We had better walk away from the house and talk," Mitford said, offering Josephine an arm and turning in the direction of a wide lawn. "Did Porterhouse insult you or harm you in any way?"

"The villain!" she said vehemently. "When I demanded my jewels, he looked very puzzled and concerned. And when Mrs. Hennessy and Caroline came out of the dressmaker's shop, he was as amiable and as charming as he used to be when he was at the Winthrops'—gracious, was it only a week ago? I am not at all surprised that I took him for a kind gentleman. But what will he do, sir? Will he run away again now that he knows we have tracked him down?"

Mitford sighed. "It is hard to say," he said. "What I would do if I were he is stay and continue to deny all knowledge of your jewels. To flee would be to own his guilt. And we have no proof that he took them."

"But he did!" she said, swinging around to face him. "I know I brought the box with me, and I know it had disappeared by the next morning. Who else could have taken them?"

He held up a staying hand. "You know that," he said, "and I know it. But there is no proof, for all that."

"Well," she said, bristling. "I am going to ride over to Deerview Park this instant and confront Mr. Porterhouse. And I shall tell everyone else there what he has done. That will be fitting embarrassment for him."

"You will do no such thing," Mitford said hastily. "It would be highly improper for a young lady to ride onto a gentleman's property unaccompanied. And I could certainly not accompany you. Your brother and sister are there."

Josephine stared at him open-mouthed, rendered speechless for the moment.

"They were hot on our trail, it seems," Mitford said, clasping his hands behind him and rocking back on his heels. "A friend of mine thought to do me a favor and lead them astray. He brought them to Deerview Park, where I suppose they decided to stay when they heard that Porterhouse was one of the guests."

"Oh, dear," Josephine said ineffectually. "Bart and Sukey?"

"I understand they are also looking for a Mr. Paul Villers,"

Mitford said. "I am afraid I gave a different name this morning and pretended to be staying in a different place from this house. So I cannot accompany you to Lord Parleigh's, you see, without their realizing that something strange is in the wind."

"Bart and Sukey," Josephine said. "Bart can lecture almost as well as Grandpapa, you know, when he is given a good enough excuse to play elder brother. And Sukey can look as sorrowful as Papa when she thinks that something I have done is not quite the thing. Oh, dear, whatever am I to do?"

"What I should have done," the Duke of Mitford said, "was take your brother aside and confess all to him. Then we could finally be free of the terrible scandal that has been threatening you."

"Are you mad?" she asked, staring at him as if she really thought he might be. "Bart would kill me. And he would kill you, which would be considerably more unjust. They must not find us. Nothing is clearer than that."

"Besides," he said with a sigh, "how can we confess the truth now, when we have accepted the hospitality of the Hennessys? The scandal would kill your reputation forever."

"Anyway," Josephine added, "if Bart found me, he would drag me off home and I would never recover my jewels."

The Duke of Mitford scratched his head and rocked back on his heels. "I am going to have to confront Porterhouse tomorrow without delay," he said, "and force the jewels from him. Then, Miss Middleton, it will be home with you as fast as horse can travel."

She opened her mouth to protest.

"There is no point whatsoever in arguing," he said. "You cannot go yourself for a variety of reasons, not the least of which is that your brother and sister would see you."

Josephine shut her mouth again.

The Duke of Mitford frowned and stared into her eyes, deep in thought. "I have an idea," he said.

She brightened perceptibly. "What?"

"I must leave here alone," he said. He rubbed his chin and thought more. "Sickness in the family. My sister's confinement. I will think of something. Something to convince the Hennessys. After I leave here, I will get your jewels, see that they are delivered to your brother, and take myself off. Then you can discover somehow that your brother and sister are at Deerview Park and be restored to them. You can persuade them of the necessity of keeping quiet about your true marital state. But your ordeal with be over, to all intents and purposes."

"But I would go with you," she said, "if you were called away. We are newly married and deeply in love."

"But I would not risk your safety in an urgent ride by curricle to London," he said. "I shall receive a summons from my sister's husband tomorrow morning."

"But I would go," Josephine said. "She is my sister-in-law, remember, and I am not at all afraid of curricles." She met his eyes. "Well, not when you are at the ribbons, anyway."

The Duke of Mitford rocked on his heels. "Would you kindly remember, ma'am," he said, "that we are not really wed? And if you choose, you can be a little afraid of curricles. And if I choose, I can be insistent that I not put your life in danger. You owe me obedience, after all."

"But I have just been told to remember that I am not your wife in reality," she said. "I owe you nothing, sir." They glared at each other for a moment until Josephine flushed. "Except for a great deal of money," she added. "I bought the most dreadful dresses, Paul, and a whole lot of accessories besides."

"You owe me nothing," he said, reaching out to touch her cheek with his fingertips. "Only this one thing, please. Allow me to free you from the tangle we have got into together. I know you would like to confront Porterhouse yourself, and I know you have the courage to do so, but you must remain here with Mrs. Hennessy and her daughter and play the part of complacent wife."

Josephine wrinkled her nose. "Well," she said, "by tomorrow perhaps we will have thought of another idea." She brightened. "Perhaps we will. Though, of course, it will be far better for you if we do not. Tomorrow you will be free of me and on your way to where you were going. You will be glad of that."

He slid his fingers down her cheek and beneath her chin.

"Where were you going?" she asked.

"Somewhere I did not want to go," he said, "to meet someone I did not want to meet."

"A lady?" she asked.

He nodded.

"You were to make her an offer?" she asked. "Perhaps she would not have been so bad after all. And she will doubtless be disappointed that you did not arrive."

He smiled. "I doubt it," he said.

"I don't." She touched one hand to the front of his coat and removed it again. "I would be disappointed." She flushed quite painfully.

"Would you?" he asked. "But you were not disappointed to have avoided your own suitor."

"That is different," she said. "He is toplofty and handsome. And a rake."

"And on whose authority do you have all this information?" he asked.

"Mr. Porterhouse's," she said. "Mr. Porterhouse knows him."

"Ah," he said. "Then we know for a certainty that the information must be reliable."

"Yes." Josephine looked doubtful. "But why would he have invented those things?"

The duke raised his eyebrows.

"Oh, dear," Josephine said. "Do you think he lied? Do you think the duke might be a decent man after all? But he cannot be. We must never forget his valet."

"Of course," the duke said. "Foolish of me to have forgotten that irrefutable evidence of his grace's depravity."

"Yes," she said, obviously still in doubt and still deep in thought. She raised her face absently for his kiss.

And the duke, who had a hand beneath her chin, could hardly refuse the invitation, though it was not consciously given. He kissed her, flickering his tongue once across her lips. But he did not prolong the embrace. And he was flushing when he looked up.

"We are in sight of the house," he said. "It is as well to give the impression that we are having a lover's conversation."

"Yes, of course," Josephine said, blushing too.

11

Mr. Porterhouse had been rather amused to meet Josephine Middleton in Ammanford. Surprised, certainly, but amused too. He had not expected her to follow him. For one thing, she had seemed to have no means with which to do so, stranded as she would have been when he had left with his carriage. For another thing, he had expected that she would be too afraid to pursue him, since she was but a young and weak female to whom he had made his intentions quite clear. Besides, he would have thought that if she did decide to follow, she would have gone in the direction of London, which any sensible person would have thought to be his destination.

However, it seemed that Miss Josephine Middleton was a far more interesting lady than he had thought. She had found a way to follow him and had done so, arriving in the vicinity of Deerview Park on the same day as he had done so himself.

She was quite a lady!

What amused him more than anything else was the manner in which she had made her pursuit. She had suddenly acquired a husband, it seemed, a Mr. Villiers. Mr. Porterhouse did not know any gentleman of that name. But who else could it be than the man who had come to her rescue at the inn? That great mountain of a man who had come bursting through the door without even opening it and had succeeded in besting him, though he was handy enough with his fives to daunt any ordinary adversary. Of course, he had been taken by surprise at a time when his mind had been on other matters entirely. And the little spitfire of a lady had lent a hand too.

Mr. Porterhouse was perhaps just a little alarmed by the knowledge that the powerful adversary of the inn was with Miss Middleton and had come, presumably, in order to get the jewels for himself. Though perhaps the man would be as disappointed as he had been if he ever got to see the pieces. But on the whole he was not unduly alarmed. The box had been disposed of, and the jewels themselves were well hidden among the belongings in his traveling bag.

It would be difficult for anyone to prove anything against him. Besides, even that uncouth giant who had attacked him would probably think twice about doing so at Deerview Park in the middle of a house party.

And of course he had a powerful weapon of his own, a certain piece of knowledge that Miss Middleton would not wish to be made public—the knowledge that she was not married or otherwise related to the Mr. Villiers with whom she was traveling. Yes, that was a powerful weapon, indeed.

Mr. Porterhouse returned to Deerview Park when he had finished his business in Ammanford without a qualm of real fear. He felt a little uneasy, it was true, when he alighted from his carriage outside the stable block of the house and caught sight of one of the grooms there—a great bald fellow whose body seemed to consist almost entirely of bulging muscles. The fellow looked familiar and aroused uneasiness in Mr. Porterhouse. But he could not place the man and could think of no reason for his uneasiness. It must just be that he had acquired a wariness of brawny males in the past week. He shrugged and made his way to the house.

Although it was only the middle of the afternoon when he arrived, most of the guests were about their own business or pleasure. It was not until he entered Lord Parleigh's drawing room prior to dinner that he saw two faces that were definitely familiar.

''Middleton!'' he said, smiling and extending a hand as he crossed the distance between them. ''And Miss Susanna. What a very pleasant and unexpected surprise, to be sure.''

Batholomew Middleton shook his hand, and Miss Susanna Middleton curtsied to him, he was interested to note. Both looked somewhat disconcerted.

''But if I had only known a week ago that you also intended to attend this house party,'' Mr. Porterhouse said, ''I would have suggested that we travel together.'' He smiled his most charming smile at brother and sister.

''Ah, yes, likewise,'' Batholomew said. They were surrounded by other guests, who could hear every word of the conversation.

"I trust you left your father and grandfather well?" Mr. Porterhouse asked Susanna.

"Oh, yes, I thank you, sir," she said.

"And Miss Middleton and your two other sisters?"

"Oh," Susanna said. "Yes, thank you, sir."

Mr. Porterhouse was beginning to enjoy himself. "And are congratulations in order for your sister yet?" he asked with a smile for them both. They were looking decidedly uncomfortable. "It was an open secret while I was staying with my cousins, the Winthrops, that his grace of Mitford was to pay his addresses to Miss Middleton soon after my departure."

"It was after our departure, too," Bartholomew said evasively.

Lord Parleigh turned from his conversation with Mrs. Hope in the group next their own. "Mitford," he said. "Yes, of course, Humphrey, I knew there was something I had forgotten to tell you when you returned this afternoon. Mitford was here this morning asking for you. He is planning to return tomorrow morning."

"Mitford?" Mr. Porterhouse said. "Here? Asking for me?"

Lord Parleigh slapped him on the shoulder. "You move in illustrious circles," he said with a laugh. "It seems he came all the way from Rutland Park to see you, having discovered that Miss Middleton was from home, and Mr. Middleton and his sister had been awaiting your arrival, too. It really is not fair, Humphrey. You handsome men get all the attention." He laughed heartily and turned to take Mrs. Hope on his arm to lead her in to dinner. Sir Thomas Burgess was extending an arm to Susanna.

For the first time Mr. Porterhouse felt a strong twinge of discomfort. What was this? First Miss Middleton herself had arrived on the scene with a fictitious husband, but a man who was nevertheless very real and a very formidable adversary. And then her brother and sister had arrived on the scene, looking for him, rather than for her. And now the Duke of Mitford, her intended husband, was in pursuit of him too. Mr. Porterhouse began not to like it. The whole business had an uncomfortable aura of conspiracy surrounding it.

And just when he was about to take his first mouthful of soup, he had a sudden memory of having to double over in the stable-yard of the Crown and Anchor Inn in order to retch from the powerful pummeling he had received from that giant who had burst into his room. And also an image of straightening up again to find himself looking into the face of a bald and muscular giant who had grinned and suggested that the next time he intended to travel by night he might drink beforehand with a little less enthusiasm.

The same giant as had been lurking outside Lord Parleigh's stables earlier that afternoon.

Mr. Porterhouse's neckcloth felt uncomfortably tight. And he found himself dabbing at his chin with his napkin and hoping that no one had noticed his soup dribbling from his mouth.

Suddenly his traveling bag did not seem a very safe hiding place after all.

There was a hint of winter in the air, Sir Thomas Burgess noticed with some regret the following day. Definitely enough of a nip to catch at one's nose and ears during the morning hours. Of course, it was having a somewhat delightful effect on the cheeks of his companion. Her normally pale complexion was healthily rosy. She had her arm linked through his as they strolled along the terrace outside Lord Parleigh's house.

He had been somewhat concerned about Miss Susanna Middleton the evening before. Whatever it was that was between her and her brother on the one hand and Porterhouse on the other, it was not something that made her at all happy. The two of them had watched Porterhouse all evening but had barely spoken a word.

It had crossed his mind that the girl was perhaps Porterhouse's rejected flirt. He was, after all, the type of man all women could be expected to sigh over. One would have to look very hard indeed to find any physical imperfection in the man.

But it was not that, either. Porterhouse had Miss Middleton's jewels, Mitford had said. The elder Miss Middleton, that was. The one Mitford was running about the country with. And the brother and sister were looking for her, but had stayed at Deerview Park as soon as Porterhouse's name had been mentioned.

It was all very intriguing, or would be so if it had not so obviously upset the little golden-haired beauty. And clearly now she was thankful for a steady arm and a sympathetic ear.

"Jo was supposed to marry the Duke of Mitford, you see," she was explaining. "He was to pay his addresses to her just a week ago. That was why Bart and I were surprised to see him here yesterday."

"I must say I had not expected to see him this far north," Sir Thomas said. "He is a friend of mine, you know."

"He is far different from what I expected," Susanna said. "We were under the impression that he was a tall and handsome gentleman." She flushed an even rosier color than the morning air had whipped into her cheeks. "Oh." She looked up at him with wide blue eyes. "I do beg your pardon. I did not mean . . ."

"I am sure you did not," he said. "If it is not impertinent to ask, ma'am, how came your sister to be with Mr., er . . . ?" He raised his eyebrows inquiringly.

"Mr. Villiers?" she said. "I do not know, sir," Her eyes looked suspiciously bright as she continued to gaze up at him. "And I wish her being with him did not have to be public knowledge. But Bart had to ask you at the inn, you see, because we might have lost them altogether. As in fact, we did, of course."

"With your pardon, ma'am," he said, looking down at her in some concern, "I am no prattler. I wish I could be of some service to you." And he wished he could too, without at the same time being disloyaal to a friend.

"She ran away," she said. "At least, we think she ran away. She said she was on her way to our aunt's. She did not wish to marry the duke, you see. I am sorry, sir, since he is your friend."

Sir Thomas smiled slightly. "So," he said, "she ran away from Mitford and somehow paired up with Villiers. Interesting."

"But perhaps he is a villain," she said. "And even if he is not, Jo will be ruined. Poor Jo. She is frequently thoughtless, you know, and Grandpapa is forever scolding her for not behaving with propriety, but she means well. She has a good heart."

"I don't believe Villiers is a scoundrel," he said. "I saw him only briefly, you know, at that inn, but he appeared to be a gentleman. He was treating your sister with deference. I would not worry unduly, if I were you."

"But why would she travel as Mrs. Villiers?" Susanna asked. "And then there is Mr. Porterhouse. He took Jo's jewels. At least, we think he took them. That is what Sam says. Sam is our coachman, you know. Or at least, he is our coachman now. He was not at the start, but he was kind enough to come with us when he discovered that Bart was driving the carriage into every pothole along the road and making me sick."

"Porterhouse," Sir Thomas said. "He greeted you and your brother like long lost friends last evening."

"Yes," Susanna said. "And poor Bart is most uncomfortable, for how can he accuse Mr. Porterhouse of stealing Jo's jewels when we have only Sam's word that they are missing at all? And yet Bart has decided that he must do just that this morning. I left him pacing about in his dressing room just a little while ago, pounding one fist against the other hand. Poor Bart. He does not like to be forced to exert himself. Oh, where can Jo be? Do you think she is in dreadful trouble?"

"I am quite convinced she is not," Sir Thomas said, watching his friend, the Duke of Mitford, approach along the terrace, and wishing there was some way of letting his companion know that her sister was safely lodged just four miles away. "Here comes Mitford."

Susanna swept him a curtsy. "Your grace," she murmured.

Mitford bowed and exchanged greetings with his friend. "Good morning, Miss Middleton, Tom," he said. "I have come in search of Porterhouse. Did he return yesterday?"

"He did," Sir Thomas said, "but was not at breakfast this morning. Perhaps he was up earlier, or perhaps he is still in bed. Middleton, I believe, has plans to speak with him, too."

"Ah," the Duke of Mitford said. "A man much in demand, is he, Tom? I shall stroll inside and see what I can see."

"They do know each other, then," Susanna said, staring at the duke's disappearing back. "I have wondered since Mr. Porterhouse left whether he just said that in order to cause trouble. His grace is not quite the way he was described to Jo, though."

"Is he not?" Sir Thomas said. "Come, ma'am, let us stroll farther. I shall talk to you and take your mind off your troubles, if I may."

"Oh," she said, looking up at him with those blue eyes that could make him quite forget that his tastes usually led him to an entirely different class of female. "You have been very kind to me, sir. And you did your best to help Bart and me find Jo."

Sir Thomas Burgess did not feel very proud of himself. He secretly cursed the bonds of friendship that forced him to keep this little creature in the misery of suspense over the fate of her sister.

The Duke of Mitford had awakened to a growingly familiar scene, and one which he had a feeling he would have to grow more accustomed to as his life progressed. Miss Josephine Middleton was kneeling on the floor beside his bed—or what he had come to recognize as his bed for the past week. As usual at such moments, her hair was all down over her shoulders and her mouth was in motion. Clearly, she had been speaking for some time.

"So you see," she was saying, "it would not do at all."

"It is not even light outside yet," he said, opening one eye, "is it?"

"Oh, yes," she said, pausing in her monologue long enough to turn her head toward the window. "But the draperies are of heavy velvet, you see, and the bed is between you and the window. And of course it is getting late on in the year again. Soon enough it will be breakfast time before it is full daylight. But by that time, of course, there is always spring to look forward to. So there is never any real reason for gloom."

The duke might have disagreed with that final statement, but he bowed to the inevitable and woke up. "You were saying?" he said politely.

"It will not do," she said. "You see, no one even knows we are here. We were supposed to be going to London. Even our servants thought we were going there."

"Yes," he agreed, "my brains were so addled with love that I forgot to let them know of our change in plans."

"So no one could send us an urgent message here," she said. "You see, do you not? We will need another plan."

She looked rather pleased with herself, Mitford thought.

"Another plan?" he said. "With regards to what, pray?"

"Oh," she said, "you are not at your best in the mornings, are you, sir?"

The Duke of Mitford continued to look at her with eyebrows politely raised. He resisted the temptation to tell her that he was considerably better on those mornings when he awoke in a bed, having slept in it all night long. If he said that, she would start offering to share her bed with him again. One experience of accepting that offer had been quite enough to prove to him that it was no viable alternative to a night spent on a hard floor.

"How could your brother-in-law send for you here when he does not even know we are here?" Josephine Middleton asked with a smile of triumph. "The Hennessys would know instantly that it was a trick."

"Would they?" he asked. "I could not say that I had written the morning after our wedding to let everyone know where we were going?"

"No," she said, "because we could not have anticipated that we would meet the Hennessys and come to Hawthorn House. It will not do, sir. You will not be able to leave on that pretext."

The Duke of Mitford sat up and ran a hand through his hair. "Well," he said, "I shall think of that later in the day. In the meantime, I shall still carry out the main part of my plan, which is to call again at Deerview Park and confront Porterhouse."

Josephine sat back on her heels. "I shall come with you," she said.

"You cannot," he reminded her. "Your brother and sister are there."

"Silly," she said. "They need not see me. We will enter Lord Parleigh's property where we will not be observed, and we will creep up on Mr. Porterhouse at a place where he will least expect us, a place where he may not call for help. We will have him at our mercy."

The Duke of Mitford got to his feet. Good Lord, Bedlam was going to seem like a sane house after a few days spent in the company of Miss Josephine Middleton.

"I shall go alone," he said. "You will stay here. And that decision is not open for argument, ma'am."

He was surprised that she did not argue. She wrinkled her nose at him instead and got to her feet.

"While I am gone," he said, "I shall think of a way of getting you back with your brother and sister as soon as possible without making your situation quite public. I shall think of something, ma'am, never fear."

Josephine gave him a beatific smile.

She was quite right, of course, he decided as he was dressing in the small dressing room that adjoined their bedchamber. It was a good thing she had thought of it. It said volumes for his own inexperience with intrigue that he had not thought of the problem himself. But he would think of something. For now he must concentrate his mind on the coming meeting with Porterhouse.

He did not on the whole expect any real difficulty. Porterhouse would discover, of course, that he was the Duke of Mitford. At first, that fact had struck the duke as problematic, but second thought had changed his mind. He was learning from his experience as plain Mr. Villiers that people had a far stronger tendency to be overawed by his ducal presence. Porterhouse would be overawed. Mitford would turn on the full force of his grandeur.

And he would speak the language that Porterhouse obviously spoke best. It was very likely that the sum of money he would offer would be far more attractive to the man than the rather modest fortune in stolen jewels he was carrying around with him. Porterhouse would not want to admit, of course, that he had those jewels, but the chances were that he would be persuaded to do so when the admission would be worth so much to him.

The Duke of Mitford had not paused to consider why he was willing to pay out such a handsome ransom for jewels that were no concern of his. The fact that they belonged to the bride his father had chosen for him, perhaps? Or the fact that having spent a great deal of his time pursuing the villain, he felt it necessary to end the episode in a satisfactory manner? Or the fact that having embarked on the first—and, he hoped fervently, the last—adventure of his life, he wished to end it in somewhat heroic fashion? He had not stopped to consider.

He set off on his way one hour later, having assured the Hennessys that he was eager to see a friend of his whom he had missed the day before. He would not take Josephine, he explained, gazing fondly at her, because the conversation would be undoubtedly male and tedious to her, and she would be so much happier in the company of her own friends.

"But you must hurry back by luncheon time," Mrs. Hennessy said, "or we will have Jo sighing and paying no attention to our conversation, Mr. Villiers, just as she was yesterday when we went shopping." She patted his hand just to show him that there was no offense in her words.

He kissed Josephine before leaving since the Hennessys clearly expected such signs of affection between them. It was a habit that must not become engrained. His mother would have an apoplexy if she ever saw him kiss a young woman on the lips, even if she were his wife, as Josephine Middleton undoubtedly would be before too much more time had elapsed. But he would not depress himself with that thought.

Porterhouse had not been at breakfast, Tom Burgess told him when he reached Deerview Park. He was out riding, Lord Parleigh told him when he went inside. And he was borne off to play a game of billiards while he waited. It was not quite the way he had hoped to spend the morning, but he could be patient. He would be waiting for Porterhouse on his return. There was plenty of time.

Josephine did not stay to converse comfortably with the ladies as the duke had expected. How could she when there was so much to be done? And how would she ever forgive herself if Mr. Villiers got himself killed on her behalf while she was sitting and talking about balls and ballgowns?

"If I may, sir," she said, smiling winningly at Mr. Hennessy the very moment the duke's curricle disappeared from view down the driveway, "I will go riding for an hour or so."

"My pleasure, Jo," he said, beaming at her. "I shall see to having a quiet little mare saddled for you. If it were not for the fact that I am expecting my bailiff, I would ride with you myself. Mrs. Hennessy and Caroline, you know, do not like to ride." He laughed heartily. "They are too afraid of coming home smelling like horse."

"Harvey!" his wife said.

"Papa!" Caroline said simultaneously.

But neither of them offered to ride with Josephine, she was much relieved to find.

"I will send a groom with you," Mr. Hennessy said.

"Please don't." Josephine smiled shyly. "You will remember, perhaps, sir, that I frequently like to be alone with my thoughts." How could they possibly remember any such thing? she thought with the merest pang of guilt. "Papa always allowed me to ride alone, provided I did not go far. And Paul has said I may."

"You wish to be alone to dream of your young husband," Mrs. Hennessy said, patting her hand. "We understand, dear Jo. And Caroline will doubtless spend the morning in her room dreaming of Mr. Porterhouse and the other handsome gentlemen she is likely to meet at Lord Parleigh's ball tomorrow night."

"Mama!" Caroline said.

Mr. Hennessy's quiet little mare did not take kindly to being prodded along, Josephine found a short while later. But under a little firm guidance it did hold to a steady canter. And indeed, it was not wise to go faster since she was unfamiliar with the terrain and indeed not quite sure of the way.

If only Bart and Sukey were not at Deerview Park, she would ride boldly up to the door. She did not care at all about possible scandal. Apart from the Hennessys, no one in this part of the world knew her anyway. What would it matter if they saw her come, a single lady in search of a single gentleman? Let them talk or think what they would.

But Bart and Sukey were there. And if Bart clapped eyes on her, he would bear her off home without further ado and scold her all the way. Bart was the laziest of mortals and loved nothing better than to sit at his ease, making fun of the foibles of the world. But when Bart felt that family honor was at stake, or the reputation of one of his sisters, then he could become remarkably like Grandpapa. It was not difficult at all to imagine the type of elderly gentleman Bart would grow into.

And then, of course, Sukey would look at her with gentle reproach all the way back to Rutland Park and try to make excuses for her behavior to an outraged Bart. No, it did not bear thinking of. She would not ride boldly up to the door.

But she did not need to do so or to slink around by kitchen entrances, as she had considered doing. By some singular good fortune, she saw Mr. Porterhouse even before she knew for certain that she must be on Lord Parleigh's land. He was riding close to a copse of trees with another gentleman and two ladies.

There was no chance to consider strategy. No time to wonder whether she should ride boldly up to the party or hide among the trees and try to attract Mr. Porterhouse's attention without being seen by the others. She had already been seen. And Mr. Porterhouse had the gall to sweep his hat from his head and made her a bow from the back of his horse.

"Mrs. Villiers, ma'am," he called as she rode closer to them, "well, met, indeed. Do join us. May I present Sir Fabian Crawley and Miss Crawley? And Lady Dorothy Brough?" He smiled around at the others. "Mrs. Villiers is a close friend and neighbor of my cousins, the Winthrops, in Northhamptonshire. And she is very recently married. Less than a week, I believe you said, ma'am?"

"Five days," Josephine said, and smiled. She hoped she was not blushing, Oh she hoped not.

She conversed with the group for all of two minutes on the state of the weather before turning to Mr. Porterhouse.

"I am afraid I was lost," she said. "I was on my way to the house. Could I beg that you cut short your ride, sir, to show me the way?"

Mr. Porterhouse bowed and smiled. There was even a twinkle in his eye, Josephine would have sworn.

A moment later they were riding away from the group.

12

Mr. Porterhouse had not had a great deal of sleep the night before. It had been a foolish theft and not at all in his usual style. It had just seemed so easy at the time to take the jewel case into his own keeping. He had not even thought of it as theft since at the time he had been fully convinced that the girl would be his too. But then that assumption had also been foolish. He had never indulged in seduction before, either. It was just that his pockets were sadly to let, and opportunity had seemed to fall into his lap when he found a rustic family which just happened to be more wealthy than he dreamed of being.

And the chit had seemed brainless enough. No town bronze. No sense of proper decorum. And facing a marriage that alarmed her. It had seemed too easy to resist.

And yet now he was stuck with stolen jewels, which were not worth near as much as he had expected, and half the world was in pursuit of him. He had seriously considered, during his wakeful night, sneaking out into the darkness and throwing the jewels down a well or into a river. He could bluff his way out of the situation if there were no evidence against him.

But he could not bring himself to do it. The pieces would not make him a wealthy man, but they would stand between him and debtors' prison, perhaps, for a while longer. The temptation to keep them was just too strong.

He should, of course, have gone immediately to London to sell the jewels. Then he would have been perfectly safe. But no, he had been too clever for his own good and turned north, imagining that any pursuit would automatically head south.

He had remembered a long-standing invitation from Lord Parleigh, who was forever holding house parties and forever inviting any chance-met stranger. It was said, indeed, that one did not need any invitation at all to Deerview Park, since Lord

Parleigh would merely assume that he had met one and invited one at some time.

He had not proved so clever after all. Miss Middleton herself, for all her rustic ways, had caught up to him, and presumably she had with her the giant who had attacked him on a previous occasion. And others had caught up to him too.

By the time morning came, he was still undecided about what was his best course of action. All instinct told him that it would be best to run, but common sense told him that that would be the worst possible thing to do since it would immediately point to his guilt.

And so he had decided to stay. And he had fallen in with the suggestion of Sir Fabian Crawley, made at an early breakfast before most of the guests had risen, that a group of them go out riding.

It was only when he was in the stables mounting his horse that something happened to cause him almost to lose his nerve. That great giant of a groom was there again, the bald man who had looked familiar the day before. And devil take it, he had been right. The man really had been one of the ostlers at the Crown and Anchor Inn. Or at least, he had assumed at the time that he was employed at the inn.

He must have been mistaken. The man must be employed by that Villiers, with whom Miss Middleton was traveling. And the groom's present assignment must be no less than to spy on his movements, since Villiers himself was not staying at Deerview Park.

Mr. Porterhouse, riding out beside Miss Crawley and making small talk with her, felt distinctly as if a noose were closing about his neck.

And then he saw Josephine Middleton and knew before many minutes had passed that she had been set to lure him back to the house.

And yet he was amused. Did they think he would crumble so easily? Did they think he was no match for a mere slip of a girl, who had fallen quite easily into his clutches on a previous occasion?

"May I congratulate you once more on your marriage, ma'am?" he said to her as they rode away from the rest of the group. "I am delighted that after all you evaded the clutches of my acquaintance, the Duke of Mitford."

"We can dispense with the small talk," she said, "since there is no audience, sir. You know as well as I that I am not married and that I came here with Mr. Villiers only to pursue you."

"Am I to feel flattered?" he asked, smiling across at her. "You rejected me once, ma'am. Am I to believe that you have had a change of heart?"

"Do you know," she said, fixing him with a severe eye, "my grandpapa has always said that lying is dangerous because sometimes one ends up living the lie so thoroughly that one loses touch with reality? I see now, sir, that he was right. I want my jewels, and I intend to have them before I return home."

He looked at her in serious concern. "That is not the first time you have said something similar," he said. "Do I take it, ma'am, that you have misplaced some jewels and imagine that I have them?"

"No," she said, "I do not imagine. I know, sir."

"In all probability," he said kindly, "you left them at home, Miss Middleton, and just imagine that you brought them with you."

"Oh," she said fiercely, "you know that is untrue, sir. I remember distinctly warning you not to bump your shins with the corner of the box in the bottom of my valise. And I was foolish enough to tell you what was in the box."

"Ah," he said. "I am afraid I do not recall the conversation, ma'am."

"You have a choice," Josephine said, sitting very straight in her saddle. "You may return the jewels to me now without any fuss at all, or you may confront Mr. Villiers with your denials."

"I am all fear and trembling," he said.

"You will be," Josephine said. "He is already at the house awaiting you. Perhaps it would be well to learn from experience and remember what resulted from your last encounter with him."

Mr. Porterhouse raised his eyebrows. But he did not reply. Mr. Seymour and the elder Miss Hope were riding toward them.

"We decided after all that we would join the ride," Mr.

Seymour called as they drew near, and he raised his hat and looked curiously at Josephine.

Mr. Porterhouse made the introductions.

"You will wish to return to the house without delay, Mr. Porterhouse," Miss Hope said. "The Duke of Mitford is waiting for you there and has been for quite some time."

"So," Mr. Porterhouse said, gazing ahead of him as the other two rode on, "you have laid a powerful trap, ma'am. The beau you pretended to despise, Villiers, your brother and sister, Villiers's groom. I suppose I should congratulate you."

Mr. Porterhouse was too engrossed in his own thoughts to take notice of the pale face and staring eyes of his companion.

"Yes," she said finally. "So I think, sir, it would be wiser to relinquish the jewels and look elsewhere for a wealthy and gullible bride."

Mr. Porterhouse made a sudden decision. "They are not at the house, you know," he said. "You do not think me fool enough to keep them there, do you?"

"Where are they, then?" she asked. "And do not say they are far away and you must ride out for them. I am not such a fool, sir. You will not escape from me again. I shall go with you to fetch them."

"My thoughts entirely," he said. "They are at my aunt's. A drive of a mere two hours, ma'am. If you will not find the journey tedious, you may ride with me and we may be done with this whole tiresome charade."

"Let us go, then," she said.

"Ah," he said, "but I must return to the house first, ma'am. And it would be wise to take my carriage since it will be rather far to ride and I fear we may have rain before the day is out."

"And how will I know that you will not ride away in the meantime?" she said.

"Ma'am," he said, "I presume that for reasons of your own you will not wish to come inside the house with me. And indeed, I do not intend to enter it myself through the front entrance. You may wait, then, in sight of the stables. I would be foolish indeed to try to escape on foot, would I not? You yourself will see me if I leave the stables and try to ride away without you. I shall take you up in my carriage a little way down the driveway where no one is likely to see you."

"I shall be waiting," she said.

Mr. Porterhouse, taking his horse into the stables a few minutes later and noting that the giant spy was still on duty there, had no doubt that she would. And he had every intention of taking her up with him and being well on his way to London with her before both he and she were missed and before anyone made the connection between the two absences.

It would be London this time. London, where he could lose both himself and her while he made negotiations with her father to marry her and save her from disgrace. Her dowry, after all, would be worth far more to him than the paltry jewels would be, though they would pay his bills until his marriage.

Josephine kept her eyes on the stables even though she tried as far as possible to stay out of sight. She was feeling a combination of elation, anxiety, and terror. Elation because she had after all and singlehandedly confronted Mr. Porterhouse and forced him into both admitting that he had her jewels and agreeing to give them up to her. How she would enjoy showing them to Mr. Villiers later that day and seeing his amazement that she had had the courage and resourcefulness to recover them without his aid at all.

She also felt some anxiety. Experience had taught her not to trust Mr. Porterhouse. She did not want to be made a fool of by him yet again. And there was always the possibility that he had a horse all tethered and ready on another part of the estate. Perhaps he was even now making his escape while she stood there waiting for him.

But she did not think so. He had not been expecting either her or Mr. Villiers that morning and would have no reason to have a horse in readiness for an escape. She did not think she had any reason to be unduly anxious. Though, of course, there was the problem of what to do with her own horse when she got into Mr. Porterhouse's carriage. She could not just turn it loose. It was, after all, not her horse. And would not the Hennessys worry if she did not return within a reasonable time after her departure? She would tie the horse to a tree, she decided, but leave it in a place where it would be seen and cared for eventually. And perhaps she could persuade Mr. Porterhouse to run back to the stables in order to send a groom with a message to Hawthorn House. Merely a message to say that she was safe and would return before nightfall.

But the feeling that tended to dominate all was one of some terror. What had Miss Hope meant by saying that the Duke of Mitford was at the house and awaiting Mr. Porterhouse? The Duke of Mitford? *Her* Duke of Mitford? Had he come in pursuit of her? And had he found her so easily? But why had he come after her? What could he want with her if he knew what she had been doing for the past week?

And if the duke was in pursuit of her, where were Papa and Grandpapa? Were they at Deerview Park too? Oh, dear, what sort of a mess had she got herself into? And all she had intended to do was go to Aunt Winifred's to ask advice on breaking the news to Papa that she did not wish to marry anyone as grand as a duke. Was it possible that so much could have resulted from that ill-conceived idea?

Well, she decided as she paced the grass at the side of the driveway, not removing her eyes from the stables, when this was all over and she was finally at home again, she would listen in patience to all the lectures she would receive. They would all be deserved. And then she was going to change. Never again would she act without thinking first. She was going to grow up and become a dignified and decorous lady. It was high time. She was fast approaching her one and twentieth birthday.

"Miss Middleton?"

The voice came from behind her and almost unseated her from her side saddle. And now look where her daydreaming had led her! She whirled about to face Mr. Villiers, who was on foot.

"What are you doing here?" he asked in exasperation.

"You are supposed to be in the house," she said. "Why are you not?"

"Will you get down from there," he said, "and tell me what on earth you think you are about?" He sounded more than exasperated. He sounded downright annoyed. Oh, dear.

Josephine set her hands on his shoulders and allowed him to lift her to the ground. She smiled foolishly up at him. "I could not stay at home," she said.

"That would appear to be the story of your life," he said. "What were you doing? Hoping that your man would just happen to come out of the stables and ride obligingly toward you?''

"And what are you doing?" she asked. "I thought you were to call at the house and confront him."

"He has been from home ever since I arrived," he said. "I played billiards and I conversed with Lord Parleigh until we had exhausted every topic known to man. But he has not come back. In the end I had to agree to stay to luncheon and made an excuse to come outside for some air. I have been walking along the driveway in the hope that he would return this way. Now I am glad he did not. In a moment I am going to set you on that horse again. But not before I have had your solemn promise to ride it home again without stopping. I have never known a more pestilential female, if you will pardon me for saying so. And you see how you have forced me into unpardonable rudeness?"

"You are a very kind man," she said, "for I know you are fearing for my safety. But you need not be anxious. I am about to recover my jewels, sir, and all without any male support at all. What do you think of that?"

She had been going to keep it a secret, she thought. It would have been so much more satisfactory to hold up the box of jewels in her hands and nonchalantly mention the fact that they were recovered. But she was stung by his typical male domineering ways.

"What?" he said.

"I am about to recover them," she said. "I found Mr. Porterhouse, you see, and have had a very satisfactory talk with him. He has agreed to return my property."

"Where and when?" the duke asked, standing very still and looking at her just as if she had two heads.

"Immediately," she said, smiling at him. "The jewels are not here, of course. I did not really expect that they would be. They are at his aunt's, a two-hour drive away. He is going to get them. And I am going with him. I do not trust him to bring them back here to me, you see."

"And that is why you are waiting here," he said. It was not a question. "He is going to take you up in his carriage and you are to go and fetch your jewels."

"Yes," she said.

"Good Lord," he said. "Good Lord!"

Josephine smiled at him in some triumph.

"Good Lord!" he said again. "How have you succeeded in living this long, ma'am, without a brain?"

Josephine's smile faded.

"I suppose," he said, "that it has not struck you that he is abducting you again?"

"Abducting me?" she said. "How foolish. He knows that I do not wish to marry him. And he said himself that he will be glad to have this whole charade at an end. That was his exact word."

The Duke of Mitford rocked on his heels. He appeared to be drawing breath to resume speech, but the sound of horses' hooves from behind them had him grabbing for her arm and drawing her off the driveway and behind the large oak trees that grew along its length. Her horse, they both noticed belatedly, was grazing on the grass at the side of the driveway.

"We must have been seen," he said in exasperation a minute later. "They were almost on top of us. I could cheerfully shake you."

He had a firm grip of her upper arms and could easily have suited action to words. He looked down at her and shook his head instead. "It is very fortunate for you that I came along when I did," he said.

Her eyes widened suddenly. "Oh, Paul," she said, "you will never guess what."

"Probably not," he agreed.

"The Duke of Mitford is here," she said. "Here. At Deerview Park. We met a Miss Hope and a gentleman whose name I have forgotten, and they said that the duke was waiting at the house to speak with Mr. Porterhouse. Whatever can it mean?"

"I don't know," the duke said, releasing her arms in order to scratch his head. "But Porterhouse did tell you that he knows the duke. Perhaps they are close friends."

"You do not think he has come after me?" Josephine asked.

"Perhaps," the duke said. "Perhaps he felt slighted when he found you gone. He is insufferably arrogant, after all, and would not take kindly to such rejection."

Josephine looked at him with wide eyes. "It is a good thing he has not found me, then," she said. "What do you think he would do?"

The Duke of Mitford shrugged. "Probably wallop you and take you back home to marry you," he said. "Dukes are notorious for having their own way, you know. Now, ma'am, what am I to do with you?"

"Perhaps if you are really concerned for my safety," she suggested, "you could follow Mr. Porterhouse's carriage. He should be along at any moment now."

"Absolutely not," he said. "If by chance I lose sight of the carriage, your doom will be certain. I have no intention of taking such a risk."

"Then I shall have to go alone," she said. "I am not chicken-hearted, sir."

"No," he said, "just brainless. I shall have to give up trying to see Porterhouse today, I see, in order to take you home myself. Only so will I be certain that you get there. You will come with me now to the stables to get my curricle. I would prefer that you not be seen, but you seem to have met a goodly number of Lord Parleigh's guests anyway. What does it matter if you also meet a few of his grooms?"

"Oh," Josephine said, "you cannot stop me. You have no right. You are not my father or my brother. Or my husband, either."

"Very well," he said, "then I will just have to turn you over to someone who is. And I think it high time I did so, anyway. I cannot imagine how I got drawn into this highly scandalous situation. Come, ma'am, we will go and find out Mr. Bartholomew Middleton."

Josephine caught at his arm as he turned away toward the driveway. "No!" she said. "Don't, please. Bart will be unbearably cross. And I will be mortified to have our meeting a public thing, as it will inevitably be in that house. Besides, think what the Hennessys will say. And I am so close to recovering my jewels. He has actually admitted taking them. I will leave it to you, then. You go and confront him now. I shall come with you. He should be in the stables himself soon."

"I will have you a safe four miles away before I do any such thing," the duke said. "And I intend taking you that four miles myself. Now. Take my arm. We are going to walk to the stables.''

Why, oh, why had she been daydreaming a few minutes before? Josephine asked herself as she took his arm obediently. If she had only heard him coming, she could have ridden among the trees and hidden from him. And soon she would have been on her way to fetch her jewels. Instead, here she was having to play the part of the helpless female again merely because a man had chosen to play tyrant. She was certainly becoming disillusioned with Mr. Paul Villiers.

She looked hopefully about her when they reached the coachhouse, but there was no sign of Mr. Porterhouse. She wished and wished that he would appear so that Mr. Villiers would be forced into a confrontation. And then she would be on hand to help too, just as she had done the last time. It was so very tiresome to be taken home like a little child while he planned all the fun for himself later. Doubtless he would find some way to set the Hennessys over her as guards the next time he left, too.

They had a slow journey back to Hawthorn House, with Josephine's horse tied behind the curricle. They spoke scarcely a word. He looked cross, she thought when she glanced at him at one point in order to make some other comment on the strange appearance of the Duke of Mitford in the neighborhood. She closed her mouth instead. She was beginning to feel just a little remorseful. He had after all been very kind to her and had given up almost the whole of a week to her affairs. He was even willing to put himself in some danger for her sake.

It was not his fault that he was a man and must forever be imagining that women could not look after themselves.

"There now," he said, when he finally lifted her down outside Mr. Hennessy's door, "you are safe despite yourself."

She would have made a suitable rejoinder if he had not led her up the steps and into the house without any delay at all. And Mr. Hennessy appeared out of his office, and Mrs. Hennessy came down the stairs, and Mr. Villiers laid a hand over hers on his arm and smiled fondly down at her.

"Josephine rode to meet me," he said. "I wonder if she will still be doing so after ten years of marriage."

"Oh," Mr. Hennessy said, "wait just five years, my dear

sir. Just five years. She will be running to meet you to tell you about the newest bauble or bonnet she has been buying.''

"Harvey!" his wife said, laughing.

"Will you, Josephine?" Mr. Villiers was asking, his gray eyes smiling warmly at her.

"Only if you insist that I go shopping, as you did yesterday," she said, watching as he lifted her hand to his lips. His breath was warm against her skin.

13

Susanna was feeling restless. She had gone inside after her stroll with Sir Thomas Burgess, but Bart was not in his room and there was nothing to do in hers except pace back and forth from the window to the door, worrying about everything her mind touched upon.

What were Papa and Grandpapa doing at that particular moment? And Penny and Gussy? Were they all worrying about Jo, and about her and Bart? But of course they would be worrying. What were they doing, though? Where were Papa and Grandpapa searching? And they would be searching, having discovered that none of the three of them had arrived at Aunt Winifred's.

And what were she and Bart doing at Lord Parleigh's home? Were they doing any good at all? They were no closer to finding Jo than they had been when they set out from home—how many days ago? It seemed very likely that she had continued north with the mysterious Mr. Villiers.

Would they ever see their sister alive again? And even if they did, what would be the extent of her ruin? Not that Susanna cared about that at all—she just wanted Jo back. But she dared not think of how her sister's life might have been ruined by the experiences of the past week.

And what about Mr. Porterhouse? They had no proof whatsoever that he had had anything to do with Jo's disappearance, though of course Sam had told them that he had been at that inn the same night as Jo and Mr. Villiers. There was even less proof that Mr. Porterhouse had stolen any of Jo's jewels. For all she and Bart knew, all of the family jewels might be lying safely at home.

So how could Bart confront Mr. Porterhouse, as he intended to do that day? He could just be starting some dreadful scandal.

Surely they should not be wasting their time at Deerview Park. They should be on their way in pursuit of Jo, though how they could do that when they did not know what direction to take, Susanna did not know.

She wished there were someone to talk to, someone who could give wise and calm advice. Bart was too caught up in the emotion of the moment. Bart always had been thoroughly easy-going except when he felt the family honor was in some jeopardy. There was Sir Thomas Burgess, of course. He was a kind gentleman; she liked him exceedingly. But she had already said more to him than she strictly ought. He was, after all, a virtual stranger.

And then, of course, she must not forget the strange appearance of the Duke of Mitford on the scene. Was it pure coincidence? Or was there some connection to Jo? But why would he pursue her when he had never set eyes on her? And why was he so different from the way Mr. Porterhouse had described him?

She was going to develop a headache, Susanna thought, if she did not get some fresh air again. Eighteen years of living in the country with a close and loving family and with a very few neighbors had really not prepared her well at all for solving such knotty problems.

It was as she walked along the terrace before the house and stepped off it onto the lawn that led to the stable block that she ran almost literally into Mr. Porterhouse, who was coming from the side of the house. He smiled at her and set down a bag at his feet.

"All alone, Miss Middleton?" he asked. "What has happened to the gallantry of the other gentlemen?"

"I am just taking the air for a few minutes, sir," she said in some confusion. She had never felt comfortable with Mr. Porterhouse. But she realized in all honesty that it was perhaps his perfect good looks and his fashionable air that overawed her.

"Ah, you are not alone," he said, smiling beyond her shoulder and making a bow. "Lady Dorothy? You are back from your ride? I am sorry I had to leave you so abruptly."

Lady Dorothy Brough joined them at the edge of the terrace. She had changed from her riding clothes into a day dress. She held a shawl about her shoulders.

"Don't mention it, Humphrey," she said. "Is his grace staying for lunch?"

"I have not seen him," Mr. Porterhouse said. "Is he here?"

"He called earlier," Susanna said. "He was looking for you, sir. But that was some time ago."

"We passed him a short while ago," Lady Dorothy said, "on the driveway. He was with the lady you introduced us to. Mrs.— I cannot recall her name. It looked to me altogether as if they had an assignation. Certainly, he drew her behind the trees when they heard us approach. Are you quite sure she is a lady, Humphrey?"

"Oh, yes," Mr. Porterhouse said, "quite sure, Lady Dorothy. You must be cold with just that thin shawl. I would hate to see you take a chill."

"Yes," she said. "I am going back inside directly. I hope he returns for luncheon, though, don't you? Life can become tedious in the country when one sees the same faces day after day. Would you not agree with me, Miss Middleton?"

Susanna flushed. "I have always lived in the country, ma'am," she said. She turned back to the house with Lady Dorothy, but Mr. Porterhouse caught at her arm.

"If you will forgive me for saying so, Miss Middleton," he said, "you seem to have lost some of the glow of high spirits that I always noticed in you when I had the pleasure of your acquaintance at Rutland Park. May I be of any service to you? Or is it presumptuous of me to ask?"

Susanna bit her lip. "It is nothing," she said.

He frowned. "Why is it," he said almost to himself, "that you make nothing seem like a great deal of something? Is it your sister? Are you worried about her?"

"What do you know of my sister?" she asked warily.

He hesitated. "I was surprised—indeed, quite shocked, ma'am," he said, "to discover when I left my cousins, the Winthrops, and was making my return to London that Miss Middleton was staying at the same inn. But she was neither alone nor traveling under her own name. Am I distressing you?"

"She did not leave home with you, then?" Susanna asked.

He looked at her in some astonishment. "With me?" he said. "Miss Middleton leave home with me, ma'am? But why would she do such a thing?"

"I thought . . ." Susanna said and swallowed.

"I was worried," he said, "especially when I heard the next morning that the two of them had turned north. I thought they must be eloping. I followed them. I am afraid I had no right to do so. Your family's business is none of my concern. But your father had been kind to me, you see."

Susanna stared at him with large blue eyes.

"Did you come in pursuit of her?" he asked. "You and your brother?"

"Yes," she said.

"It was fortunate that Lord Parleigh is an acquaintance of mine," he said, "and that I was able to come here, so close to where she is. But I must confess that since I arrived back from my aunt's yesterday and found you and your brother here, I have not known what to do. For to betray your sister is perhaps the wrong thing to do. But I cannot bear to see your distress."

Susanna's eyes widened still further. "You know where she is?" she asked.

He nodded and gnawed at his top lip with his teeth. "She is staying with old friends," he said. "The Hennessys."

Susanna stared at him. "Caroline Hennessy?" she said.

"I believe that is the daughter's name, yes," he said. "They live a few miles away. And now already I feel that I could bite my tongue out. Your brother's anger will be a terrible thing, I feel sure. I would not wish such an ending on Miss Middleton's romance, indiscreet as it undoubtedly is."

"Jo is just a few miles away?" she said.

He moved a step closer to her. "Perhaps it would help if you went to her, ma'am," he said. "Perhaps she would realize the foolhardiness of her behavior if she were to see you."

"Oh, yes," Susanna said, tears springing to her eyes.

"Perhaps you should see her before your brother knows of her whereabouts," he said.

"Bart would be very angry with her," she said.

"Let me take you to her, then, ma'am," he said. "It will be a load off my mind to know that she has been restored to one member of her family at least. Perhaps she will consent to your sending for your brother and all will be well after all."

"You will take me to her now?" Susanna asked. "And miss your luncheon, sir?"

"How could I eat," he said, "after having seen the tears in your eyes? I am only sorry that I could not force myself to speak up sooner. Come, ma'am, some of the grooms have gone for their own luncheon, I have observed. But no matter. I shall hitch my horses to my carriage myself if my coachman is not in the stables, and we will be on our way without further ado."

He took her by the elbow and picked up his bag before hurrying her across the grass to the stables.

The blue and yellow carriage was making its way down the driveway ten minutes later, the curtains lowered over the windows.

Susanna, seated inside it, sat tensely watching her hands as they twisted and clutched each other in her lap. She was not thinking about possible travel sickness but about her sister and what she would say to her when she saw her again. But she knew she would not say anything at first. She would throw herself into Jo's arms and forgive her everything.

And Mr. Porterhouse sat beside her, a slight smile on his lips. So he had been right. Or partly so. It seemed that the Duke of Mitford and Miss Middleton, alias Mrs. Villiers, were indeed in league against him, and doubtless that giant of a rogue, Villiers, too. But they had not been clever enough for him. It had been too careless of them to hold a meeting on the driveway while they awaited him. Too careless of them to allow themselves to be seen. And too careless to allow their groom to go for luncheon before his departure.

Doubtless the lady would be mystified and somewhat alarmed to find that his carriage swept past without waiting to take her up.

But he had a prize that was almost as valuable. It was doubtless true that Miss Susanna Middleton's dowry was not as large as her elder sister's. But she was, after all, Cheamley's daughter and Rutland's granddaughter. They would pay a goodly sum to see her safely married and ruin averted. And he still had the jewels, for what they were worth.

Besides, he thought, examining the profile of the girl beside him, the younger sister was more lovely than the elder. Yes, his first experience with theft and abduction was not turning out too disastrously after all.

Sir Thomas Burgess, standing at the window of his dressing

room, watched the golden-haired beauty cross the lawn toward the stables with Porterhouse. And the latter, he noted with a frown, was carrying a bag.

He stood a long time in the window until the carriage appeared, driven by Porterhouse's coachman. The curtains were drawn across the windows, he could see even from a distance. The carriage turned toward the driveway and disappeared from sight.

Sir Thomas continued to frown and stare after it for a few minutes longer.

"If you must know," the Duke of Mitford was saying to Josephine, "I plan to offer him money for the return of your jewels. It is the type of persuasion he will understand. I do not doubt that the whole thing can be settled without any fuss or violence whatsoever."

"What?" Josephine knelt up on the bed and watched her companion pace the floor of their bedchamber. They had retired there when Caroline had been borne off to her mother's dressing room so that her maid could add new flounces to the ball dress she planned to wear the following night. "You plan to offer him money for what is not his? I will not hear of any such thing."

The duke scratched his head and turned to look at her. "I suppose," he said, "that you think a few firm and fierce words will have the man cringing and rushing to relinquish his treasure. I suppose you still believe that he was going to take you to the jewels before I was unkind enough to drag you home."

"I do," she said. "He must realize that the game is up, after all. It must have been a nasty shock to him yesterday to find that I had caught up to him."

"I am quite sure he was shaking in his boots all night long," the duke said, "if he wore them all night long, that is. If you will pardon me for saying so, ma'am, I would point out that you seem to know very little of the world."

"And perhaps you know too much," she said. "Paying for the return of stolen property, indeed. You would merely encourage him in future thefts. Besides, however would I repay you? I have already told you that I am in debt for the next month. And it will take me several more months to repay you for what you have already spent on my behalf. I certainly have no intention of paying for my own jewels, sir.''

"And I have no intention of asking you to do so," he said. "All I ask is a little common sense.''

"Well." Josephine climbed down from the bed and came to stand in front of him, her hands on her hips. "I see you are intent on insulting me, sir. And of course you have me at a disadvantage for you have been kind enough to give up a week of your time to affairs that are none of your concern. And you have been willing to allow me to get deep in debt to you. But for all that, it is ungentlemanly of you to insult me. And really, you know, I did not need you. I could have managed quite well on my own when I discovered the theft. You offered your services. I did not ask for them.''

"What in the name of all that is wonderful were you doing at that inn, anyway?" the duke asked. He had almost never lost his temper. There had never been any need. But he was losing it now. "But I don't know why I need to ask. You were willing to accept my protection when you did not know one single thing about me. And you were willing to drive off with Porterhouse this morning when he had spun you such an unlikely story that a child would have seen through it. Why do I need to ask your reason for coming away with him in the first place?''

"And why did you come with me?" she asked, her eyes blazing back at him. "You did not know me, either. And you were on your way somewhere else—to some poor lady who is probably still looking for you. Though I would tell her if I could that she has had a fortunate escape, for you are just like all the other men and have to have your own way. Why did you come to the salon with Caroline and me after luncheon? Could you not see that she wanted to be alone with me for a while so that we could talk as we used to do? Did you have to act like a jailer?''

"I dare not let you out of my sight," he said, exasperated. "If I do, you will doubtless go tearing off again and get yourself kidnapped or ravished. I have to keep you within my sight.''

"And why should you care anyway?" she asked. 'What is it to you if any of those things happen to me? You will be well rid of me. You will be able to go about your own business again.''

"So I will," he said. "How very pleasant that sounds. It seems to me that until a week or so ago life was tranquil and sane. Perhaps what I think I remember was but a dream. Perhaps life has always been this mad. But I think not. I think life used to be different."

"Oooh," she said, her nostrils flaring, "don't let me stop you from going back to your life then, sir. Go back by all means. I shall do quite well where I am, and I shall get my jewels besides. I do not need you or your domineering ways. Or your insults or your sneering."

"I do not sneer," the duke said.

"Yes you do." Josephine glared at him. "But leave me your card before you go. I would never have you say that I did not pay my debts. I shall pay back every farthing you have spent on me, sir, including the price of this unspeakable garment." She caught at the wool stuff of her new dress.

"Will you stop talking about money?" Mitford said irritably. He passed a hand across his brow. "Do you think I care about the paltry sum I have spent in the past week? Do you think of nothing but money and jewels?"

"If I had spent money on you in the last week," she said, "you would worry about it too, sir."

"How absurd!" he said.

"Yes," she said, "it is absurd, is it not, to know that a lady can have some pride? You are looking at me, sir, rather as if I am a worm beneath your feet. I am not. I am a woman. A person. And I will pay you back the money. And if you spend one penny in recovering my jewels from Mr. Porterhouse, I will never forgive you. Not ever, because I would never be able to repay that kind of money. You must be wealthy, I think."

Mitford blew out air from puffed cheeks. "So I am to let you do any foolhardy act that comes into your head," he said. "What I ought to have done, ma'am, was turn you over to your father that very first night. Or explain the whole thing to Mr. Hennessy the second. Or put you into your brother's care yesterday. Or today. You must go home. Though your father has my profoundest symapthy. You are unmanageable. He should have walloped you long years ago."

"Well." Josephine's hands were back on her hips. "Well." Lost for words as she was, she had to let out her fury in another way. She lifted one hand from her hip and dealt him a stinging blow across one cheek. "And don't ask me to say I am sorry, either," she added.

The duke's face turned livid so that the red marks left by four flashing fingers stood out in marked contrast. He held himself stiffly erect. "So, ma'am," he said, "it seems that you have forced me to my senses at last. Why have I talked constantly about what I ought to have done and yet have never done any of it? It is time for me to write a note to your brother. If you will excuse me." He made her a stiff bow.

"Oh!" Josephine's hands had flown to her mouth and she regarded him with two large and horrified eyes. "Paul, don't. Don't turn all cold on me. Oh, don't. It is not fair. I was angry and so were you. I did not mean it. Not any of it. Oh, please forgive me."

"I shall find out Mr. Hennessy," he said, "and ask for paper and pen."

"Paul." She caught at one of his arms with both hands. "Please don't. Oh, please don't be angry with me."

"I am not angry," he said. "Not at all. Only restored suddenly to common sense. I told you a few minutes ago that you were lacking in it. But I have been without it for days. I shall write to your brother without further delay."

"Paul," she said, linking one arm through his and smoothing her free hand over the lapel of his coat, "tell me you forgive me. Don't look at me like that. You look like a king viewing the lowliest of his subjects. You look like the Duke of Mitford's valet. Don't. Please say you forgive me. Smile at me." She smiled at him.

His shoulders sagged suddenly and he sighed. "I am not angry with you," he said, "only aghast at what I have allowed to happen in the past week. I should never have started it. Your father had come to your rescue, and I allowed you to hide from him in my own room. Good Lord."

"Don't," she said. She had both hands on his shoulders and lifted one of them to brush back some wayward curls at his temple. "Don't start to feel guilty. You were merely helping me. You have been very kind. Smile at me."

"Kind!" he said, closing his eyes briefly.

"Smile at me," she said.

He looked at her and shook his head slightly. "Do you have any sense of decorum whatsoever?" he asked. "Do you have any idea what you have got yourself into, Miss Middleton?"

"Smile at me," she said, "and say you forgive me."

The Duke of Mitford shook his head and sighed again. "Words are wasted on you, are they not?" he said in exasperation, and kissed her instead of wasting more.

"Say you forgive me," she whispered. "I did not mean to strike you. Truly I did not. Say you forgive me."

"I forgive you," he said, reaching for her lips with his own again. "I did not mean to look at you as if you were a worm, you know. And I did not mean to look like Henry."

"Henry?" She had her fingers entwined in his curls and was watching his lips, very close to her own.

"The duke's valet," he said. "You did say he was Henry, did you not?"

"Did I?" She closed her eyes and opened her mouth at the approach of his. She set her body against his almost before he put his arms about her and drew her close. "I don't remember. Paul. Oh, Paul."

"Mm," he said, and his tongue teased her lips, and one hand moved up between them to touch her breasts, full and warm beneath the soft wool of her dress. His tongue accepted the invitation of her opened mouth, and his hand fondled and kneaded as she drew the upper part of her body away from his.

"Paul," she whispered, her fingertips moving through his hair when his mouth moved down over her chin to her throat. "I am not sorry. Perhaps I should be, but if I had not come I would not have met you. I would hate never to have met you."

He raised his head and looked down into her half-closed eyes. "Ah, but you should be sorry," he said. "And I should be horsewhipped. Whatever are we about now? Good Lord, what are we about now?" He put her from him, set one hand over his eyes, and shook his head vigorously.

"Paul." She touched his sleeve again.

"No," he said. "I am going to find paper and pen. No more foolishness, ma'am. And no more delaying." He walked purposefully across the room and flung the door open only to find Mr. Hennessy on the other side, his hand raised ready to knock.

"Ho," he said with a booming laugh, "I was almost afraid to knock. I know what those silences after a noisy argument usually mean. And it was a noisy argument, to be sure. Your first, I take it, but not by any means your last." He laughed again. "I would have left you to your reconciliation, but I thought this might be important." He held up a sealed letter. "It came from Deerview Park. I undertook to deliver it into your hands myself, sir."

Mitford took it and looked at it. "I thank you, sir," he said. "Perhaps I could beg the use of your study after I have read it? Josephine is planning to rest."

"Any time, any time," Mr. Hennessy said, looking past the duke to wink at Josephine. He turned away and Mitford closed the door again.

"What is it?" Josephine asked, coming across the room toward him.

"From Burgess," he said. "A friend of mine staying at Parleigh's."

He read quickly and then folded the letter with care, his eyes on what he was doing.

"What is it?" Josephine asked again.

"Your sister," he said quietly. "It seems that Porterhouse has her. He has gone off with her. Your brother and Tom have gone in pursuit."

"Sukey?" Josephine was whispering. "He has kidnapped Sukey?"

The duke turned to her with sudden decision. "The letter is from my brother-in-law," he said. "We have to return to London immediately. My sister has just given birth. To a boy. We will have to hope the Hennessys do not realize the impossibility of my having received it. Pack your bag."

"I am going to kill him," Josephine announced, "with my bare hands."

"Use your bare hands to pack your bag," the Duke of Mitford said firmly. "I shall see that my curricle is at the door in fifteen minutes' time."

14

Josephine, still boiling with indignation, clung to a fistful of the Duke of Mitford's coat and urged him onward.

"You do not need to slow down at every bend in the road on my account," she said. "I am quite accustomed to riding in a curricle by now, sir, and even if I were not, I trust your driving. Besides, I cannot wait to get my hands on the villain. Oh, just wait. He will be sorry he was ever born."

"It was fortunate we met that farmer a few miles back," he said, "so that at least we know Porterhouse was making his way back to the Great North Road. But we have to use some small modicum of common sense, Miss Middleton. If I do not slow for the bends, we would both be tossed into a hedge and never get to the highway ourselves."

"But this road is nothing but bends," she said in some frustration, clinging more tightly as they swayed around yet another one. "Where do you suppose he is taking her?"

"To Gretna," he said, "or to London. Who knows? If I were he, I would make for London. There are many places there to hide. And he can possibly force a larger dowry from your father if he can threaten not to marry your sister than if he has already done so."

"Threaten not to marry her?" Josephine turned from her intent stare at the road ahead to gaze at her companion in disbelief. "Threaten? Papa will kill him rather than let him marry Sukey. *I* will kill him."

"And your sister may have to live in disgrace for the rest of her life as a result," he said quietly.

"In disgrace," Josephine said. "How absurd. Who says so?"

"Society, I am afraid," he said.

"Society is an idiot," Josephine said indignantly.

"Perhaps," he said. "But it is an idiot we have to live with."

"Nonsense," she said. "I have no intention of doing any such thing. Marrying a man merely because one has been abducted by him, indeed. I have never heard anything more foolish in my life."

"Somehow, Miss Middleton," he said, "you have turned the meanings of sanity and insanity so topsy-turvy in my mind, that I am no longer confident of knowing the difference. Am I going too fast for you?" Her free hand had joined the other in clinging to his coat.

"No," she said resolutely, "you may spring the horses if you will, sir. Do you think the Hennessys believed your story about your sister?"

"If they have believed everything else we have told them in the past few days," he said, "doubtless they believe this too. And you did go into quite convincing raptures at the prospect of seeing your new nephew."

"I am going to feel very guilty writing to them from home," she said, "to tell them that this has all been a lie. It does not seem right to have so deceived them."

"Don't write too soon," he said. "Just leave it for a while."

"I shall," she said. "Doubtless I shall be busy for a week or so listening to Grandpapa's lectures."

"I can see the Swan Inn ahead of us," he said. "We have made good time."

"But how will we know which way to go?" Josephine asked. "If he was wise, Mr. Porterhouse will not have stopped at the inn. Oh, the villain. My fingers itch to be at his throat. At least he could have kidnapped me. I am the one who has been pursuing him. He might have left Sukey alone. I will never forgive him for this. I will kill him."

"Probably," he said, "your brother will have relieved you of the pleasure of doing so by getting there before you. I would not worry unduly, Miss Middleton. He and Burgess would not have been far behind Porterhouse and your sister. It is fortunate that Tom saw them leave."

"Who is this Burgess you talk of, anyway?" Josephine asked, but she did not wait for an answer. She leaned eagerly forward as the curricle drove into the courtyard.

Mitford lifted her to the ground before turning with her to speak to the ostler who had come forward to see to the horses.

"We are in pursuit of a carriage that came along the same country road as the one we have just emerged from," the duke said.

"Ah, yes, sir," the man said cheerfully, "that would be the blue and yellow carriage that turned north. The lady and gent inside were headed to Scotland for a purpose if you was to ask me." He favored Mitford with a broad smile.

"The villain," Josephine said. "So he *is* taking her to Gretna. But he will not get there in time. I swear he will not. Come, sir, we will leave immediately, and I will kill him."

"There was another carriage too?" the duke asked.

"Not that I know of, sir," the ostler said, turning to his work.

"There is not time to change the horses," Josephine said. "We will change them later. Let us be after him."

The Duke of Mitford turned to her. "Go inside and order some tea," he said. "We will pause here for ten minutes."

"Ten minutes!" Josephine said. "In ten minutes we can be a few miles down the road, sir."

"Ten minutes," he said firmly.

Josephine frowned as she scurried inside the inn and allowed herself to be ushered into a private parlor. What was it about Mr. Villiers that sometimes had her rushing into obedience almost like a frightened child? He never raised his voice as Bart sometimes did, or blustered as Papa did when he was too embarrassed to be angry, or lectured as Grandpapa did. He just looked at her with those level gray eyes and spoke to her in such a way that she thought a mountain would probably move if he told it to.

There was no reason at all why she should have obeyed. How could he expect her to cool her heels in an inn parlor sipping tea while Sukey was being borne away to Gretna Green to be married to a slimy villain whose only concern was to get his hands on some of Papa's and Grandpapa's fortunes? And it seemed that everything depended upon her. No other carriage but Mr. Porterhouse's had passed this way. Bart's must have gone astray.

Josephine did not order tea, but she did remain in the parlor for all of five minutes, pacing the floor and swearing that she was going to kill someone, though whether she meant Mr. Porterhouse or the duke even she could not tell. She was saved from the torture of the remaining five minutes by the entry of Mr. Villiers.

"Well," he said, "I have had the truth."

"Let us go," Josephine said, marching across the room toward him. "How many days will it take him to reach Gretna?"

"He is going to London," he said.

"Oh, nonsense," she said. "You heard the ostler."

"Yes," he said. "He was very eager indeed to give us the information, was he not? He even described the carriage before we did."

"Well," Josephine said, "it is a very distinctive carriage and one in very poor taste."

"The man was well paid," he said, "to throw us off the scent."

Josephine regarded him with open mouth.

"I am afraid Burgess and your brother fell into the trap," he said. "They went tearing off north. We will head south when you are ready."

"Ready?" Josephine's voice was almost a squeak. "Why are we standing here talking?"

His right sleeve might bulge out of shape forever after, the duke reflected as he drove his curricle along the highway a few minutes later. Josephine Middleton had taken her usual fistful of its fabric in order to steady herself. She was staring intently ahead of them as if she expected to see Porterhouse tooling along just down the road. Mitford only hoped they could come up with him some time that night.

Before the girl was ravished.

"How did you find out the truth?" Josephine asked, looking at him with sudden suspicion.

"By persistent questioning," he said. "I suspected the truth."

"Did you knock the ostler down?" she asked. "Or did you pay him?"

"I questioned him," Mitford said.

"Oh." The duke could feel her eyes on his profile for a long and silent moment. "You paid him, did you not?"

"There are some people," he said, "with whom money talks far faster than anything else, including a fist. If one uses a fist, you see, sometimes one has to revive the victim before he can talk."

"And now I am even more deeply in your debt," she said, her voice aggrieved. "How much did you pay him?"

"It is not at all the thing to ask a gentleman such a question," he said.

Josephine stared at him. "Stuff and nonsense," she said. "How much did you pay him?"

He took his eyes off the road long enough to level a look at her. "Are the members of your family used to such language and such demands from you, Miss Middleton?" he asked. "Do you always bully people into giving you your own way? I am not accustomed to being spoken to in just that way, and I have no intention of answering your demand. The sum I paid the ostler was between him and me. It need not concern you at all."

"I begin to think you are worse than Papa and Grandpapa," she said, fixing her eyes on the road ahead and lifting her chin to a stubborn angle.

"I begin to hope that I am," he said. "And if you wave to these rowdy dandies on the roof of the stage, I shall throttle you, ma'am."

"Oh!" Josephine was so outraged that she scarcely noticed the whoops of appreciation and the whistles and catcalls from the passing vehicle. "I will do whatever I wish, sir. The next time a stage passes, I shall stand up and wave both arms. See if I don't."

The duke forebore to comment.

"Will we never come up to them?" Josephine asked after a few minutes of stony silence. "Sukey will be so very frightened."

"Porterhouse will doubtless think himself safe and will not be in a mad dash," Mitford said. He reached across and covered her free hand with his gloved one for a brief moment. "We will come up with him tonight even if we have to drive on into the darkness. We will save your sister, never fear."

"I just want one chance to get my hands on him," Josephine said. "One chance, that's all."

The Duke of Mitford opened his mouth to say something but closed it again. There was really no point whatsoever in fighting premature battles.

No more than a couple of hours later, the ostler at the Swan,

who was congratulating himself on having made more in one
day than he earned at his job in one year emerged from a stall
to find a vaguely familiar looking bald-headed giant bearing
down on him. One fearful glance beyond his approaching figure
showed the ostler an equally familiar carriage with two grim
gentlemen descending from it.

He turned to smile cheerfully at the giant and made a valiant
effort to keep his knees from knocking together.

"Forgetting yer directions, are you lad?" Sam asked, not
breaking his stride as he lifted the grinning ostler by the lapels
of his coat and proceeded on his way into the stall with him.
"Don't know yer left 'and from yer right? Or up from down?
Or inside from outside? Or north from south?"

The ostler, his grin frozen to his face, his feet dangling a few
inches from the ground, found silence his best defense.

"Let's arsk the question again," Sam said, "for sake of
clarity, us 'aving misunderstood yer the first time around p'raps.
Which way did 'e go, lad?"

The lad, who was fifty if he was a day, swallowed with great
difficulty. "I said south," he said with a squeak.

"Ah." Sam lowered him so that the tips of his toes scraped
tantalyzingly against the ground. "It's on account of the 'ardness
of my 'earing, then, lad, that we went the wrong way. No
matter, then. All is well."

"I wondered," the osler said, "when I saw you turn north
after I had distinctly said south."

"Did yer?" Sam said, lowering a relieved ostler all the way
to the ground. "Just out of cooriosity, lad . . ." He leaned down
and suddenly the whole world turned upside down for the
luckless ostler. His head dangled the same few inches from the
ground as his feet had done a minute before. He could only hope,
if he was rational enough to hope any such thing, that Sam had
a firm grasp on his ankles.

Sam did. He shook his victim so that his head did not once
bump against the ground. There was a metallic shower.

"Ah," Sam said, retaining his hold on the ostler's heels and
staring downward. "I used to 'ave a job like yers, lad, only
farther south. It didn't pay as well down there. Not near as well.
Pick up yer earnings now before someone comes and steals
them."

He lowered the ostler gently down onto his head and released his hold of him. The man was scrambling around gathering up gold coins when Sir Thomas Burgess and Bartholomew Middleton appeared in the doorway.

"I don't suppose you need any help, Sam, do you?" Sir Thomas asked, looking inside with some interest.

"Not at all, sir," Sam said. "We was mistook, as we thought, sir. The lad said south. Just funny that it sounded like north."

"Perhaps he needs a lesson in elocution," Bartholomew said grimly. "I am in just the mood to give it personally if you would care to stand back, Sam."

"Nothing I would like better, sir," Sam said. "But we 'as better things to do, beggin' yer pardon, sir. The little lady will be frightened. And she will be sick if 'e 'as been driving 'er through all the potholes."

"You are right," Bartholomew said, allowing himself one regretful look at the ostler before hurrying back to the carriage.

Sir Thomas looked down at the man, who was still searching for one lost coin. "Has anyone else been inquiring after that same carriage?" he asked. "And think carefully before deciding to feed me a lie. There will be no money for your answer, by the way."

The ostler dared one glance at Sam. "A gent in a curricle," he said. "With a lady. They went after them, sir. South, that is."

"The, ah, gent paid well, then, did he?" Sir Thomas said before turning away.

Sam finally lifted his foot away from the missing coin. "I might be back for yer job, lad," he said, "if it pays this well."

Although the journey to the Great North Road was all of seven miles long, Susanna did not suspect the truth until they reached the Swan Inn. Even the fact that Mr. Porterhouse was very reluctant to stop on the two occasions when she felt too bilious to continue did not seem totally strange to her. He was anxious to take her to her sister before Jo could take it into her head to move on again.

But Susanna recognized the Swan Inn when she peered through the curtains, which had been drawn across the windows for some mysterious reason. It was the place where she and

Bart had met Sir Thomas Burgess and been informd that Jo was on her way to Deerview Park.

Was this the way to Mr. Hennessy's house?

"You must not look out through the window," Mr. Porterhouse said, taking the curtain from her hand and replacing it across the window. "There are those, ma'am, who would think it not quite the thing for you to be traveling without a maid. I must have a care to your reputation."

"But when will I see Jo?" she asked.

"Soon," he said as he made to descend from the carriage. "You must stay here, Miss Middleton. You must not show yourself."

Susanna stayed though she would dearly have liked to descend for a few minutes and a few breaths of fresh air. And indeed, she wished to descend for another reason. She was beginning to feel uneasy. She would have liked to ask someone where Mr. Hennessy lived.

But whom would she ask? She was but eighteen years of age and had done no extensive traveling during her life. She would not know whom to ask or quite what to say. And it was true that anyone of fashion who might be staying at the inn would probably be outraged to see that she was alone without chaperone or maid.

"But where are we going?" she asked Mr. Porterhouse when they were on their way again. She could not see out through the window, but she was sure they were on their way south, along the road she had traveled with Bart.

He reached across the carriage and squeezed her hand. Susanna edged away from him. "I will take care of you," he said. "You must not be afraid."

"Not be afraid?" she said. But Susanna was not the girl to say the obvious or to beg and grovel when she knew both to be useless. "Ah, now I understand."

"Do you?" he asked with a half smile.

"I feel sick," Susanna announced, a hand over her mouth.

Mr. Porterhouse swore—something he had not done on the two previous occasions—as he leaned forward to knock on the panel for his coachman to stop.

"I am afraid," Mr. Porterhouse said when he bundled her inside again after scarcely half a minute outside, "that that will be the last stop, ma'am. You must control your impulses."

Susanna retched miserably—and dryly—against a large handkerchief for the rest of the afternoon and evening, and for part of the night until the coachman came to the door to declare that there was not a glimmer of moonlight and that he was not going to risk his neck by going one yard farther that night. He had stopped outside a cozy looking inn.

"Well," Mr. Porterhouse said, "pursuit is doubtless half a day or more behind us by now. We can spare a few hours." He looked across at Susanna. "You are my wife, ma'am. I will expect you to behave accordingly. If you do not, you will doubtless scandalize the good people of the house, and I will be forced to discipline you as any self-respecting husband would discipline a wayward wife." He smiled.

Susanna lifted her chin and descended the steps of the carriage without assistance, pointedly ignoring his outstretched hand. She entered the inn quietly and ascended without a murmur to the room to which Mr. Porterhouse escorted her.

"Ah," he said, closing the door quietly behind him, "we will deal well together, I see."

"Lay one finger on me," Susanna said, turning to face him with calm expression and hands clasped quietly before her, "and I shall scream the roof down, sir. You may explain the noise, if you wish, as that of your wayward wife, and you may beat me into submission. But for all that, I believe you will be the laughingstock in this inn."

Mr. Porterhouse grinned slowly. "Very well," he said. "You will have your way for now. I can wait, ma'am. I can be patient."

"And now," Susanna said, "I wish to refresh myself and sleep. You will leave the room, if you please. You will, of course, lock me in, but you will not enter until it is time to leave in the morning. If you do, I shall scream the roof down. Good night."

Mr. Porterhouse looked at her appreciatively, and chuckled. "Good night, ma'am," he said. "Sleep well."

It was very late. And the night was as dark as it was possible for a night to be. The Duke of Mitford had reduced the speed of his curricle a few hours before and was leaning forward in his seat as if the position could help his eyes to penetrate the darkness ahead. Josephine was clutching one of the capes of his coat and clinging firmly to the rail at her other side.

"But you must not stop," she had said several times since darkness had fallen, though the duke had not once suggested they they should.

"There is another inn ahead," he said now. They had traveled in silence for an hour and more, all his attention being needed for the task of driving his curricle. "Perhaps we will have better fortune there. If they have not seen him, then I am afraid it must mean that he has taken another road again."

"Then we will go back and find it," Jospehine said. "But we will not stop. Promise me we will not stop."

"We will not stop," Mitford said grimly. "We will not stop until we have found them."

"Will we be too late?" she asked. But her words whipped up her wrath again. She did not wait for an answer. "Oh, the wretch. Just wait until I have my hands on him. If he has harmed one hair of Sukey's head, I will kill him. I will kill him anyway."

"Get down for a moment," the duke said when he drew his curricle into the yard before the inn. "You will need to stretch your legs. I am afraid you have been up here for hours. You must be very weary."

Her legs buckled under her for a moment when he lifted her down to the cobbles, but he kept a firm hold of her waist to steady her, and she kept her hands on his shoulders.

"You are cold," he said. "Go inside and warm yourself. It seems that no one is in a hurry to offer us services out here. I shall go in search of a groom who can perhaps tell me if a blue and yellow carriage has passed this way."

"Do so," Josephine said. "But none of your ten-minute stops, if you please, sir. Two will do quite nicely." She strode off in the direction of the door that led into the taproom.

The room was in semi-darkness, the customers having all betaken themselves to bed an hour or more before. Only one candle burned, though there was an additional glow from the fire in the hearth. And only one gentleman remained. He was slumped in a chair that had been pulled close to the fire. His feet were crossed on the hearth before him. His head was dropped forward in sleep.

Josephine stood quietly in the doorway staring at him. Then she looked about her. It was true that no one seemed eager for their business at this hour of the night. There was no sign of a landlord or barmaid or any other servant. Not that that mattered in the least.

Her eyes finally came to rest on the opposite side of the hearth from the one on which the gentleman's boots were stretched. She crossed the room and picked up the heavy iron poker that was lying there. She examined its end in almost leisurely fashion and tested its weight in her hand. She seemed satisfied with her examination.

She turned toward the sleeping gentleman, who had begun to snore quietly. She watched him for several unhurried moments before lifting the poker and prodding him gently in the stomach with the end of it.

The snoring stopped and he made sleepy murmurs of protest.

"It is time to wake up, sir," Josephine said quietly.

He opened his eyes.

"It is the time of reckoning," she said, raising the poker slowly so that it pointed directly between his eyes. "It would be a pity to sleep through such an important moment in your life, now would it not?"

When he lifted one hand as if to push the poker away, she moved it forward by a fraction of an inch so that its tip rested against the bridge of his nose.

"Don't even think about it," she said.

Mr. Porterhouse lowered his hand.

15

Perhaps it was a good thing that his decision to travel incognito had made him a little more cautious than usual, the Duke of Mitford thought. He normally traveled with almost empty pockets, relying on his secretary or his valet to handle such mundane matters as paying his bills. Unaccustomed as he was to having to look after all his own needs, he had left home this time with far more money than he could have been expected to need. Far more.

But what a blessing his caution and inexperience were proving now. Indeed, another few days of this mad adventure would put his pockets in grave danger of being to let. He had just spent yet another small fortune on yet another ostler whose sense of honor was quite as mercenary as the ostler's at the Swan had been.

The man's denial of having seen anything resembling a blue and yellow carriage in the past week had quickly melted away at the sight of gold. And suddenly it seemed that he had not only seen the carriage but had put it away for the night but two hours before.

Porterhouse and Miss Susanna Middleton were, it seemed, guests at that very inn.

How to handle the matter was the next question. They had been there for two hours. The chances were that more than the poor girl's honor had been ruined in that time.

What was he to do? Somehow he must release the girl from Porterhouse's clutches as quietly as possible. It was bad enough that her honor and virtue had been ruined. It was of the utmost importance that the fact should not be advertised to the interest of every chance traveler who had taken up his abode in the inn that night.

And then there was Porterhouse to deal with. Punishment must be meted out, but in the form of a challenge or a thorough drubbing? The man did not deserve the honor of a challenge. But how was either to be accomplished without arousing every sleeper in the house?

And how was Miss Josephine Middleton to be kept quiet throughout the proceedings? Indeed, she was likely to be the biggest problem of all, determined as she was to get her own hands on Porterhouse—the unrealistic and thoroughly irritating little baggage.

What he would have to do, the duke decided as he approached the door of the taproom, was try to lure her into a private parlor for tea. He would have to say that the horses needed changing. And then he must go about his business as swiftly and as silently as possible.

He drew a deep breath and pushed open the door. And released the breath and closed his eyes briefly. The madwoman was standing there, not three feet from a man who could break every bone in her body without exerting himself, if he so wished, a poker pointed at his head.

All Mitford's plans flew out through the doorway as he closed the door quietly behind him.

"Do you seriously think you could do me harm with that thing?" Mr. Porterhouse asked, amusement in his voice.

"To be quite frank with you," Josephine said, neither her eyes nor her hand wavering, "I am not quite sure. I daresay that my wrist may not be strong enough to hold the poker steady enough to pierce your brain if you decide to move forward. But I suppose any movement may deflect its course and embed it in one of your eyes. Yes, I think that may very well happen."

Mr. Porterhouse chuckled. "What I shall do in a moment," he said, "is take that poker from you and use it across your oh-so-lovely derrière. I would advise you to put it down."

"Well," Josephine said, while the Duke of Mitford held his breath and closed his eyes again, "we shall see which of us is right, will we not? In the meantime, you will tell me where my sister is."

"Your sister?" he said, beginning to raise his eyebrows but changing his mind. "She is upstairs sleeping, ma'am. I am taking her home. To ask your father if I may pay my addresses

to her, of course. A lovely woman, your sister, Miss Middleton.''

"You are a worm and a toad," she said. "I fully intend to
kill you.''

"Do you?" he said, lifting a hand to the poker and twisting
it away from him. He rose to his feet, grinning. And only then
was his eye caught by the other occupant of the room.

"I would not try harming Miss Middleton in any way
whatsoever if I were you," the Duke of Mitford said quietly,
his eyes narrowing.

Mr. Porterhouse stared at him for a long moment. He released
his hold on the poker. And then his grin returned.

"Well," he said, "if it is not the brave giant who can heave
doors off their hinges. What happened, Villiers? Did you get
caught out in a rainstorm and shrink?"

But before either Mitford or Josephine could answer, a sleepy
looking and hastily dressed landlord appeared, grumbling at the
late arrival of his new guests.

"Yes, I will take a room for the night," the duke said, without
removing his eyes from Mr. Porterhouse. "This lady will be
staying with her sister, who is already abovestairs in the room
taken earlier by this gentleman. Perhaps you would provide her
with another key?''

"But . . ." Josephine said.

"You will wish to join your sister," the Duke of Mitford
said, using his firmest ducal manner. "She will be awaiting you
in some anxiety at such a late hour, I am sure.''

"Oh!" Josephine said after a short pause, during which she
had glanced in some frustration at the landlord, who was
yawning and scratching his chest, not much interested in what
was going on before him, it seemed.

"You may put down the poker," the duke said, without
looking at either her or it. "You will not need to poke the fire
into greater life tonight, having a room to retire to.''

"Oh!" Josephine said after another pause.

The landlord had set a key down on the counter before him.

"Good night," the duke said.

"Good night, ma'am," Mr. Porterhouse said, a look of some
amusement on his face.

Josephine did not answer. She dropped the poker to the hearth with a clatter, snatched the key from the counter, and stalked up the stairs, her back bristling.

"And here be your key, sir," the landlord said.

"Thank you," Mitford said without turning. "Please leave it on the counter. This gentleman and I are going to take a turn outside before retiring for the night."

The landlord yawned and scratched again and shrugged at the strange eccentricity of the quality. He disappeared into the back regions from which he had come.

"Are we?" Mr. Porterhouse asked. "Are you sure that is wise, Villiers? Will it be good for your health? Night air, and all that?"

"A certain amount of vigorous exercise induces a good night's sleep," the duke said, opening the outer door and motioning the other to precede him through it. "I intend to have a goodly amount of vigorous exercise."

Mr. Porterhouse crossed the room indolently and looked down at the duke. "A little out of your class this time, wouldn't you say?" he said.

"We shall see," the Duke of Mitford said. "There is much provocation. The honor of two young and innocent ladies is not something to be taken lightly."

"You refer to Miss Susanna Middleton and, ah, Mrs. Villiers, I assume?" Mr. Porterhouse asked.

"Perhaps we should continue the discussion outside and a little way from the inn," the duke said, motioning through the door again, "and with fists rather than words. I find myself somewhat nauseated by the idea of conversing with you, Porterhouse. I prefer to converse with gentlemen."

Mr. Porterhouse's smile faded. "Perhaps you will not be able to do even that tomorrow, Villiers," he said. "Or the next day or the next." He strode out through the door.

There was no answer to Josephine's gentle tap on Susanna's door. When she turned the key in the lock and opened the door, it was to find her sister standing very straight at the foot of the bed, fully clothed, and looking as if she would have hurled something if only there had been something to hurl. A single candle burned on the washstand. Clearly, she was not as enterprising as her sister. The water jug and bowl, perfectly adequate weapons, were in their accustomed places.

"Sukey!" Josephine said.

"Jo!"

They were in each other's arms then and dancing each other around in a circle.

"Did he harm you?"

"Wherever have you been? Bart and I looked everywhere."

"I'll kill him if he touched a hair of your head."

"I feared we would never see you again."

"You will never know how relieved I am to have found you."

"We thought you must have gone to Scotland."

"I was beginning to think he had turned off this road and we would have difficulty finding him."

"But where were you, Jo? And how have you found me now?"

"Just tell me if he harmed you. I'll kill him."

"And, Jo, who on earth is Mr. Villiers?"

They stared into each other's eyes.

"Sukey," Josephine said, "why did you leave Deerview Park with him?"

Susanna frowned. "You know about that?" she said. "But where were you, Jo? Were you at Mr. and Mrs. Hennessys', as he said? That was where he said he was taking me. I was very foolish to get into his carriage with him, was I not?"

"Yes," Josephine said, "but no more foolish than I was to do the same thing a week ago. Did he harm you?"

"No," Susanna said. "I told him I would screech the roof down if he did not leave me here alone. And I would have, too."

"I was unable to do that when I was with him," Josephine said. "Everyone was singing downstairs, I seem to recall. But Mr. Villiers came to my rescue."

"Oh, Jo," Susanna said, "Who is Mr. Villiers?"

Josephine stared at her open-mouthed. "Oh, dear," she said, "he is getting himself killed on my account. And on yours, but that does not signify, for if I had not dragged him half across England he would not have known that there was need to fight on your account. And I daresay there would not have been, either, for if I had not come, you would not have come after me.''

"Jo," Susanna said, looking quite her old self again, "you are not making sense, dear.''

"He is getting killed," Josephine said, striding to the window and pulling back one curtain to peer out into the darkness. "And it serves him right, too, for he got rid of me in his usual sly manner and sent me up here to you. That was most unfair, you know, for no one has more of a grievance against Mr. Porterhouse than I. If anyone is to have the pleasure of killing him, it really ought to be me. Oh, there they are.'' Her voice immediately lost its note of indignation. "He will be killed, Sukey.''

Susanna peered over her sister's shoulder. "Where?" she asked.

"Over there," Josephine said, pointing off into the darkness. "They are fighting. Oh, dear me, they are fighting and he will be killed. All on my account. I will never forgive myself. He is the dearest, kindest gentleman.''

"But where are you going?" Susanna caught at her arm as she turned from the window and made for the door. "You are never going down there, Jo. Oh, no, really you must not. You must not. Please, Jo.''

But her elder sister tore her arm from her grasp. "If he has hurt Mr. Villiers," she said, "then I will kill him for sure, Sukey.'' Her voice was shaking.

Susanna was left protesting to empty air.

Josephine paused only long enough in the taproom to grasp the poker she had discarded a few minutes earlier. Then she marched out through the door into the stableyard and without pausing, on through the gate at the other side.

Mr. Porterhouse was hovering over Mr. Villiers. That she could see at a glance even if the night was dark and they were somewhat removed from the lights outside the inn. And he was so much larger and more powerful. In one more moment he would kill him.

Over her dead body! she thought as she strode forward, lifting the poker as she went.

She did not break stride. "Now we will see how much damage

it will do,'' she cried, using both hands to bring the weapon down across Mr. Porterhouse's skull with a satisfying thud.

He crumpled up and measured his length on the ground between her and the duke.

"I could not have him killing you,'' she said somewhat lamely.

He rubbed at his nose with one hand. "That is the second time you have robbed me of the satisfaction of finishing off an opponent,'' he said. "Thank you.'' He flexed his right hand. "He was already unconscious to all intents and purposes. All that was needed was the one nudge more to topple him down.''

"Oh,'' Josephine said, resting the point of the poker on the ground before her, "how splended you are. I never doubted for one moment that you could defeat him yourself. You are a great hero, sir.''

"You could not have stayed upstairs with your sister, I suppose,'' he said.

"And allowed you all the pleasure of dealing with Mr. Porterhouse alone? Never,'' she said. She looked downward at her fallen foe with some regret. "I just wish it were possible really to kill him. But it is not, is it?''

"Alas, no,'' he said.

"What is on your face?'' Josephine asked, raising one hand to it. "It is dark.''

"Blood, I would imagine,'' he said. "But no matter. I will doubtless survive. How is your sister? Has she been harmed?''

"No,'' Josephine said. "Sukey is quite strong-willed even though she is only eighteen years old. She advised Mr. Porterhouse to leave her room, and he did.''

"Good Lord,'' Mitford said, staring at her. "Can there possibly be two of you?''

"What are we going to do with him?'' Josephine asked, leaning on the poker and gazing down at the unconscious body of Mr. Porterhouse. "Leave him there?''

"No,'' the duke said. "There may be awkward questions in the morning. I would ask you to take yourself back upstairs, ma'am. I shall see that the man is packed into his own coach and sent on his way. I do not particularly wish to set eyes on him again after tonight. Do you?''

"I shall go and find a groom to help you,'' Josephine said.

She found one slim and strong hand clasping her by the upper arm.

"You will go inside," he said, "and upstairs to your sister's room. If you are wise, you will go to bed and get some sleep. But wise or not, you will stay in that room. And you will go there now."

Josephine glowered at him, opened her mouth to speak, and closed it again. "You are just like Papa, only worse," she said at last. "At least one can reason with Papa."

"Which presumably means that you can twist him about your little finger," he said. "On your way, ma'am."

She turned away from him indignantly. But she turned back and grinned before making her way to the inn. "Do you think he will have a headache in the morning?" she asked.

He smiled. "I rather think he will wish he had been born without a head at all," he said.

Sam was holding the ribbons of Sir Thomas Burgess's newly repaired carriage, that gentleman's own coachman making a valiant and not entirely successful effort to keep from nodding off beside him.

"I'll arsk 'ere," Sam said as yet another inn came into sight. The coachman yawned and sat up.

"Oh, Lordy, yes," the ostler at the inn said with a look of gloom at the giant who vaulted down from the seat to confront him. It would be fair to wager that he was not to get a wink of sleep that night. He might as well give up the attempt. "He left here not ten minutes since."

Sam took a not ungentle grip of the man's lapels. "If yer lying, lad . . ."

"Oh, Lordy, no," the ostler assured him, with a sideways glance at the two gentlemen who were descending from the carriage. "It was not ten minutes since, I swear."

"He is trying to evade us by traveling through the night," Bartholomew said grimly. "Well, he will find out if a ten-minute start on us is a safe one. Spring them, Sam."

Sam climbed back to his seat, all eagerness to obey. Sir Thomas took a few steps closer to the terrified ostler.

"You have seen a gentleman's curricle also this night?" he asked quietly.

The ostler nodded.

"Perhaps I will be too late to kill him myself after all," Sir Thomas muttered as he climbed back inside the carriage.

If Sir Thomas's coachman had had difficulty staying awake for the past few hours, he had no such problem for the following half hour. He sat bolt upright in his seat, clinging to it with both hands, staring off into the darkness with eyes that were starting from their sockets. In a night that was not the lightest on record, Sam sprang the horses.

The luckless coachman reverted to sanity only when the blue and yellow carriage came into sight lumbering along the highway ahead of them. Not that its colors could be discerned in the darkness, of course, but who else would be mad enough to be traveling in a private carriage at night?

"Here, here," Mr. Porterhouse's coachman protested as the other carriage came thundering alongside him and swerved in toward him, forcing him to stop. His hands reached for the sky. "Don't shoot."

Sam did not deign to give him an answer, and Sir Thomas's coachman looked too baffled to do so. By the time Bartholomew and Sir Thomas had leaped from the carriage, Sam already had the door to the other open and was reaching inside.

Mr. Porterhouse appeared lapels first. Sam held him against the side of the carriage, his feet a good few inches from the ground.

"Where is my sister?" Bartholomew's head was inside the carriage as he asked. "Where is she, you villain?"

"Answer the question." Sam gave the lapels a shake. "Where's the little lady?"

"How would I know?" Mr. Porterhouse said weakly.

Sam shook him again. " 'ow?" he said. " 'ow? I'll show you 'ow."

"Set him down, Sam, if you please." Bartholomew was standing in the roadway, his feet set apart, his fists clenched.

Sam reluctantly set his victim down on his feet and stepped back.

"Where is she?" Bartholomew did not raise his voice, but there was quiet menace in it.

"To which sister are you referring?" Mr. Porterhouse asked with weak derision in his voice.

A moment later his head smashed back against the side of the carriage and Bartholomew lowered his fist to his side again.

"Where is she?" he asked.

Mr. Porterhouse's eyes remained closed for a few moments. "Both sisters are at the last inn we passed," he said. He looked at Bartholomew with a weary sneer. "Together with Miss Middleton's protector, Villiers. One female was not enough for him, it seems."

He was rewarded with another fist to the jaw. This time he kept his head back against the carriage and his eyes closed.

"Liar!" Bartholomew said between his teeth. "Where is she?"

Sir Thomas Burgess cleared his throat. "I have reason to believe that he is probably right, Middleton," he said. "I have been asking along the way and have realized that Villiers and your elder sister were also in pursuit. And they were ahead of us."

Bartholomew continued to stare stonily at the half-conscious Mr. Porterhouse.

"And if you will look more closely," Sir Thomas said, "I think you will see that Porterhouse has already been well worked over tonight. A pity. I fully looked forward to the pleasure of helping you kill him. But it is hardly gentlemanly to challenge a man who can scarce stand on his feet."

"Who fought with you?" Bartholomew asked. "Villiers?"

Mr. Porterhouse sneered without opening his eyes. "Someone was cowardly enough to hit me over the back of the head while we were fighting," he said. "Your lady sister, I believe, Middleton."

"Jo?" Bartholomew said. "Good for Jo. She and Sukey are both back at that inn?"

Mr. Porterhouse shrugged. "That is where I left them," he said.

"If you are lying, I will catch up to you again," Bartholomew said. "Believe me. Sam, you may put him back inside the carriage. He looks incapable of climbing inside himself. And he will certainly be so in another few seconds' time."

His fists pounded at Mr. Porterhouse's face twice each. And then he lowered them in disgust.

"You are right, Burgess," he said. "It seems almost ungentlemanly. Sam?"

But Sam did not immediately do as he was told. His hands on Mr. Porterhouse's lapels this time held the man upright. "There is still the small matter of the lady's jewels," he said. "You will tell Sam where they are, so Sam don't 'ave to beat the hinformation out of yer."

"In my bag," Mr. Porterhouse mumbled. "Worthless pieces, anyway."

Sam lifted him inside the carriage and deposited him on the seat. He took the bag from the opposite seat and drew out a palmful of jewels from the bottom. "They'd better all be 'ere," he said. "Else I'll be coming after yer."

Mr. Porterhouse did not answer.

Sir Thomas Burgess was standing in the open doorway as Sam withdrew. "I am more sorry than I can say that my friend Villiers got to you before I could, Porterhouse," he said amiably. "I will only say this. I spend a large portion of each year in London. I do not wish to encounter you there. Ever. If I do, I shall be sure to find some pretext to slap a glove in your face. And if we should find on our return to the inn that Miss Susanna Middleton has been harmed in any way whatsoever, I shall find you out wherever you choose to hide yourself and slap that glove in your already bruised face."

Mr. Porterhouse neither replied nor opened his eyes.

"You need not exert yourself," Sir Thomas said kindly. "I shall close the door for you and instruct your coachman to drive on. Good night to you."

Mr. Porterhouse did not see fit to return the greeting.

The Duke of Mitford could not sleep. For one thing, he was sore and aching all over. And he supposed that it was no small miracle that he did not hurt a great deal more than he did. Only the careful physical conditioning of years had enabled him to get the upper hand in his fight with Porterhouse.

For another thing, he had heard the sounds of an approaching carriage and had seen through his window that it was Burgess's and that both Burgess and Middleton were its passengers. It had moved off before he could pull on his shirt and go down to them. But perhaps it was just as well, he thought, that they had not found out that the Misses Middleton were at the inn. The brother doubtless needed the satisfaction of dealing with Porterhouse himself. The duke could almost pity the man.

But what if they did not come back again? What if Porterhouse had turned off the main highway, and they did not find him? That left him in charge of two young ladies who were no relations of his. It would be his responsibility to convey them home to their father. A tricky business, indeed. It was not quite the way he would like to meet the viscount.

Not that there was going to be any easy way of meeting the viscount, of course.

And when and how was he to let Miss Middleton know who he really was? He had uncomfortable memories of the poker she had wielded earlier and of the triumph in her eyes as she had stood over the man she had felled.

Then there were her jewels. He had remembered them a full fifteen minutes after sending Porterhouse on his way. He would still have to go after them—and dissuade Miss Middleton from accompanying him.

Mitford stood looking out through the window and sighed. How uncomplicated life might have been. He might have made his way to Rutland Park with all the pomp and comfort that usually characterized his journeys. And he might have discovered on his arrival that Miss Middleton had taken herself off elsewhere. He might have made his way back to London and resumed his life as it had always been—safe, decorous, predictable, dignified, comfortable.

And dull.

The duke smiled unwillingly into the darkness just as Sir Thomas Burgess's carriage returned to the stableyard.

He pulled on his shirt and buttoned it with hasty fingers. But when his hand was on the doorknob, he turned back and added his waistcoat and his coat.

Bartholomew Middleton was frowning and impatient. He was calling for the landlord, and his fingers were drumming on the counter as the duke descended the stairs. Sir Thomas Burgess was closing the outer door.

Bartholomew snapped to attention when he saw the duke. "Mitford!" he said, and smiled foolishly.

Ah, yes, of course, the duke thought as he mentally switched persona. He felt for his quizzing glass, which was not there. He gave Middleton a cool stare instead.

"Middleton?" he said. "Burgess? Is one to have no sleep here?"

Bartholomew laughed. "Oh," he said, "Sir Thomas here was returning to London, and I decided to come with him."

"I am in rather a hurry," Sir Thomas said. Mitford caught his eye and looked away again. "We decided to travel part of the way through the night."

"Ah, quite so," Mitford said.

The landlord appeared from the nether regions, scratching and yawning and looking somewhat more irritated than he had looked earlier.

"I wish to know if my sister is a guest here," Bartholomew ssaid. "Miss Susanna Middleton. Ah, with her maid."

"That would be the fair-haired lady," the innkeeper said, having disposed of a particularly protracted yawn. "With her sister, as I understand it."

Bartholomew laughed heartily. "Oh, dear, no," he said. "That's a good one. Molly my sister? She does like to put on airs, though, does she not?"

"Upstairs," the landlord said. "Third door on the left. The door will be locked, though. You will be wanting a room for yourself, sir?"

"Ah, yes, certainly," Bartholomew said. "I will just go on up to assure my sister that I have arrived safely." He smiled broadly at the Duke of Mitford. "Always a worrier, Susanna, you know. She is probably not sleeping for worrying about me."

The duke moved to one side of the stairs and watched Bartholomew take them two at a time.

"What happened?" Sir Thomas asked tensely. "Did he touch her, Paul? Did he ravish her?"

"I gather," Mitford said, "from what her sister has told me, that she showed him the door in no uncertain terms. He was taking his ease here in the taproom when we arrived."

Sir Thomas's shoulders visibly sagged with relief. "You did a good job of work on Porterhouse," he said. "But you might have left something for Middleton and me, Paul. Most unsporting of you. Sam has the jewels, by the way, and is guarding them with his life."

The duke rocked back on his heels. "I am mentally bracing myself," he said. "At any moment now Miss Middleton is going to find out from her brother just who I am. I am not sure whether I should clap my hands over my ears or my arms over my head. Or perhaps both."

"She still doesn't know?" Sir Thomas said. "Are you mad, Paul?"

"Oh, undoubtedly," his friend said. "Pardon me, Tom, but I am about to take the coward's way out and withdraw to my room, if I can reach it in time. This is best faced in the morning. I shall see you then—if I survive for long enough, that is."

He turned and climbed the stairs while his grinning friend and the long-suffering landlord stood looking after him.

16

The duke had just fallen into a doze some time later—a half an hour, an hour, perhaps, he was not sure—when there was an urgent scratching from somewhere close by. Mice? No, too loud. Rats?

He woke up fully.

"Paul?" A whisper of breath from the direction of the door, and the scratching resumed.

Oh, Lord. There was no way of deferring it until the morrow, then. He might as well have stayed in the taproom and faced it all before trying to sleep for what remained of the night— and that could surely not be too long. It had already seemed a week long.

He made his way to the door in the light of the moon and realized only as he was opening it that both his feet and his chest were bare. Wonderfully exposed targets for her wrath.

"Paul." Josephine rushed into the room. "I thought this was your room. Oh, I would have been most embarrased if it had not been."

What? No poker? No pistol? No water jug or bowl? She was also barefoot. She had a shawl wrapped about her nightgown. Her hair was streaming down her back.

The Duke of Mitford closed the door quietly and leaned back against it.

"Paul," she said, turning to face him, all wide eyes and mobile mouth. "You have to leave. Now. You must not wait until morning. They will kill you."

"They?"

"Bart is here," she said. "It seems that he has been chasing after Sukey, too. And he caught up to Mr. Porterhouse after he left here. And he punched him too, though it was no fun at all, he said, because Mr. Porterhouse was quite incapable of fighting back. And now he is here and has given me a thundering scold.'' She giggled suddenly. ''All in a whisper so that no one in any other room would hear.''

The duke stood away from the door only so that he might clasp his hands behind him and rock on his heels.

''I told him you had gone,'' she said. ''Once we had found Sukey, I told him, and you had punished Mr. Porterhouse, you decided to continue on your way. He thinks you are gone. You must leave, or he will kill you in the morning.''

''Ah,'' he said. ''Who else is going to kill me?''

She put both hands up over her mouth, and her eyes grew rounder. ''The Duke of Mitford is here,'' she said.

''Here at this inn?'' He raised his eyebrows.

''He was here when Bart arrived,'' she said. ''Bart only just stopped himself from blurting out that I was here too. I am supposed to be tending my sick aunt, I believe. I am going to have to remain hidden upstairs until he leaves, horrid man. What is it about him? Is he really following me, or is it just coincidence that he pops up wherever I go? He quite gives me the shudders, I declare.''

The Duke of Mitford drew a deep breath and clasped his hands even more tightly behind him. ''Miss Middleton,'' he began.

''Oh,'' she said, coming closer and spreading her hands over his bare chest before removing them hastily again, ''you must go, sir. You really must. They must not find you here tomorrow morning. They will kill you, I swear they will. And I should hate that of all things.''

The duke watched himself turn utterly and despicably craven. ''Perhaps it would be best,'' he said more to himself than to her. ''There has to be a better time and place than this. And you are safe with your brother. He will be able to escort you home in safety.''

''And my jewels have been recovered,'' she said, ''so you need not feel obliged to go after them for me. Is it not absurd that we completely forgot about them in all the excitement over Sukey?''

''I suppose that means that your sister is more important to you than your jewels,'' he said.

''But of course,'' she said. ''Well, of course she is. You must go. If Sukey wakes up or if Bart wakes up, you may even now be in danger. Please go.''

"Yes," he said. "I shall."

But how could he be expected to get himself dressed and on his way when her hands spread over his chest again and when she looked at him with those big eyes?

"Thank you," she said. "You are a very kind gentleman. You have done so much for me. I am sorry that I have taken so much of your time and been such a burden to you. But I am not sorry that it all happened, though I know I should be. I am not sorry I met you.''

"Well." When had his hands moved up to cover hers? "I am not sorry, either. Though I think perhaps both of us will be before too much more time has passed.''

"No," she said. "I will always remember you. I will. Paul." Her voice had become a high, thin thread.

"I will see you again," he said, lifting one of her hands to his mouth and kissing the palm. "By that time you will doubtless not want to see me.''

"Paul."

Had she sagged against him, or had he drawn her there? The answer was unimportant. She was there. That was all that mattered. And her arms had lifted about his neck and his had encircled her—the shawl must have dropped to the floor.

And her mouth was open and warm and inviting beneath his own. And her breasts were taut against his chest, only the flannel of her nightgown between them.

"Paul."

His mouth was at her throat. His hand was toying with the idea of opening the buttons at the front of her nightgown. And he was walking her backward until she could walk no farther. And he was stooping down to lift her onto the bed.

And joining her there. And lying half on top of her, his hands smoothing back the hair from her face. He was kissing her and reaching into her mouth with his tongue for more of her.

"Josephine."

And one hand was caressing her breast through the nightgown, his thumb rubbing against the taut nipple so that she moaned.

"Paul. Oh, Paul."

Her hands were roaming over his back and down to the band at the waist of his breeches. And her fingers were reaching beneath it. Warm and teasing.

He was opening the top button of her nightgown, and his hand was moving flat inside it, across the delicate bones of her shoulders. And he was aching for her. On fire for her.

And remembering who she was.

And who he was.

Oh, Lord!

"Paul." She reached for him as he rolled off her to the side of the bed. She was all languorous heat and invitation. The hussy.

"Good Lord," he said, his voice not as steady as he would have liked to hear it. "Good Lord, what are we about now?"

"Oh, yes." She sat up in a panic, her fingers fumbling with her top button. "You must leave, and I am keeping you. Yes, you must go. You must."

He stood up beside the bed and reached down a hand for hers. "Yes, I will leave," he said. "You must get back to bed before you are missed. Take care of yourself on your way home. Or rather, let your brother take care of you. Will you? Will you promise me?"

"Well, of course," she said, looking blankly at him. "Why should I not let Bart look after me? Not that I need looking after, of course."

The duke sighed. He held out his right hand in a gesture that struck him as ridiculously formal, considering what had just gone before.

"Au revoir," he said.

Josephine put her hand in his and looked at it there. "Good-bye, Paul," she said. "I am not sorry even for that, you know." She nodded her head in the direction of the bed. "Am I not a shameless hussy?" She flashed a smile up at him and looked down again. "Good-bye."

She stood meekly at the door while he opened it for her and took a quick look to right and left outside. Then she slipped past him without once looking up and disappeared along the corridor.

The Duke of Mitford stood looking after her before shutting

the door quietly and blowing out his breath from puffed cheeks.
Oh, Lord, what fireworks there were going to be when they
next met!

Did the woman know nothing? Did she not realize that
whether he were simply Paul Villiers or the Duke of Mitford
he was honor-bound to seek out her father and make an offer
for her?

Did she expect that he could fade out her life and retain his
self-respect and his name of gentleman?

Whom was he more dreading meeting? Her father or her?

And how could he even contemplate marriage with her? His
life would never be the same again.

He paused in the act of buttoning up his shirt and stared into
the darkness for an interested moment.

Did he want his life to be the same again?

The Earl of Rutland and Viscount Cheamley were on the road
north. They were following a very faint scent, if the strange
details they had been given at the Crown and Anchor were
anything to judge by. Yes, there had been such ladies, the
servants there had claimed after listening to descriptions of
Josephine and Susanna, all trying to talk more loudly and
convincingly than everyone else. And such a gentleman. Though
they had not been all traveling together. There had been a blue
and yellow carriage—one groom declared dogmatically that it
had been blue and green—and a gentleman's curricle, and a lady
who had been suffering from travel sickness. There were jewels,
too.

There was that gentleman who had vomited in the stables,
too, someone had added helpfully and apparently irrelevantly.

And Sam had gone to drive one of the carriages—without so
much as a by-your-leave. They were all agreed on that, and
the innkeeper also added wrathfully that if Sam thought there
would be a job awaiting him when he returned from traipsing
over England with some nobs who were all chasing after one
another, then he would have a rude awakening.

The earl and the viscount dismissed Sam as having nothing
whatsoever to do with their search. A blue and yellow carriage
they would believe in—Mr. Porterhouse's, and a travel-sick

young lady—Susanna. But a curricle? What did a curricle have to do with anything? And jewels?

After a week, the two gentlemen supposed, one could not expect the servants at a public inn to remember anything with great clarity. It need not have been a week, of course, but it was amazing how much time could pass while one dithered in a wrath, and a panic, and a puzzle; and when one rushed off on wild goose chases.

Lord Cheamley had twiddled his thumbs and fumed and paced for all of one day at his sister's, waiting for Jo to arrive, and afraid to leave for home again in case she came to the house by a different way, the moment he had left. Lord Rutland had spent a similar day at home, wondering when his son and his grandson and two granddaughters would decide to return home, and wondering what on earth he was to say to the Duke of Mitford when he arrived.

He was more relieved than he could say when the duke did not arrive.

When Lord Cheamley had arrived home the following day, it was to find that not only Jo, but also Bart and Sukey had taken themselves off and disappeared in the direction of nowhere.

Jo had not wanted to marry the duke, Augusta had told them. She had been in a panic at the very thought.

That was why she had decided to go to her aunt's, the two men agreed. But no, if Jo really had taken fright—but why would she take fright at the thought of becoming a duchess with forty thousand a year?—she would doubtless want to run farther than Winnie's. The foolish girl must have gone to her grandmother in London.

That was it. And Bart and Sukey must have realized it and gone after her. That was why their note had been rather vague, saying only that they were going to meet Jo and accompany her home. But why had they not written the truth? Didn't Bart know better than that?

The viscount had gone, tearing off to London, only to come tearing back again after four days with the news that neither their grandmother nor their maternal aunt had seen either Bart or Jo or Sukey for almost two years.

Mr. Porterhouse had left the very same day as Jo, Penelope had said.

And so the truth, or at least some vague glimmering of the truth, had finally broken through the bafflement and the panic. Jo had eloped with Porterhouse rather than marry a duke, and Bart and Sukey had gone after them.

This time the earl accompanied his son. And the viscount, questioning the servants at the Crown and Anchor Inn, realized that if his daughter and Porterhouse really had spent a night there, it must have been the same night he had spent there on his way to Winnie's.

And so they were on their way north, keeping a gloomy eye open for two familiar carriages coming the other way, returning from Gretna Green.

They were having a late breakfast at a posting inn.

"Jo, Jo," the earl said with a sigh. "Why didn't she just come to us and explain? Instead she has married over the anvil."

"I thought Porterhouse was a decent sort," the viscount said. "But I don't call eloping with a girl who often doesn't know if her head is facing forward or back, a decent thing to do. You don't suppose Bart and Sukey caught up to them in time?"

"It has been seven days," the earl said. "She will be ruined even if they caught up to her before Gretna. I wonder what was so wrong about Mitford? She had never even set eyes on the boy."

"Perhaps that was the trouble," his son said.

A young man at a nearby table had been sipping his coffee and fidgeting for a few minutes past. He finally threw his napkin to the table and strode over to stand beside theirs.

"Pardon the interruption," he said, "but I am Mitford."

If he had not been quite so full of distress, Mitford thought, he would have felt amusement at what he saw. The two men gaped at him. The elder's fork was halfway to his mouth. And then both scrambled to their feet, and he found himself looking up at them.

"Mitford?" the elder man said.

The duke bowed. "Do I have the honor of addressing the Earl of Rutland and Viscount Cheamley?" he asked.

And he wondered why the urge to stand up and make himself known had won over the almost equally strong urge to pull his collar up about his ears, slink from the dining room, jump into his curricle, and spring his horses.

The two men were laughing heartily and making a very poor imitation of two gentlemen who just happened to be out on the Great North Road for the benefit of their health.

"Allow me to inform you," he said, "that your daughter is safe and not a half day's journey ahead of you on the road. Coming this way. Both your daughters, in fact. And your son."

Both gentlemen sank back to their chairs.

"You have seen them?" the viscount said.

The duke bowed. And this was definitely the tricky part. For if it would have been a relief to his conscience to confess all and risk being taken apart limb from limb in the public dining room of an inn, he must also remember that he would be compromising Josephine if he told even one small part of the truth.

And that little lady was such an accomplished liar and seemed to revel so gleefully in hopeless and tangled intrigue, that there was no knowing what story she would tell her relatives when she finally came up to them. The brother and sister were unknown quantities. He did not know whether they were normal human beings or formed from the same mold as Josephine. From what he had heard of Miss Susanna Middleton the night before, he rather thought that the latter might be closer to the truth.

"I came across them at Lord Parleigh's—Deerview Park, that is—a few days ago," the duke said. "The three of them were pursuing a Mr. Porterhouse, who had stolen Miss Middleton's jewels, it seems."

"Deerview Park? Jewels?" The earl was frowning.

"And Jo was with Bartholomew and Susanna?" the viscount said, his face brightening considerably. "She was not with Porterhouse?"

"Absolutely not," the duke said, a hand straying to his quizzing glass. "That would have been most improper, I believe."

"And they are on the way back?" The earl's frown deepened. He looked somewhat blankly at Mitford.

And the duke remembered why it is always so unwise to tell lies. What on earth was he doing at Deerview Park when he was supposed to be at Rutland Park making an offer to one Miss Josephine Middleton? He clasped his hands behind him and rocked on his heels.

"Actually," he said, "I heard about the stolen jewels and the pursuit when I stopped at the Crown and Anchor Inn on my way to Rutland Park." He bowed to both gentlemen. "I joined the pursuit in the hope of being of some assistance. Miss Middleton has recovered her jewels, and no harm has come to her, I do assure you."

Oh, Lord, he was going to find himself in very deep and very hot water if Josephine decided to tell the full truth and his double identity became known to the two flushed and bewildered looking gentlemen who were gazing at him, their breakfasts growing cold on their plates.

Not to mention the hot water he was going to be in when Josephine saw him again.

"This is a rather public setting," he said, "and I am sure you will want to be on your way as soon as possible to assure yourselves that what I have told you is true. My lord." He addressed himself to the viscount. "If I may, I will present myself at Rutland Park next week to speak to you about your daughter and to make my offer to her if I meet with your approval."

He was alone with his cool coffee again ten minutes later, after a great deal of hearty laughter and hand-pumping and a great many assurances that there must be a good explanation indeed for Jo's chasing about the countryside with her brother and sister. Jo was, apparently, a quiet and a dutiful girl under normal circumstances. Mitford had sent them on their way with a description of Burgess's carriage, in which the Middletons were traveling.

Quiet? Josephine?

Dutiful? Josephine?

A waiter looked uneasily at the lone gentleman in the dining room, chuckling aloud to himself though there was no one else except the waiter within thirty feet of him. He decided after all not to approach the gentleman with fresh hot coffee.

Not that the Duke of Mitford laughed for very long. Oh, Lord, he was in for trouble. Adventures were certainly not comfortable affairs.

Her grandfather's description of her as a quiet girl certainly seemed to hold true for Josephine that morning. She sat next to Susanna in the carriage, one hand holding to the strap, and seemed totally oblivious to the conversation flowing about her.

Bartholomew looked at her a little uneasily from time to time but refused to relent. She had deserved every second of every minute of the tongue-lashing he had given her that morning. In fact, he felt rather pleased with himself. He was not sure he would have believed anyone who had told him he could rage with marvelous eloquence for twenty minutes, without pausing except for the occasional necessary breath.

Josephine had watched him the whole time with raised chin and uncharacteristically still tongue. Sukey had dissolved into tears after the first half-minute.

And Susanna watched Jo sorrowfully and ached to take her hand and tell her that all would be well. But Bart might begin scolding again if she did. And besides, there was a stranger in the carriage with them. A stranger who could make her heart flutter and her breath quicken, it was true, and who had proved to be a very kind gentleman indeed. But nevertheless, a stranger.

Besides, she had her queazy stomach to contend with.

Josephine did not notice any of the three of them. She would never see him again, and that was the only thought that had any reality to her that morning. He had had to leave in a greaty hurry before she had been able to fully steel herself to his leaving. And this morning she was feeling bereft, a great emptiness somewhere deep inside her.

And so she sat quietly. And remembered the hot embrace of the night before, and knew that she would never see him again, let alone touch him like that.

She wished they had not come to their senses so soon, she thought rebelliously. She wished there were more to remember. She wished they had made love. And she was not going to blush or feel guilty at the thought, either.

"Strange that both the Duke of Mitford and Villiers had disappeared by this morning," Bartholomew said with a frown.

"Ah, yes," Sir Thomas said.

"I would have liked to have a word with Villiers," Bartholomew said testily.

"Yes," Sir Thomas said. "But it was good of him to bring Miss Middleton so quickly in pursuit of Miss Susanna."

Bartholomew said no more.

''Papa!'' Susanna cried suddenly, craning her head to see out of the window. ''That was Papa's carriage.''

Bartholomew turned sharply to the window and was soon pounding on the front panel for Sam to stop.

Josephine swallowed and closed her eyes briefly.

''Come on, little lady,'' Sam said a moment later, throwing open the carriage door and reaching inside to lift Susanna to the roadway.

But he looked around in some surprise as another carriage— one that had been tooling along in the opposite direction—made a sharp turn in the road and pulled up behind theirs. And then everyone was spilling out of both carriages, and everyone was talking at once, each fresh voice at a slightly higher volume than the one before. Sam stood and scratched his bald head.

And so amid hugs and laughter and scoldings and threatenings the story they had agreed to that morning was told—all of them standing at the edge of the king's highway for all the world to observe.

Mr. Porterhouse had been taking Jo to Aunt Winifred's when he had suddenly seized her jewels and made off without her. Jo had stayed at the Crown and Anchor Inn for the night and been found there the next morning by her brother and sister. The three of them had pursued Mr. Porterhouse, come up with him a few days before at Deerview Park, followed him back along the great North Road, and recovered the jewels just the night before.

''Oh, and Sir Thomas Burgess was at Deerview Park and was kind enough to help us,'' Bartholomew added, gesturing to the man who was still sitting quietly inside the carriage. He made the introductions.

''So, all is well, you see,'' Susanna said, an identical smile on her face to the ones on Josephine's and Bartholomew's.

''But what about the Duke of Mitford?'' the earl asked, frowning.

The identical smiles all persisted for the moment. None of their owners recognized the cue. What about the Duke of Mitford?

''He was at Deerview Park, too,'' Sir Thomas said, climbing down to the road and looking casually about him. ''He is a friend of mine. He had come out of concern for Miss Middleton, I believe. He left before us.''

''Yes,'' three voices said. And all resumed their smiles.

Sam was seated at the roadside, sucking on a blade of grass and watching the world go by long before his charges and the other two gentlemen decided to divide into two groups again and resume their journey south.

Josephine was taken into her father's carriage and was subjected to a far lengthier and even more eloquent scolding than the one she had received from Bart earlier.

Which seemed somewhat unfair when one considered the fact that they knew far less than half of what Bart knew.

But by far the worst of it all—ten thousand times worse than all the scoldings doubled and then tripled—was the news that the Duke of Mitford had met Papa and Grandpapa on the road and had announced his intention of calling upon her the following week.

Paul. Oh, Paul.

She would have cried, except that she never cried.

17

"Jo?" Augusta stood in the middle of the schoolroom, looking hopefully at her sister's back.

"No, not today, Gussie. I am not in the mood." Josephine continued to stare listlessly from the window. "Besides, you know we are expecting visitors."

Bartholomew, who was sitting in his favorite chair reading a book, looked up and stopped swinging the leg that was dangling over one of the arms. "And you know that Papa has promised a walloping if Jo is not here when they arrive," he said. "And if Papa should happen not to keep that promise, Jo, I will positively keep it for him."

"Stuff and nonsense," Josephine said without looking around, but with something of her old spirit. "I would push your front teeth down your throat if you tried, Bart."

Her brother chuckled and returned his attention to his book.

"Sukey?" Augusta asked, the hope still in her voice.

Susanna was sitting staring from another window, her chin in her hand. She did not look around, either. "No, Gussie," she said. "I have the headache."

"Again?" Augusta wailed. "You had the headache yesterday, Sukey."

"Oh, come along, then," Penelope said, putting down her embroidery with some impatience. "I will come walking with you, Gussie. You can be such a pest."

Bartholomew put down his book. "I'll come, too, Gussie," he said, getting to his feet and pulling affectionately at one of his youngest sister's braids. "I need to have the cobwebs blown away. And I do not have to stay to make polite conversation with Lord Ainsbury and the Countess of Newman." He looked for the expected sharp retort from his eldest sister, but merely shrugged when she said nothing.

"Oh, will you, Bart?" Augusta brightened visibly. "And you will not scold every step of the way as Penny always does, will you?"

Bartholomew grinned and winked over her head at Penelope, who looked as if she were about to explode with wrath. "I shall walk between the two of you," he said, "one on each arm, and if you are to come to blows it will have to be through my body. Come along, then. Perhaps we will be able to find out what Jo and Sukey are finding so fascinating through the windows."

There was a lengthy silence after they left.

"Why does he still want to marry me, do you suppose?" Josephine asked eventually, though it was not clear whether she spoke to her sister or to the beech tree that she stared at.

"He thought you were nursing Aunt Winifred last time," Susanna said. "He probably admires you, Jo."

"But he followed me almost every step of the way," Josephine said. "Did he not realize it? Was it really just coincidence? Sir Thomas Burgess and Papa said he followed me."

"He must not have taken a disgust of you, anyway, Jo, if he made arrangements with Papa to come here again," Susanna said.

Josephine sighed. "And to send his mother and his grandfather on ahead of him," she said. "Oh, I hate him, Sukey. But I cannot refuse him, can I?"

Susanna echoed the sigh. "You could say no, I suppose," she said.

"What?" Josephine finally withdrew her attention from the scene beyond the window to look at her sister. "After I disgraced myself so the last time? And after all of Bart's scoldings and Papa's fumings and Grandpapa's lecturings? And your tears? No, I cannot refuse, Sukey. I can only be grateful, I suppose, that someone is still willing to marry me."

Susanna sighed again. "He did say he would ask Papa if he could call on me here," she said. "But he won't, will he, Jo? Once he returns to London and sees all the grand ladies there, he will forget all about me. Won't he?"

Josephine frowned. "Are you talking about Sir Thomas Burgess?" she asked. "He was kind enough to bring Bart in search of you. And he did kiss your hand at the inn the morning after you were found. And sat across from you all day in the carriage until we came up with Papa. And lifted you down the twice you were forced to stop. He is a handsome gentleman. Do you like him, Sukey?''

"He asked me if he could call," her sister said. "And when I said yes, he said that he would ask Papa. But I daresay he did not. He was just being gallant."

"That would not be gallant," Josephine said, "to raise a girl's hopes only to dash them again. If he said he would come, then I think he will."

"Do you really think so?" Susanna said with anxious hope in her eyes.

Josephine sighed and returned her gaze to the window again. "Oh, Sukey, I don't know," she said. "I don't know anything any more. Except that the Duke of Mitford's mother is coming here today and he is coming tomorrow. I wish I were dead."

"But perhaps he will not be too bad," Susanna said. "When I met him at Deerview Park, he seemed quite a proper gentleman, Jo, if a little stiff in his manner. But I daresay it is not always easy to be a duke."

"I wonder where he is now," Josephine said, her eyes glazed.

"I daresay he is on his way here," Susanna said. And then she looked more closely at her sister. "Oh, you don't mean his grace, do you? You mean Mr. Villiers."

Josephine said nothing.

"Do you love him, Jo?" Susanna asked. And after a silent pause. "Oh, poor Jo, you love him."

Josephine said nothing.

"Oh, Jo, is it not dreadful?" Susanna said.

Josephine drew a deep breath. "Perhaps we should run away, Sukey," she said. "Do you think we should?"

"Oh, Jo," Susanna looked at her sister with gentle reproach. "We cannot. Where would we go? To Aunt Winifred's?"

Josephine laughed. "There is not much point, is there?" she said. "We cannot possibly go and find them. It would be most unladylike. And what if they did not want us when we had done so? Think of the humiliation, Sukey."

They sighed simultaneously, caught each other's eye, and giggled.

"Can you imagine their faces, Sukey?"

"We have come, sirs," Susanna said dramatically, spreading her arms and batting her eyelids.

They snorted with mirth.

"Do you think she will be glad to see me, Paul? She is very young and had had no chance at all to look about her yet."

"What I should have done right at the start was tell her who I was. As soon as she told me she would be forced to marry the Duke of Mitford if she went back home, I should have told her who I was."

"And of course the sight of me might merely serve to remind her of a week that I am sure she would as soon forget."

"That was my first mistake. Of course, I made so many after that that there would be no point in even trying to count."

"Perhaps I ought to have waited a little longer. Maybe until spring. Don't you think, Paul? Of course, by then someone else will probably have spoken for her."

"Well, there is no point in sighing over the matter now, I suppose. What is done is done. I have told so many lies in the past few weeks, Tom, that the thought of them just about makes my hair stand on end."

"I could say, I suppose, that I am merely accompanying you. I could be very casual and civil about the whole thing. Do you think I should?"

"She will kill me. That is an incontrovertible fact. The method she will choose is the only mystery. I did contemplate bringing that suit of armor that stands in the hallway of my townhouse, you know, Tom. But I could not figure out how I was to climb in and out of the carriage with it on."

Sir Thomas Burgess and the Duke of Mitford were seated side by side in the latter's traveling carriage, holding a conversation that was more two parallel monologues than communication. They were on their way to Rutland Park.

"One advantage to traveling with a duke," Sir Thomas said, withdrawing his attention from his own private thoughts for a moment, "is that one is accorded the best possible treatment." He chuckled. "Did you notice how last night's landlord kept bowing, Paul? I feared at one point that the poor man's forehead was going to scrape the floor."

Mitford grinned. "The same man seems to have forgotten that he allotted a box of a room with a cracked ceiling and pea-green wallpaper to a Mr. Paul Villiers just two weeks ago," he said. "He showed not a glimmering of recognition last night, even though Mr. Villiers made a spectacle of himself by driving off with a young lady who had not arrived with him and who was loudly proclaiming that she was going in pursuit of her jewels."

Sir Thomas chuckled again. "One would have expected the lady to be quite cowed after her brother caught up with her," he said. "But not she. She kept insisting that she was not at all sorry she had gone after Porterhouse and that she would do so again the next day if the need arose. At least she did until Middleton took her aside for half an hour. After that she was quiet enough."

The duke closed his eyes and shook his head. "She is not at all my kind of lady," he said.

"For which I must be eternally grateful," Sir Thomas said.

"She will turn my life upside down."

"Yes, thank goodness."

"She will make the most unlikely duchess in history."

"Probably, yes."

"She will embarrass me every day for the rest of my life."

"Undoubtedly."

"Do you think there is any way I can persuade her to have me, Tom?"

"A tricky business," Sir Thomas said. "She seems to have as much fondness for Villiers as she has an aversion to Mitford. Who are you going to be when you present yourself at Rutland Park?"

"Oh, Lord," Mitford said, "with my mother and my grandfather and all her relatives there in force, I don't have much choice, do I? I'll have to be Mitford."

"May the good Lord help you, then," his friend said with a laugh.

"Thank you, Tom," the duke said. "You realize, do you, that your own suit is likely to prosper better if mine does?"

Sir Thomas sobered instantly. "Do you think she will have me?" he said. "Not that I am intending to make her an offer so soon, of course. But will she welcome the acquaintance and be willing to continue it later?''

"I'm sorry," Mitford said, "I can't help you, Tom. The only time I saw the girl was when she was bobbing curtsies and tripping all over herself to confirm my lie that her sister was nursing their aunt. She looked at the time as if her eyes were about to pop from her head.''

"She is the most beautiful creature I have ever set eyes on," Sir Thomas said.

"Ah, well, then," Mitford said, "undoubtedly she will not have anything to do with you, Tom. Perhaps one of the other sisters will do. There are two others, you know." He laughed at his friend's indignation.

They both resumed their mental contemplation of the unknown ordeals ahead.

Oh, Lord! Mama and Grandpapa insisting on preceding him into the country so that they would be on hand for the betrothal celebration, Mitford thought. It was enough to make him break into a cold sweat. He had told so many lies!

Miss Middleton had been called away from home to the sickbed of an aunt, he had reported. And yes, indeed, it sounded as if she must be all they had expected her to be. Her devotion to duty when it had meant postponing listening to such an advantageous marriage proposal was highly to be praised. A serious and demure young lady, without a doubt.

And yes, he had been received with courtesy, indeed with affection, by both the Earl of Rutland and Viscount Cheamley. Both had assured him that Miss Middleton was favorably disposed toward the match. All that remained to do was return to Rutland Park when Miss Middleton would be sure to have returned in order to make the offer official.

What bouncers! Josephine Middleton serious and demure? He doubted she knew the meaning of the words. Devoted to duty? Ha! Mama and Grandpapa would have an apoplexy apiece when they finally came to know her, as they surely would if she could be prevailed upon to have him.

Not, of course, that they would have to live with the hussy. That was to be his pleasure.

Angela knew the truth, at least. He had admitted to her that he had at least met Miss Middleton. She had looked pale, but pleased with herself on his return to town. As it had turned out, the lie to the Hennessys had not been such a big one, after all. Angela had given birth to a son the day before his arrival in London.

"Oh, Paul," she had said, after showing off her child to him, "you need to be happy too. And you are doomed to become betrothed to a lady who deems it more proper and dutiful to tend a sick aunt than to listen to a marriage proposal. Oh, Paul!"

"Well," he had said, "that is a bit of a white lie, you know, Angie. In fact, if the truth were known, it is a whole lot of a whopper of a black lie. She is about as improper and undutiful a hoyden as you seem to wish for me."

Angela had looked distinctly interested. And then, of course, the whole truth had come out. The whole sordid, horrible truth.

She had been smiling radiantly by the time he had finished. "I am so glad," she had said. "So very glad, Paul. You are going to have some of the happiness you deserve after all. She sounds quite delightful."

"Angie?" he had said with a frown. "Have you been listening to a word I have said?"

"And you love her," she had announced.

"Love her!" The Duke of Mitford had stood up and begun to pace the floor. "Love her, Angie? Are you mad? She is about as unlikely a duchess as I could possibly find."

"Good," she had said as if he had just declared undying affection for the lady in question. "Oh, good, Paul. I am so glad. I am so happy," she had told the oblivious infant in her arms. "Uncle Paul is going to marry a most improper lady and a most unlikely duchess. Uncle Paul is going to be as happy as your mama, sweetheart."

Not for the first time Mitford had wondered if he were the only sane mortal in the world, or if perhaps he were the only insane one and did not know it.

In love with Josephine Middleton, indeed.

"Do you think she will kill me, Tom?" he asked now. "Will she at least listen to me first, do you suppose? Oh, Lord, I am not looking forward to this at all, you know."

Josephine did not like embroidering. Indeed, she liked it so

little that she had refused to do any since she had left the
schoolroom years before. But she was embroidering now—a
cloth that Susanna had started earlier in the autumn and a cloth
that the Countess of Newman had commended her on.

Josephine sat with her eyes lowered to her work and her mouth
uncharacteristically closed and still. Grandpapa had advised her
to speak as little as possible, and Papa had threatened her with
dire consequences if she so much as hinted at the events of the
past two weeks.

The Countess of Newman was, of cousre, just the sort of lady
who always made Josephine feel tongue-tied. She was soft-
spoken and dignified and very kindly. The perfect lady, in fact.

Susanna watched her sister and made an effort to take the
burden of the conversation upon herself. Just the three of them
were in the salon together, Penny and Gussie having been judged
too young to be present.

Susanna was glad of the distraction to her mind. Very glad.
The Duke of Mitford had arrived more than an hour before.
And with him was his friend, Sir Thomas Burgess.

The latter had come, of course, only because he was his
grace's friend. She had known that. It was perfectly natural that
his grace should bring a friend with him on such a long journey.
She must not refine upon the matter at all. Neither she nor Jo
had set eyes on either gentleman.

But Susanna jumped anyway and her heart began to thump
painfully when the door opened to admit the butler. It would
be Jo's summons to wait upon Papa. Poor Jo!

But it was not for Jo at all that the butler had come. It was
for her. She was the one asked to step downstairs to the library.

Susanna patted her hair with shaking hands as she descended
the stairs, and smoothed out the folds of her gown. She wished
now that she had changed into something more becoming. But
she had been afraid that to do so would be to tempt fate.

And of course, when she entered the library it would be to
find that Papa had some perfectly ordinary errand to send her
on. Or perhaps one of the Winthrops had arrived to take her
walking. Not that they would come today. They knew that the
Duke of Mitford was coming.

Susanna curtsied as soon as she entered the library. His grace
was standing in front of the fire, his hands behind his back.

Perhaps it was only the firelight behind him that made him look very pale. He certainly did not look particularly arrogant, Susanna thought, furiously trying to fill her thoughts with something. And they had only Mr. Porterhouse's word that he was arrogant. Susanna thought he looked rather nice. Perhaps Jo would grow to like him. There was another gentleman standing by the window. She did not turn her head to see who he was. Grandpapa was sitting by the fire, Lord Ainsbury at the other side. Papa was at his desk.

"Here is a gentleman of your acquaintance, Sukey, come to inquire about your health," the viscount said.

Susanna curtsied in the direction of the window without raising her eyes.

"I have said he might take you walking on the terrace, child," her father said, "it being a pleasant day, even if there is a brisk breeze. I have sent a maid for your cloak."

"Yes, Papa," Susanna said.

"If you wish to walk, of course," Sir Thomas said.

"Oh, yes," she said, bobbing another curtsy and feeling remarkably foolish for doing so. "That would be very pleasant, sir."

"I will send for Josephine, your grace," the viscount said as Sir Thomas stepped forward and offered Susanna his arm. "You may speak to her in here. The rest of us will retire to the billiard room."

"And not even set our ears to the panel, boy," Lord Ainsbury said with a hearty laugh.

"Though you must not keep us in suspense beyond the half hour," the Earl of Rutland added with a chuckle.

Susanna did not even notice his grace turn one shade paler.

"May I hope that you are none the worse for your ordeal?" Sir Thomas asked as he placed Susanna's cloak about her shoulders.

"Oh, no, I thank you," she said. "We found Jo and all arrived home safe and sound. That is all that matters."

"I have been afraid that you would be troubled with bad dreams," he said.

"Oh, no." Susanna risked her first peep up at him as they stepped outside onto the terrace. "I am not given to bad dreams, sir. I really came to no harm at all. And what did happen was a result of my own foolishness.''

"I would say it was a result of your fondness for your sister,'' he said.

"Jo is so very impulsive,'' she said. "Sometimes I worry about her.''

They walked in silence for a few moments.

"I hope you do not think it presumptuous of me to appear here like this,'' he said, "and to ask your father if I might walk with you.''

"Oh, no,'' she said. "I am honored, sir.''

"Are you?'' he said. "You were not hoping last week when we parted that you had seen the last of me?''

Susanna swallowed, "No,'' she said.

"Dare I hope that you were expecting me?'' he asked.

"Oh,'' she said hastily, "I was not expecting you, sir.'' She flushed hotly. "That would have been presumptuous.''

"Miss Middleton,'' he said in a rush, "I have scarce thought of anyone else since I first set eyes on you outside the Swan Inn.''

"Oh,'' she said.

"And is that not foolish?'' he said. "I must be ten years your senior. I must appear as an old man to you. I am seven-and-twenty.''

"Oh,'' she said, raising her eyes to his again. "I am eighteen, sir. I believe I look young for my age.''

"Nine years, then,'' he said. "It is a large gap in age.''

Susanna said nothing.

"Is it too large?'' he asked.

Susanna bit her lip and regarded the ground before her feet.

"If I were to ask your father if I might court you,'' he said, "would you be horrified? Disgusted?''

"No!'' she said, and this time she raised large eyes to his and kept them there. "No, of course, I would not. Are you going to ask Papa?''

"May I?'' he said, taking the hand that had been resting on his arm and raising it to his lips. "Do you wish me to?''

"Yes,'' she said, flushing again. "If you wish to, of course, sir.''

Sir Thomas grinned suddenly. "I am terrified, you know," he said. "I have never done this before. And if your father favors my suit, for how long will you expect me to court you, Miss Middleton? For a year? Six months? Three? When will you be ready for me to ask for your hand?"

"To ask for my hand?" Susanna said. "Will you wish to, sir?"

Sir Thomas still smiled. "Wrong tense," he said. "There is nothing future about either my feelings or my intentions, ma'am. But you are very young. I will not rush you or ask again how long I must wait. I will be content to court you, to come to visit you occasionally."

Susanna swallowed awkwardly. "My feelings are not future either, sir," she said.

He looked at her with interest. He still held her hand. "Are they not?" he said quietly. "And what are those feelings? But that is an unfair question, is it not, since I have not explained what my own are. Let me be specific, then. I love you, Susanna. I was at first dazzled by your beauty, and then I came to admire your courage and fortitude and your devotion to your sister. And finally I came to love you for yourself. Will you tell me now what your feelings are?"

"You were kind enough to care for both Jo and me when we were not your concern at all," she said. "And you were honest enough to confess to Bart that you had led us deliberately to Deerview Park, thinking that Jo and Mr. Villiers were going to Scotland. You need not have told us that. We would never have known. But it is not just gratitude I feel. I feel grateful to Bart too and to Mr. Villiers, though I have never met him. But I love you."

Sir Thomas lifted her hand to his lips again. "One more confession," he said. "You have met Villiers. Both at Deerview Park and in the library here a few minutes ago."

She frowned. "But there was no one else there except Papa and Grandpapa and Lord Ainsbury and his grace," she said. But as she gazed at him, light dawned in her eyes and they grew wider. "Oh, dear," she said, "Jo will kill him. She will really not take kindly to being so deceived, you know."

"He is mortally afraid of the meeting," Sir Thomas said with a grin.

Susanna was smiling slowly. "But how very wonderful," she said. "Jo is in love with Mr. Villiers, you know. I mean, with his grace. She has been pining for him for days."

"Will you marry me?" he asked. "Is it far too soon to ask that? I have no experience at all in this sort of thing. Will you permit me to speak to your father? Or would you prefer me to wait?"

"Yes, I will," she said quickly. "And no, I would not, if you please, sir."

"Well, then," he said, "I can only hope that my friend Mitford's suit will prosper as well as mine today. And I can only envy him for having somewhere as private as the library in which to make his offer. He will be able to kiss his lady. I will have to wait for another occasion to kiss mine."

Susanna blushed and lowered her lashes.

"Perhaps," he said, "I will ask your father for the use of the library too when it comes time to make my formal offer. Tomorrow, perhaps? And then I will kiss you."

"Yes," she whispered.

"Sometimes," he said with a smile, "it is hard to wait for tomorrow."

"Yes," she said.

18

Lady Newman had smiled and nodded and assured her that she was looking very pretty. And she knew she was looking her very best. Betty has insisted that she sit far longer than usual having her hair done. And she was wearing the rose-pink dress that always had Papa calling her his pretty half-pint. Not that he had called her by that old pet name a great deal in the past week. In fact, perhaps he had not called her that even once.

Oh, dear. She had disappointed him a great deal. She must do better this time. Josephine squared her shoulders and raised her chin. He was tall and blond and blue-eyed. And arrogant. She gulped. And had chased her half over England, though she was still not sure if he had done so by coincidence or design.

She schooled her features to blandness as a footman opened the door into the library for her. She lowered her eyes and stepped inside—a lamb to the wolves, a Christian to the lions' den.

The Duke of Mitford gripped his hands behind his back and schooled his features to blandness, and prepared to duck—a batter at cricket, without bat or pads, a victim to be used for target practice.

She looked so very familiar and yet so different—tiny, demure, neat. Mitford passed a tongue over dry lips. He had missed her. Life had been almost tranquil for the past week. Almost dull.

And then she looked up, and he wondered how he could have thought her different at all. Her face lit up and her mouth went into action. She hurtled across the room—in most unladylike fashion and with a most unladylike purpose. She came rushing straight into his arms—had he opened them to receive her? He must have done, because there she was against him, not an inch

212

of air between them from shoulders to knees. And his arms had wrapped themselves right about her.

He had come. He had come! Looking so very dearly familiar that she could have wept buckets if she were given to tears and the vapors.

"Paul!" she cried, flying across the room to him before he could disappear and prove himself to be a mirage. "Paul, you have come. Oh, how wonderful. I was quite convinced that I would never see you again. And it has been such a very dull week without you. Nothing but scoldings and lecturings. But none of that matters now. You have come."

It must be more than five minutes since he had combed his hair, she thought, feeling it with her fingertips, running her fingers through it. It was all definitely unruly. And how could she have ever thought that he was not quite handsome but only nice? He was so very much more than nice. She stopped talking and smiled at him.

"I told you I would," he said. "Did you not believe me?"

Tell her now. Now! Immediately. With not another moment's delay. Tell her. She was looking at him with large and shining gray eyes. She was smiling at him with an eagerness he had seen before, usually when she was about to suggest some mad, harebrained scheme. But she had stopped talking.

He kissed her. And knew something that he had been suspecting all week, something that he had hoped was not true, something that had filled him with a certain dread. Something that both Tom and Angela had told him was so. Oh, Lord, it really was so. Though how he could have fallen in love with such a very improper little hoyden quite escaped logical understanding.

Not that he was quite occupied with logic at this precise moment, of course. He was kissing her again as he had kissed her twice before—in a totally improper manner, in a manner he had never even employed with Eveline, or with anyone else, of course. Except with this little pest, who should have clamped her lips firmly together and not allowed it even to begin.

Not that she should have allowed him even near her lips. Lord. Oh, dear Lord.

If she kept her eyes very firmly closed and kept her arms very tight about his neck and her body pressed very close to his, if she held her mouth open to his and allowed his tongue to continue its magic, if she wished very, very hard—if, oh, if.

Josephine abandoned herself for long and deliberately mindless moments to her love. And he felt so very right, so very dear.

"Paul," she said eventually, "you have come. You should not have come. Oh, I wish you had not done so. I was beginning to forget you."

"Were you?" he said, gazing into her eyes, a mere few inches from his own. Tell her! Oh, Lord, he was doing this all wrong. "So soon? I want you to marry me. Will you?"

The eagerness came back into her face for a fleeting moment only to fade right away again.

"Oh, Paul," she said. "I cannot, you know. The Duke of Mitford is come here today and I am to listen to his addresses and I am to accept him. I have promised Papa."

"I have your father's permission to offer for you," he said. No, don't do it this way. This is the road to sure disaster.

Soon now she would wake up. Oh, surely she would. She kept her arms clasped about his neck. If she let go for even one moment, he would fade away and be replaced by that horrid duke. "Papa has said I may marry you?" she said. "You mean I have a choice, Paul?"

He licked his lips. Well, here it was now. No longer any chance of avoiding it. And serve him right that it was the worst of all possible moments. "No," he said. "Only the choice of yes or no, Josephine."

"But . . ." she said.

And he could see it coming every inch of the way, just as if it had to work its way up from her toes through her body and into her face. For a moment he found himself wishing that she were seven feet tall.

He had examined the room very carefully with his eyes before her arrival. It was the worst possible room for such an encounter. Hundreds of books, among other things. It was rather like standing in the middle of a circle of heavy guns, all manned by enemy gunners.

Her first choice was the paperweight on the desk. Fortunately, the duke discovered over the next few seconds—or was it hours?—Miss Josephine Middleton had a very poor aim. She did not come even close with any of the weapons she chose, and she chose many. Any one of them would have decapitated him if it had crossed paths with his head.

She had never been so humiliated in her life. Never! All that time trotting about the country with him, telling him how much she hated the Duke of Mitford. And all the time he was laughing at her, allowing her to dig her own grave—handing her the shovel, even.

Oh, he was a horrid man. Horrid. A zillion times more horrid than she had ever imagined.

Oh, she would die of mortification. She would dig a hole for her head and put her head in and never pull it out again. All the time she had thought the duke was following her about. And all the time he had been leading her about. By the nose.

"Oh, how could you!" The paperweight from Papa's desk went zooming past his shoulder. "Get away from me!" The paperknife flew past his other shoulder. "You toad!" A book died even before it had time to fly past him. "Get out of here. I hate you."

And so on. She did not know what she screamed. It rained books in the library.

"Josephine . . ."

"Don't you Josephine me!" A cushion finally hit a glancing blow off his shoulder.

They would have the whole household in there in a moment witnessing the Duke of Mitford's proposal to the Honorable Miss Josephine Middleton. Mama and Grandpapa would discover just what sort of a demure and proper young lady she was. Good Lord. She would wreck every book in the room. They would be wading in books soon.

"Josephine. Enough!" he commanded eventually in his best ducal voice. But the voice was not enough to quell this particular little termagant. He had to step right up to her, catch her by the wrists, and twist them behind her back. "Enough now," he said, feeling her bosom heaving against his chest.

"Unhand me," she said, all ice now that her body had been put out of action. She glared fiercely into his eyes. "Or I shall spit in your eye."

"Oh, no," he said, "don't do that. I should hate that."

"Unhand me, then," she said.

"Josephine." He tightened his grip on her wrists. "What was I to do? You had told me that if you were back home again you would have had to marry me. The duke, that is. It would have been most ungentlemanly to have told you the truth then. It would have embarrassed you."

He could hear breath being drawn into her. He could feel her breasts pushing more firmly against his chest.

"Embarrassed?" she said. "And how do you think I feel now, sir? Pardon me—I mean, how do you think I feel now, *your grace*? Charmed to know what a prize cake I have been making of myself? And how dare you hold me like this against my will! Unhand me immediately."

"Josephine!" he said, his head tilting to one side.

She did not even have a hand free to put up over her eyes. And she was pressed so firmly to him that she could not even dip her face against his neckcloth. Oh, she would die of humiliation. She would. All those things she had told him about himself. Had she told him that he was tall and blond and blue-eyed? Had she? She could not remember. She would die if she had. Oh, dear, and oh, gracious, she had told him he was a womanizer! She ruthlessly suppressed the thought.

"Mr. Porterhouse lied," she said. "He said you were tall and blond and blue-eyed."

"Alas," he said, and he had the gall almost to smile, "the man is a born liar, Josephine. You might have known that he meant small and mousy and plain."

"Your hair is not mousy," she said indignantly. "It is a wonderful brown. And you are not plain. You are—nice. And if you were tall I should feel like a veritable infant tripping along at your side."

"You are planning to trip along there in the future, then?" he said. And she almost exploded with wrath when he tipped his head still more and kissed her neck beneath one ear.

"I am not!" she said firmly. "And I do not recall giving you permission to touch my person, sir—your grace."

The Duke of Mitford choked, his mouth still against her neck. "Jo!" he said. "I will not ask you if you have heard the one about the stable doors and the bolting horse. Everyone has heard that one. Don't you think it is time you forgave me?"

"You dare to laugh at me?" she said. "And you ask for forgiveness? Never. I hate you."

"I don't think you do," he said, daring to approach her mouth with his own. She would probably bite his nose off. "I don't think you do. I think you love me . . ."

"*Love* you?" She injected as much scorn into the word as she could muster.

". . . as I love you."

"What did you say?"

"I don't think you do," he said.

"After that."

"I think you love me."

"After that."

"Ah." Mitford raised his eyes to the ceiling and frowned. "Did I say something else?"

"Tell me!"

"Mm," he said, looking back into her eyes. "As I love you."

"You don't!"

"Yes, I do."

"You don't."

"Do."

"You don't."

"All right, then," he said with his best ducal hauteur, "I don't."

"Paul?"

"Josephine?"

"Do you?"

"Do I what?"

"Oh!" She twisted away from him with one mighty jerk and grabbed a volume from the shelf behind her with a wrist that bent beneath its weight. "Do I have to throw it?"

"What is it?" he asked.

She looked at the cover. "Plato."

"Better not, then," he said. "Put it back and I'll tell you that I love you. Shall I?"

She put the book back with a great deal of care, turning to face full against the shelf.

"I know why you came," she said. "You think you compromised me, and now you have come to do your duty."

"*Think*?" he said. "*Think*, Josephine? Good Lord, we

traveled half over England in a curricle together. We spent—
how many nights?—in a room together. We have indulged in
embraces that have no business being indulged in outside of a
marriage bed, and that would doubtless be considered highly
improper even there by any delicately nurtured female. And
you think I *think* I have compromised you?"

"I am saying no," she said. "You are released from your
obligation, sir—your grace."

"Paul," he said.

"Your grace," she said firmly.

"What will your father say?" he asked. "And your grandfather? Didn't you promise them?"

"Oh, dear," she said.

"And how will I face my mother and my grandfather?" he
said. "They think you a proper and dutiful and demure young
lady, you know."

Josephine snorted.

"Precisely," he said. "Let us try it again, shall we?" He
set firm hands on her shoulders and turned her to him. Then
he went down on one knee before her.

"Miss Middleton," he said. "will you do me the honor of
becoming my wife and my duchess? On the understanding that
I love you dearly, of course, and am willing to be plagued by
you for the rest of a lifetime?"

Josephine giggled. "You do look remarkably silly," she said.

"I know," he said. "And I am living in agony at the
possibility that our fond relatives are going to walk through that
door at any moment and see me at it."

"Oh," she said, a hand flying to her mouth as she looked
about her. "And just look at the mess in here, Paul. They will
wonder what on earth has been going on. Oh, Papa will kill
me."

The next few minutes found them rushing about the library,
setting all to rights again. And not a moment too soon. There
was some throat-clearing outside the door, and it opened to admit
a smiling Countess of Newman, an anxious looking Viscount
Cheamley, a beaming Lord Ainsbury, and an equally beaming
Earl of Rutland.

The Duke of Mitford took Josephine's hand in his.

"Well?" Lord Ainsbury said, rubbing his hands together, "Am I to congratulate you, boy?"

"What a very charming couple you make," the countess said, smiling warmly. "And so well suited. Such a quiet and lovely girl, my lord." She smiled at the viscount.

"We have been so busy getting acquainted," the Duke of Mitford said, smiling down at Josephine, "that I have not been given my answer yet. What do you say, Miss Middleton? Will you marry me?" He raised her hand to his lips."

And looked down into her upturned face and held his breath. For if she said no this time, he would accept it and go away from her. And his life could be quiet and predictable and decorous again. And very dull. There would be no more adventures if Josephine Middleton were not there to share them with him. He smiled at her.

He was very sly. She had noticed that about him before. Very sly. For all his quiet, unassuming manner, he had a way of getting what he wanted. She had the feeling that if she married this man, she would find herself also obeying him for what remained of her life. And she had never really obeyed any man, or thought ever to do so. The alternative was freedom. But freedom without Paul. A life without Paul? It sounded very dreary.

"Yes, I will, your grace," she said. And she could feel herself blushing.

Noise broke out around them and everyone seemed to be laughing and slapping everyone else's back. And Paul's eyes smiled all the way into hers, and his hand still held hers. And she felt safe. And at home.

There would be time enough later, she thought, as Lady Newman swept her into a warm hug—oh, plenty of time—to punish him for that totally mortifying deception he had perpetrated against her.

The Duke of Mitford was forced to relinquish the hand of his betrothed so that the Earl of Rutland might pump his and attempt to break every bone in it. But there would be time enough—a lifetime of time—to hold her and kiss her and love her to his heart's content. And to try to make her into something resembling a duchess.

Though not too closely resembling, he thought as he recovered his hand only to have it seized anew by the grandfather. No, not too close at all. He had had one adventure with Josephine, and he had, he realized with some surprise, enjoyed it quite immensely.

Perhaps they would have more adventures together. Perhaps, after all, she was just the duchess for him. Just exactly as she was. And when she next took to hurling books at his head, well then, he would imprison her against him again and kiss her into submission.

He caught her eye across a press of relatives' bodies and a babble of hearty congratulations, and smiled ruefully.

He could hardly wait.

And then he found himself closing his eyes briefly as she smiled back at him and—yes, actually, the hussy winked.

His future duchess!

His smile broadened and he stretched out a hand toward hers.

27 million Americans can't read a bedtime story to a child.

It's because 27 million adults in this country simply can't read.

Functional illiteracy has reached one out of five Americans. It robs them of even the simplest of human pleasures, like reading a fairy tale to a child.

You can change all this by joining the fight against illiteracy.

Call the Coalition for Literacy at toll-free **1-800-228-8813** and volunteer.

Volunteer Against Illiteracy. The only degree you need is a degree of caring.